BOUNDARIES, AND OTHER FICTIONS

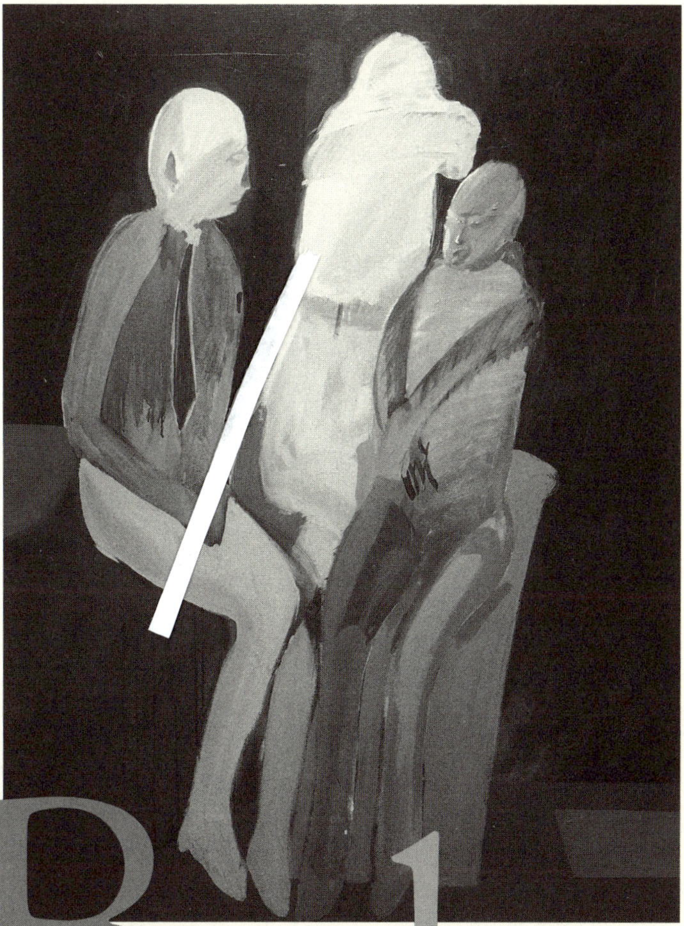

Boundaries

BOUNDARIES, AND OTHER FICTIONS

Robert Rawdon Wilson

The University of Alberta Press

Published by
The University of Alberta Press
Ring House 2
Edmonton, Alberta T6G 2E2

Published in Australia in association with Mattoid/Grange.

Copyright © The University of Alberta Press 1999
ISBN 0-88864-322-5
Printed in Canada   5   4   3   2   1

A volume in (cuRRents), an interdisciplinary series. Jonathan Hart, series editor.

Cover image: "Between F" by Jim Davies (1979). Used by permission of the artist.

CANADIAN CATALOGUING IN PUBLICATION DATA

Wilson, R. Rawdon.
    Boundaries, and other fictions
    ISBN 0-88864-322-5

    I. Title.
PS8595.I5854B6 1999   C813'.54   C99-910436-5
PR9199.3.W49858B6 1999

All rights reserved.
No part of this publication may be produced, stored in a retrieval system, or transmitted in any forms or by any means, electronic, mechanical, photocopying, recording, or otherwise, without the prior permission of the copyright owner.

∞ Printed on acid-free paper.
Printed and bound in Canada by Hignell Book Printing Ltd., Winnipeg, Manitoba.

The University of Alberta Press acknowledges the financial support of the Government of Canada through the Book Publishing Industry Development Program for its publishing activities. The Press also gratefully acknowledges the support received for its program from the Canada Council for the Arts.

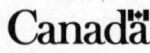

To Aaron Shawnandithit Tronsgard

Contents

QUEANG-QUEANG'S BEACHES
In Chicomuscelo, Once — 3

TRANSGRESSIONS
Boundaries — 13

THE QUEENSLAND MUNDUNGUS
Paracursions — 29

UNDERSTANDINGS
Making Do — 47

DELIQUESCENCE
Shultz on Discovery — 59
On Intolerance — 64
On Sexual Disgust — 68

THE FALCON'S TEARS
Processes — 83

TRACES
Rethinking Ludopolis — 97

CROSSING BOUNDARIES
Mapping Toronto by Darkness — 127

SELF-ENHANCEMENT
141 Apprehensions
THE BLACK THONGS
153 The Scarlet Crab
EVIDENCE
169 Methods
IMAGINING WHAT IS NOT
183 Clinks and Thuds
QUEANG-QUEANG'S TALES
197 Smoked-glass
ACADEMIC ADVANCEMENT
211 Parable
INFINITE PLURITUDES

METAFICTIONIST METAFABLES

You are standing on an edge. There is only blackness below. You are tottering. Your standing is uncertain. The edge has begun to dissolve. There is only the black emptiness. You see a spark rise from the depths. Then there are two or three. They rise disturbingly at a swifter, yet swifter rate. Now there are more. Sparks of light begin to swarm about you. You think that they are rising vortically, whirling and spinning. The lights thicken. Like autumn leaves or swarming gnats they are everywhere about you. The blackness is now a nearly solid light. It spins with the massive force of a galaxy. Beginning to speak, your voice fills with its reflections.

Swiftly, above the scrub the bright birds sweep and dive. Shadows swirl over the ground. Stunted trees stretch raggedly. The birds fly low, close to the ground, only infrequently rising to the tops of the squat, ugly trees. Their feathers are luminous. Their wings are muscular and steady. Their eyes, like hidden suns, are sunken. As they fly, they sing melodiously. Their sharp bell-tones fill the opaque air. The radiant birds, their short wings beating furiously, wheel in narrowing circles. They are almost lost in the dark scrub.

QueAng-QueAng's Beaches

QueAng-QueAng has a coastline, a harsh littoral that stretches along the sea from one point on the map to another, but it does not have beaches. It does not have beaches because the people of QueAng-QueAng have no concept of play. They have no room in their lives for swimming, for picnics, for sunbathing, or for surfing. The people of QueAng-QueAng say that they are serious and do not open their lives to fun. Fishermen draw their boats upon the sand, and women often look for anemones in tidal pools from which they make dark purple and red dyes. No one goes to the sea to swim. They tell foreigners who ask that it would be frivolous to waste time in swimming or in playing in the surf. On certain days when the sky is empty of everything but light and the sun burns with red ferocity, young theological students may hire a carriage that will be drawn by peasants over the sand. The carriages are black and completely sealed. Inside, there is neither light nor breeze. The young men have themselves pulled at great speed along the sand, from one headland to another, and back. They do this only to demonstrate that there are no beaches in QueAng-QueAng.

The real reason there are no beaches, one traveller writes who knows them well, is that no one has ever imagined a beach before or what could be done on one. The people of QueAng-QueAng do not have a word in their language for fun. The single word that even begins to translate "play" applies only to the flighty actions of puppies and very small children. They believe in conformity. They do not tolerate deviance. They dress sombrely alike. They always tell the same stories. They weave patterns that are different, but somehow always the same. There are only a few patterns in life, they say, and these are all one pattern in any case. Even if God were to be seen surfing, the people of QueAng-QueAng would not emulate Him.

In Chicomuscelo, Once

In the *Constitution of Athens,* Aristotle remarks that after the battle of Salamis, Themistocles became a "leader of the people" though this was never an official institution of the Athenian polity. I have often speculated about the nature of this unofficial leadership. What form did it take? Did Themistocles exercise specific kinds of power that were different from those exercised by the archons? Did everyone recognize that he was a leader? Or was this knowledge limited to his friends and admirers? Was he an unofficial figurehead or an unofficial power? Perhaps his non-constitutional leadership extended no further than a privilege of plucking a few choice figs or dates from market baskets. For reasons that I shall make clear, I have always experienced a sharp interest in the question of unofficial (unchosen, unappointed, and unelected) roles. Like Themistocles, anyone may find himself playing an unofficial role: not a leader perhaps, but a symbol or a champion.

[Tyler Haynes remembers studying the *Athpol* at the University of Chicago some years ago. They sat twice a week, the three of them (Tyler, a dreary graduate student in Classics, and Professor Chambers), in a small seminar room in the depths of the Harper Library and tried to interpret that intractably empirical document and to place it within the conceptual framework that Aristotle's canonical works create. When they came to the passage about Themistocles being an unofficial "leader of the people" Professor Chambers couldn't make any sense out of it. Neither of his two students were any help, of course, but that very night Tyler was eating at the Athens Restaurant up on Halsted. While he was sitting at the bar with his friends he overheard a conversation at a nearby table. A man loudly proclaimed that someone named Papadopoulos could buy and sell every other Greek businessman in Chicago. "Papadopoulos is the top Greek in town," the man shouted. Now that's it, Tyler thought, that's all Aristotle meant. After Salamis, Themistocles was simply the Top Greek in town. He reported his discovery at the next meeting of the seminar but (stuffy types, both) neither Professor Chambers nor the graduate student in Classics was persuaded.]

The reason that I have this interest in unofficial roles stems from an experience I had travelling in Mexico a number of years back. It's also an interest that has a lot to do with the Russian thinker M.M. Bakhtin. Bakhtin has quite a bit to say about unofficial roles: masks and carnivals, for example. He makes some remarkable suggestions about the ways people borrow each other's voices for the purposes of parody and travesty. If you were looking for a theorist to make sense out of an idea like "unofficial," you couldn't do better than to read Bakhtin. Try *Rabelais and His World* to start with. But Bakhtin worked into my thinking a long time after I acquired my interest in unofficial roles. My Mexican adventure had come years before.

About one in the morning I had boarded a bus in Guatemala City on my way to Mexico City. I was tired of that bleak mountain city, with all its tensions and disparities. I would like to call it a sepulchral city despite the vivid colour of the marketplace except that Conrad uses "sepulchral" to describe Brussels and García Márquez to describe Bogotá. But that's the right word in any case. [What I was doing in Guatemala constitutes another story (a good one) but not one that I will allow to perturb this that I plan to tell.] So I was happy when the bus appeared and I could board. It was a fairly large vehicle by Central American standards, not a VW microbus at least, like those cramped little torture-buggies I had come to hate back down the road in Nicaragua. I managed a seat by a window near the front and watched the lights of the city glint in the blackness as we crawled up the mountains. I fell asleep fairly early on, scarcely waking when we stopped in villages. Somehow the seat next to me stayed empty until we reached San Cristóbal Totonicapán about half past three. Then a young man got on and immediately took the aisle seat next to me. He squirmed for a minute or two, unzipped his windbreaker, found a cigarette, and then turned to me and asked in thin, flat Spanish, ¿fósforo? The single word displayed an unmistakable English accent so I suggested that we might get along better speaking our native idiom. He turned out to be an American seaman who had jumped some small cargo ship in Champerico and was trying to make his way home to North Carolina.

We reached Paso Hondo on the Mexican side of the border a little after nine, just a few kilometres short of Chicomuscelo, where I wanted to see a famous church. There wasn't much there beyond the harsh Chiapas landscape, full of limestone escarpments, scrub, straggly trees, and rocks, all stunningly random. After we had passed through customs the agent shut his little shed, climbed into his jeep, and drove off. It felt lonely as an Arctic wind blowing ice-flakes, there in the blistering morning sun. A small cantina across the road from the customs-shed offered the only refuge from the sun and emptiness, so we headed for it. We had a three-hour wait for the bus to Mexico City. And I still hoped to find a local ride into Chicomuscelo.

The cantina was just a canvas stretched over red poles, open in the front and along the sides and pulled down to within a few feet of the ground behind. There were some tables and chairs and a bar to one side. Four men were sitting at one of the tables drinking beer. We sat down at a table just inside the shade of the canvas, several tables away from the men who sat silently watching us. We must have seemed fascinating: gringos coming from somewhere and going somewhere else, carrying bags and suitcases. The American seaman even had a camera slung over his shoulder. No doubt we provided more to watch than the empty road, the rocks, or the thornbushes. But they didn't say anything or even, so far as I could tell, shift their positions when we entered. [The four men are important to this story, though they remain utterly passive throughout. If I wanted to tell it a certain way I could invoke familiar archetypes: the winds, the elements, the corners of the earth, the heart's chambers, the rivers of Paradise, the rivers of Hades, the four horsemen, the four letters in the name of God, the four quarters of Brahman, the quaternity itself. As universals, always hungry for incarnation, archetypes enhance narrative, but I want those men simply to sit there, as they did, sombre, silent, foursquare.] They were distinctly Mayan, impassive, almost unblinking, ochreous. Their dark clothes and low, wide-brimmed hats made me remember the Gypsy men in Spain whom you often see, elegant and stiff, waiting in cafes for the chance to buy or sell horses. I never learned what, if anything, those Mayan men were waiting for. They sat there, four bottles of *Negra Modelo* on the table, watching, peering.

In Mexico, and sometimes in Guatemala, when you enter a cantina or a bar it is common to find little saucers on the tables holding jalapeño chilies nestled in rock salt. It is a bit like putting out plates of potato crisps in Europe or peanuts here. They start a thirst and keep it going. When we sat down the first thing that caught my eye was the *platito* of jalapeños, like fat green slugs on their cloudy bed of salt crystals. I had always fancied myself possessing something like an iron palate when it came to hot chilies so I picked one up, glad that it was there, and began to nibble it. The American was tired and he sat morosely, silent as a movie cowpoke, looking out towards the road. It didn't matter much since during our waking moments on the bus we had just about exhausted our tiny store of mutual talk.

While we sat there, indifferent and mostly out of things, looking and being watched, the woman who ran the cantina came up to take our orders. She must have been out in back because she carried a chicken under her left arm, her right hand twisting its neck, as if our presence had interrupted her in the act of execution. She was a rather tall Mayan woman wearing a long skirt of those bright red and green, tightly woven geometric patterns that you see commonly in Guatemala and southern Mexico. She wore a scarf, almost like a mantilla, around her shoulders, and her black hair was tied up in a bun. I badly wanted a dark Mexican beer but before I could order one, she shot me a hard look, a bit hostile and challenging. It was my nibbling that damn jalapeño that had aroused her.

¿*No le pican?* she asked sharply. I should have said that, yes, they did burn, at least a bit, but that I liked them that way. Instead, I said that, no, they didn't burn, that they were as sweet as harvest grapes. That was just a bit of *machismo*, of course, brought on by the challenge in her look, and by the four stolid men watching each nuance of our transaction. Behind the bantering smile I was putting on for the woman's instruction, I could feel the high, stinging burn, not actually unpleasant, of fresh jalapeños, unpickled and unbottled. The woman gave her head a short toss, let the chicken down (it immediately ran off, its untwisted neck jabbing high in the air, making for the opening at the back), and headed purposefully past the bar and out into the rock-strewn space behind the cantina. My only thought was that we were not getting the beer we wanted. The American paid no attention to what was happening.

What *was* happening? Well, I could see that a challenge to my pretenses had begun. Pretenses have their cost. I regretted not having admitted freely that the chilies burned, but it was too late to switch masks. I would have to live up to the assertion that, for me, jalapeños were as sweet as grapes. I watched the woman climb a small hill covered with scrub and thornbushes. Near the top of the rise she stopped, hoisted her long skirt a bit, and knelt down to pick something from a bush. I watched her stand up, examine whatever she had in her hand, and then turn back towards the cantina. Abruptly, I understood that I would be put to the proof, a test of disturbing unexpectedness. [Here, too, archetypes suggest themselves. You stand always in the shadows cast by the giant shapes, the mythic configurations, that sweep onwards through our culture. You can't avoid them so perhaps they should be allowed their sway. I might have imagined myself then as Beowulf readying himself to dive into the fen or to enter the dragon's lair. Or Hercules. Or Theseus. Or Ned Kelly, his armour already on, his hand on the pub's door, that final morning in Glenrowan. Anyone who faces a challenge that has been forced upon him stands, momentarily, in those shadows. Like Thor in Jotunheim, the palace of the Giants, I watched the duplicitous horn being brought.] The woman returned, her right hand held forward in a clasped fist. The four men watched without comment.

¡*Tome!* she exclaimed happily. I looked into her opened fist to see what I should take. In her palm there were several small round berries, some green, some red. I had never seen anything like them before. Quickly I attempted to work out which was more likely to be the hottest. It seemed obvious that red would be the hottest so I concluded, in the instant that a smile permitted me, that green would actually be the hottest and chose one, bright red pellet. I held it in front of my mouth, still smiling, while the woman peered intently into my eyes. Then, as casually as I could manage, I popped it in.

¿*Le pica?* she inquired, probing into my eyes for signs of weakness, for pain and fear. I smiled and replied easily, *un poco, nada mas, me pica un poco*. Inside my mouth a horrible, agonizing fire had taken root. It seemed as if I had poured acid down my throat. Nothing in my experience had ever been like that searing, corrosive burning that penetrated into every space from lips to throat, even between my teeth. My gums, my tongue, my palate felt as if they were dissolving. My skull had begun to emerge from behind its flesh. But I wore the smiling mask that my foolishness had chosen. From distantly behind the agony that filled my mouth, only the slightest hint of tears in my eyes (and these, it might have been, there only because my good humour was irrepressible), I watched the woman's face turn sour. Disbelief flitted in her eyes.

I had won. I had mastered my pain, refused to let it be seen, and held the senseless mask. I had shown those incredulous Mayans that a gringo could eat the hottest chilies. A victory without point, as foolish as the unconsidered assertion that had prompted the challenge, it made me feel deeply triumphant. Then the American awoke out of his torpor. Throughout he had been oblivious of the heroic transaction that had been taking place so close to him, his eyes fixed emptily upon the road. Now he looked up and saw only that the woman was holding something in her still open hand, evidently some delicacy, a treat. He reached out silently and picked two of the fireseeds, put them in his mouth and bit down. There was a brief instant in which his eyes sprang widely open and seemed to bulge, then he let out a roar, staggered up from his chair and, howling like a tormented tomcat that wanton boys have arsesoused with turpentine, lurched over to the table where the four, sombre, unblinking men sat. He snatched up a bottle of *Negra Modelo* and drank it in a continuous swallow. The men did not move or comment, but the woman clapped her hands and cried out, ¡bueno!

There had been a comic coda to my heroic encounter. Everyone (except the American) could now feel bliss. The American had demonstrated that gringos really couldn't eat chilies. Clearly, I was an exception. [I like to imagine that today, when other versions of this story are told in the cantinas around Chicomuscelo and Paso Hondo, it is always explained that I could not have been truly a gringo: surely a *señorito* from the north or (more to the ways of narrative) a descendant of Hernán Cortéz.] Nothing could diminish my sense of triumph. A comic coda, or an interlude in the very midst of things, allows the heroic agent to step outside himself and to join in the laughter, the benefits of distance suddenly bestowed, even if only briefly or illusorily, in the whirligig of plot. Remember the jokes in *Hamlet*. Remember how the final act begins.

Later, on the bus to Mexico City, I reflected on the adventure I had just lived through. I decided that I had won something significant though no one would ever admit this. I had met a challenge thrust upon me unexpectedly from a hostile source and I had overcome it. So, in that moment, the bleak landscape of Chiapas flowing by, I determined that I would afterwards call myself The Chili-eating Champion of Southern Mexico. Of course, it is an unofficial title, conferred by no one, but it is authenticated by the nature of narrative. This is how stories are told. Ask any good story-teller. Now when I go to a Mexican, Indian or Sichuan restaurant I always take the occasion to tell how I won my title. Some friends may have heard it more than once, but that, too, is the way of stories. [Now that was the best place to close my narrative: an artificial break so cunning that it must seem natural (almost as crafty as Spenser!). But there remains the problem of unofficial roles and the purpose of the allusion to the *Constitution of Athens* with which I began. After the encounter, having given myself my unofficial title, I stood in the shadow of Themistocles. Chili-eating Champion has never been an official institution in Chicomuscelo, no one will recognize it, but it is nonetheless real. I took it, occasionally choose it as a mask, and invariably discover, at least in the carnivalities of eating, that my friends will grant it. The functions of masks, as any reader of Bakhtin will know, are multiplex. One is to make narration more fun: to help perplex the narrative line a bit.] A man who likes words can't have too many titles.

TRANSGRESSIONS

Someone asks me did I know that the people of QueAng-QueAng drink the eyeballs of living animals using a slender metal straw. The trick, that only practice can teach, is to pierce the eyeball through the iris to the exact centre and then drink the vitreous gel in many tiny sips. In QueAng-QueAng, they also execute blasphemers in a similar manner. The community kneel and angrily pierce the condemned person's body with their metal straws. When the execution has been finished nothing much is left but skin and bones. These dry in the desert air until, withered and empty, they blow away into the bleached horizon. The condemned, like husks, are soon forgotten. I do not know how to answer. I do not understand the people of QueAng-QueAng. I try to remember Montaigne, but he offers little help. Finally, I decide that, no matter what, I shall not go there. I shall leave the people of QueAng-QueAng to their private intensities.

Boundaries

Tommy Joe pivoted the Remington .12-gauge in his right hand, grabbed the barrel with his left, and swung the gun upwards into the Chinese clerk's face. An expression of shocked surprise flooded the young man's eyes. There was a sharp cracking noise as his teeth broke. Blood spurted from his nose. He clutched his face, moaning, and sank out of sight behind the counter. Across the store, by the freezer, a small boy watched bug-eyed, mouth gaping. Next to the pet food, a large woman had fallen to the floor praying. Her striped skirt had rucked up onto creamcheese thighs. Blue veins splayed upwards. Her Miss Clairol hair burrowed, a fuzzy, discoloured mop, beneath a shelf of cat food. Lorne could hear her mumble, over and over, "Christ Jesus, O Christ Jesus, help me." He kept his Colt .22 swinging back and forth between them. Out of the corner of one eye he had seen Tommy Joe waste the clerk. He was now behind the counter scooping the till. He would also take the man's wallet and all the lottery tickets.

A minute afterwards they had jumped into Lorne's blue 1974 Mustang and spun away. Two blocks and three quick turns later, Tommy Joe braked the car abruptly and Lorne, on cue, clambered out of the passenger's seat, ran to the rear and tore off the paper plates. As far as he could tell, no one in the early winter gloom had seen them. Now he would scrunch down beneath the dash while Tommy Joe aced them out of the neighbourhood and, following a twisting route that he had worked out from a city map and then practised twice, took them along McKnight Boulevard and out onto the Deerfoot Trail heading north. They would be ahead of the Calgary police by minutes. Tommy Joe had said that there was no chance that the RCMP would close the highway over a convenience store robbery with no more damage than a broken face. But, cutting risk, he would turn off onto a secondary road at Balzac, heading east towards Kathyrn. Lorne would come up for air then. After the initial getaway burst, Tommy Joe never drove fast. He would pull out a pipe and light up. It was the only time that he smoked, but the pipe made a solid impression of a man driving alone, thinking, perhaps counting up the sales for the day, or dreaming about his kids. Beneath the dash of his own car, Lorne stifled in the smoke and dust, waiting his chance to breathe openly.

Later they drove through Three Hills and then whipped around at the junction east of town and drove back to buy gas. They laughed when they saw that the RCMP were next to the gas station. Coming from the opposite direction, they would look like any tourists driving up from Drumheller and heading on to the David Thompson highway. Lorne gestured across the road at a Bible college. "T Joe, it's time to get religion. Mend your ways or face the wrath of the Almighty."

"I've faced it many times already. A whole bunch, damn it. I faced it in Nam and I faced it in the brig. I reckon I'm a regular hoodoo from facing it. I face it every day in this goddamn cold country. I ask myself what I'm doin' hanging on here and when I'm goin' to have me the good blessings to go home. Then I face it for sure."

It had been this way of talking that had touched Lorne. He had never loved an American before, never even liked one, but now his mind was held and his body ran with longing. He had always remembered with a queasiness close to fear, his only trip to the United States. He remembered the people crowding ahead in lines, the hard looks, the dangerous incomprehension of rednecks when he said that he was

Canadian. ("Some kind of Yankee, 're you?") And he remembered the walls that shut around each person. He felt then, at eighteen, riding a motorcycle through small American towns, like some unregarded creature trapped on a pool table, cowering from the death-threat in each volcanic carom. Nothing he had experienced, absolutely nothing, his degree from Western, his decade working in Toronto, his three years in publishing in the real London, no, nothing, had made him ready to fall in love with an American. More oddly yet, he also knew, tasting deliciously the outrageous irony, Tommy Joe was an American so vulgar, so nearly illiterate, so flint-like in his dealings with others, that Lorne sometimes felt vertiginously afraid. But he fell in love with the voice. He had fallen in love with the self-assurance, the mocking edge, the quick, harsh stories that grabbed the craziness of things.

Cruising the bar in Niagara-on-the-Lake, Tommy Joe had been telling stories. His voice, like a knife's blade flashing in the uncertain light, hardly slowed down for more than two hours. Guys came and left after hearing him hold forth, but Lorne sat transfixed. The Yank, six or seven years younger than himself, with long, dark hair and headband, excited him. He felt warmth heating upwards, but also a racking tension like cresting a giddying hump on a roller-coaster just before the downrush. More drawn than intimidated, he sat there sipping a watery Budweiser and listening to the first American he had ever loved. In his nasal accent, the Texan spun out yarns in knotted links. His voice wrapped itself like gritty honey around each flat, long syllable.

"I don't much care if there has been a pardon for deserters, I'm never goin' home. That whole country down there is crazy about killing. I'll just stay here in this neighbourly old snowfield and make my way. When I lived down there, they sent me to Nam, pounded my ass in the Camp Pendleton brig, and just generally I didn't never get to have no kind of fun."

Someone had said that he certainly could tell stories well. "I'm a sweet-talker, for sure. I reckon that back home we're all mostly sweet-talkers. It's something you just learn how to do, like shootin' rabbits maybe or jackin' off." A drag queen in plum-tone blush guffawed appreciatively.

Then the American had dropped some change, and Lorne leapt down from the bar stool and picked it up for him. Kneeling by the American's feet, gathering the scattered coins, Lorne noticed that he was wearing incised leather boots, the pattern of two crossed whips lashing rigidly upwards from arch to calf beneath a hard black polish. The sweet-talker smiled and patted Lorne on the shoulder.

"You're a right sweet little Canuck," he said. "My ol' pappy used to say, 'If a man'll pick up your gear for you, then he'll sure carry your tackle too'. I reckon you'd like to carry my tackle for a spell."

Lorne had blushed hard. A couple of the other guys in the bar snickered, but Lorne felt ambiguously pleased. He liked the confidence with which the American spoke, the masterful flow of the stories in which the fantastic and the anecdotal wove together. He liked the slow cadences, the twang and grit, and the impression of distance, of having come from over the horizon. He had met Americans before, many times, in London or Toronto, but this was the first one who made him glow. This was the first one he ever heard say, "I'm just a lonesome whippoorwill," and then laugh as if he were displaying a secret plumage. He was also "just a piece of driftwood on the sea." Lorne hadn't been certain what "tackle" meant, but he was willing to find out. He would carry it all right.

They had driven up the Queen E towards Toronto in the early morning, passing a few trucks and the occasional car. Tommy Joe sprawled in the passenger's seat, telling Lorne about the U.S. Marines. And Viet Nam. Oh, man, that had been pure hell. More miserable than having warts, or pus-running cankers, on your prick. Lorne tried to visualize the jungles, the elephant grass, the stench of rotting flesh. Huge bursts of napalm exploded before the mind's eye and small, brown people, their skin hanging in burned strips, grimacing but silent, stumbled from what had been a village. Tommy Joe swung his M-16 back and forth, herding the maimed peasants, or he carried a grenade launcher as he approached the village, his mouth twisted tightly in an anticipatory smile. He walked point on a recon patrol, his eyes flitting ahead and sideways, always alert for punji sticks. He saw a leg tangled in a tree, no body, and fired until it hitched sideways and fell. He watched the earth erupt in a black cloud, streaked momentarily by deep red flashes, and a friend lay sprawled on the trail, his insides, silver and blue, pouring out in the sunglare. He shot a Cong sapper through the left eye and watched the brains stream down his cheek. Then he cut off the man's ears, tucking them swiftly into an inside pocket to trade later, back at Cam Ranh, for hash. Lorne sensed adventure, barely comprehensible as yet, surge and writhe like a cable loose in a deep current. When they reached Toronto, he took Tommy Joe to his apartment without even asking. It had seemed happily inevitable.

They woke up in the late afternoon, summer light stabbing through the drapes in thousands of tiny needles. Lorne turned on the radio, permanently set for CBC FM, hoping for light classical music, but Tommy Joe scanned the dial back and forwards looking for country and western. He boogied rhythmically in a tight circle, humming, almost inaudibly, "you're just tryin' to find the best deal in town." Turning the volume up, he yelled excitedly, "Hank Williams!" In amazement, for the first time in his life, Lorne listened to the drawn-out vibrato, husky but mellifluous, gliding robustly through an athletic portamento. Scoot it on over, tote it on over, sneak it on over, the big dog, the fat dog, the new dog's movin' in. Tommy Joe gave him a hug, as if his enthusiasm couldn't be bounded.

"Boy, we're fixin' to be a team. We're goin' to plain flabbergast the wooden Indians in this hick town. We're goin' to find us a brand-new recipe."

They danced a few steps together, Tommy Joe leading. Lorne pressed his right hand against the American's back, stroking gently through the flannel plaid, feeling the cord-like muscles, the raised blades of the shoulders. He felt like a kid, new things bursting in the air around him like Catherine wheels, wild but unsteady. He had never desired anyone, man or woman, quite this way, fierce, happy, himself a whippoorwill, but neither lonesome nor (yet) skimming the clouds. The tackle he had agreed to carry was turning out to be surprisingly various.

The first two convenience stores they robbed were in North York. Lorne felt freezing drops of sweat dribble down from his armpits. His thigh muscles quivered uncontrollably. Tommy Joe would position him near the entrance so that he could cover other customers or shout if anyone came in sight. He chose the stores with care. They were always deserted, only a single terrified clerk behind the counter, or at most a couple of teenagers pissing with fear in the corner. He carried a Remington shotgun that he had sawn off himself and gave Lorne his own Colt .22 to wave and point with. Neither one of them ever loaded ammunition. Start shooting folks, Tommy Joe had said, and the coppers would run you down, just like a couple of raggedy ass 'possums, but just beat them up, neat like, paying attention to what you do, and the police wouldn't be feeling much sweat.

"Pistols scare the livin' shit out of folks." Tommy Joe shook his head like a man with water in his ear, smiling. "I don't rightly know why. Seems like a shotgun would make more of a mess, but somehow it just don't seem so righteous."

They got away easily. Tommy Joe always studied the hit carefully, and the funny plates worked. He knew the probable customer patterns, the streets leading away, and the nearest expressway entrances. Tommy Joe in command, they made an efficient team. But what good are convenience stores, Lorne had wondered. It didn't seem that a hundred dollars or less, the occasional lottery ticket with a small pay-off, made any sense. Why take such big risks, he nagged, for small dollars?

"It's good for the soul, I reckon. Just take it as dry runs for the big one." Tommy Joe had said this philosophically, like a man estimating which crow would fly first from a powerline. "Just remember, I don't take nobody's advice. I'm feelin' mostly blue, but flyin' my own course. Just you love me half as much as I love you."

Lorne listened in amazement to learn that he was in training for a major bank robbery. A bank, Tommy Joe thought, a bank in Vancouver, or a credit union, if he could spot the right one and choose his own time. He had slipped over the border in 1967, travelling up from San Diego one day before his travel orders that would have sent him back to Saigon, and he had lived in Vancouver for months before heading east. He knew it, he said, at least as well as he knew Santa Fe.

"I liked them mountains. They always did remind me of when you drive north from Albuquerque. Though I reckon they're different enough. Them San Juan Mountains. A man could lose himself both places."

Slowly, Lorne had discovered the tackle he had agreed to carry. "The future looks so dark and cold," Tommy Joe would sing, laughing. Cheer up, he told Lorne, they were a team now. A sweet team. They could knock over every raggedy convenience store between Toronto and Vancouver and the police would never get even a sniff. What a great trip, Tommy Joe would rhapsodize, a great trip and just themselves, two lonesome whippoorwills, to enjoy it. Lorne had his new Mustang serviced and tried to imagine how he might consider himself someday, if they did pull things off, with retrospective pride.

Tommy Joe snorted. His hilarity made Lorne feel warm and good. "Did you see that sucker?" They were cutting back down to the TransCanada through Tuxford, leisurely, like two sportsmen on vacation. The Mustang's Ontario plates were fully in view. If anyone looked, they had fishing tackle conspicuously displayed on top of the sleeping bags in the back seat. "His eyes just opened up like two hot nookies. He didn't believe that pistol even when he saw it." Lorne stretched out in the passenger's seat. Ronnie Milsap was singing, "It was almost like a song." Tommy Joe wouldn't stand for the CBC except for the newscasts.

"They're all so easy, Lorne ol' buddy, they're all easy as young gals. I guess I love it here just because folks are so polite. They say 'please' and 'thank you' and then just stand still and smile when you poke some righteous weapon in their face. I don't reckon I've ever seen so many nice-mannered scaredy-cats in one place in all my life. President Ford can just keep his pardons. I'm staying here to have me a good time. Then I reckon I might just build me a little cottage in the valley and give up the honky-tonk life."

Lorne understood that he loved Tommy Joe's competence and self-confidence. "I wish I could be as sure of myself as you are of yourself, T Joe," he would say. Then the hard edge, the quick look like a pistol's muzzle, would strike him. "You're just a little Canuck. You can't never be too sure of yourself." And he realized that he loved the edge, swift and harsh, as well. He remembered the fear he had felt when he travelled, the one and only time, to the United States. Everywhere people had flashed knives from their eyes.

He had made a motorcycle trip when he was eighteen. He and his best friend, Philip, had ridden down to Kentucky at a time when Philip, who had a favourite uncle in Lexington, was thinking about going to university there. They let a younger kid, whom they always called dismissively the supernumerary, ride his bike with them. They rode into Kentucky, crossing the iron bridge at Madison, in a flurry of three English bikes. (At eighteen, Lorne would reflect, happiness, bliss even, comes easily, in flurries.) When the magneto blinked out on Philip's bike, they stopped in a small town to fix it. The local men hung around the garage where they were working, watching them taking the magneto down, making comments. It hit like shock in a horror show to grasp suddenly from their desultory talk that they didn't believe that Philip's bike, a 500 cc Triumph Speed Twin, was a real motorcycle. He had never quite figured out what exactly they thought it was. Perhaps they thought it was some kind of Whizzer, or more likely they merely declined to acknowledge it. The local men stood in a partial circle around the three of them as they crouched over the magneto, an unfriendly chorus, making derisive observations. When the comments began to pick up momentum, turning to jeers, coalescing like threads of dirty smoke, Lorne had felt his guts knot, fear spreading thickly upwards. Both Philip and the supernumerary seemed oblivious of the hostile atmosphere, but later they had agreed that the situation had been dangerous. No one should take a Kentucky redneck, showing his hatred for something he didn't understand, too confidently. Well, Philip grimaced, you wouldn't want to laugh at one, would you?

After he and Philip had roared, fleeing really, out of the town, the supernumerary, younger and more idiotic than even they were, had stayed around to show off, revving his motor and then slipping the clutch. Looking back over his shoulder when the road had curved slightly, Lorne saw the kid's headlights leap into the air while dozens of local men in overalls watched. He knew instantly that the supernumerary was showing off, rising up on the rear wheel, hurtling bird-like out of town. Later they explained to him that, if he ever acted so stupidly again, they wouldn't let him ride with them. The rednecks, hating them enough, might have sent a posse on their track. (Years later, seeing *Easy Rider* for the first time, Lorne had sat through the final scene, gnawed by terror, remembering that moment.) Once, early in their relationship, Lorne had told Tommy Joe this story.

And Tommy Joe had laughed. "T Joe, really, it was like a whole different world. I mean they simply didn't know what motorcycles were. They said they knew what Harley-Davidson bikes were, but they couldn't make the connection. They couldn't see that our English bikes belonged to the same category. No connections at all. They even found some local expert who came over to the garage and studied our bikes. He looked right at my AJS and said, like he had been handing down a judgement from a pulpit, 'That ain't no motorbike'." Tommy Joe just laughed. He might never have heard anything so funny. His sympathies were all with the rednecks.

"Lorne, sweet little buddy, they were just good ol' boys who didn't appreciate having Yankees, or whatsoever, coming into their town and sashaying about. You come into a town with something nobody's never seen, and it's like puttin' on the dog. Just maybe you youngsters needed to be taken down a peg or two. So they was lettin' you know they didn't cotton to your ways."

Lorne thought that Tommy Joe had missed the point about the motorcycle story, but perhaps there were two points. Strangers crossing boundaries might be anyone or represent anything. He had never asked himself what those Kentucky rednecks might have thought that he and the other two intended. What inferences would they have drawn? What does anyone know about a stranger's inwardness? They went into stores in small towns where no one had ever seen them before, always smiling and polite, and then Tommy Joe would swing the sawed-off .12-gauge out from under his windbreaker, and abruptly the person in the store would have to look death in its smirking mouth. It would all be over in less than a minute and they would be gone. Tommy Joe never hesitated, reversing the shotgun and bringing the butt down sharply, to strike the clerk, girl or boy, across the side of the neck or over the bridge of the nose. It never required more than a single blow. That was something else that he had learned in the U.S. Marines.

What memories did they leave behind? What had the boy in the Mohawk station in Regina remembered about them when he picked himself up? What had they represented to him when they drove up, nameless out of the dark, and parked the car just beyond the arc of light around the pumps? Strangers looking for a map? or a place to piss? Had they looked even a little like death? Strangers were always, had to be, Lorne thought, blankly opaque. Those rednecks had known instinctively that aliens, perhaps dangerous ones, had come to town. In their own minds, closed and dim but rational, they had been dealing with pure strangeness, with many-faced danger. It is always there, Lorne now knew, behind a stranger's smile.

Tommy Joe and Lorne were driving south in the early morning sun, the level Saskatchewan fields stretching languidly towards infinity. Toronto had become, in dream-like dissolution, a tiny place. The long slanting rays slashed across Tommy Joe onto Lorne's lap. He glanced sideways searchingly. Tommy Joe's profile was still dark, though the brilliance of the sun on the other side gave his nose and chin a back-lit outline, like an aura. Lorne imagined the ten or twenty years in Kingston, his final pay-off, that he would receive if he wasn't extremely lucky. He had bought into all this without thinking. And all because he had fallen in love, because he could not turn away from the other man's determination never to be intimidated, never to slow down. "When the Lord made me, he made a ramblin' man," Tommy Joe would sing, and Lorne would think that, yes, he was like a bird, perhaps more hawk than whippoorwill, or a piece of driftwood, or the wind itself.

He had overborne the older man, teaching and bullying at once, and Lorne loved him for it. Not to be intimidated, never to be put down, to take no one's advice: this was the other face of the competence and verbal grace he had loved when they first met in Niagara-on-the-Lake. The crow's-nose, at once dark in its shadow and golden in the sunlight, seemed to point straight ahead toward all the world's flush horizons.

"When tears come down like fallin' rain." Tommy Joe was singing under his breath. "Don't never stay too long in one place, Lorne ol' buddy, don't never hit more than a couple of places, don't never make patterns. And don't never kill nobody. Most of all, I reckon, don't *never* push your luck." He pronounced "never" with the accent on the first syllable, drawing it

The crow's-nose, at once dark in its shadow and golden in the sunlight, seemed to point straight ahead toward all the world's flush horizons.

"When tears come down like fallin' rain." Tommy Joe was singing under his breath. "Don't never stay too long in one place, Lorne ol' buddy, don't never hit more than a couple of places, don't never make patterns. And don't never kill nobody. Most of all, I reckon, don't *never* push your luck." He pronounced "never" with the accent on the first syllable, drawing it out high and twisting.

Tommy Joe reached over and squeezed Lorne's upper arm. Lorne could feel the fingertips push into his muscle, through to the bone. Tommy Joe often showed his affection this way: it would hurt, but pleasure would flow from the arm into Lorne's body. The American's spare, springsteel body shed warmth, like a hot-running racing motor, when he touched or caressed. Lorne looked over at him. His neck thrust from the blue-and-black plaid shirt's open collar. His long black hair, held against his skull by a black headband, his face, all dark surfaces and chiselled edges, concentrated upon the road. "On to Calgary, sweet buddy o' mine. This time next week Vancouver'll spread her legs for us." He pinched Lorne once again, his good spirits bursting. "The future don't look so dark an' cold no more."

Now, having hit and fled Calgary safely, in the late afternoon of the next day they were slowly heading back along the East Coulee road to Drumheller. Between his thighs, Tommy Joe balanced a small cactus he had dug from the ground at Rosedale. Laughing together like small boys, they had walked over the swinging bridge that miners had once used to the smouldering heaps of slag, climbing and throwing rocks. Tommy Joe had made the bridge swing in frightening arcs so that Lorne was forced to cling unsteadily to the suspension cables, laughing and yelling. Tommy Joe waved his hand out the car window towards the stratiform bluffs that overhung the north bank of the Red Deer river.

"Never would have thought to find me a cactus in Canada. Never would have thought to find something called a hoodoo neither. Except for them knobby hoodoos, lookin' just like a Mormon grandaddy's cock, it's just so like the country north of Pecos that I'd half expect to find me a rattler in my boots."

Lorne curved his arm along the back of the driver's seat. He tried to imagine the two of them knocking over a Vancouver bank. Himself standing at the entrance, wearing a balaclava or perhaps the blonde wig that Tommy Joe had bought in Thunder Bay, he points his .22 fiercely and makes the customers lie face down on the floor while Tommy Joe, leaping the counter, sweeps up the cash in the tellers' drawers or forces his way into the vault. He doesn't want to believe in the reality of the big heist, but he knows that he will go through with it if Tommy Joe makes the move. He has liked driving from one province to another, the practice runs, hitting randomly one town or another, but most of all he likes being with Tommy Joe. He has wanted to see only aimlessness beneath a fiction of practising for the big hit, but now Tommy Joe, aiming purposefully, is stalking in narrowing circles. It all seems oppressively surreal. In his fantasies he towers over the cowing customers and bank employees.

"Sweet buddy, we're going to make ourselves some dollars." Tommy Joe is bubbling. "I'm feelin' real lucky, like we can't miss if we try. I'm the real hoodoo here, riding down in black on this cattlemen's town, busting up Wells Fargo afore they know what kind of black wind has done blown through. We're goin' to tear this rinky-dink town right open. We're goin' to hit us a bank today. Can't you just see it, Lorne, honey?"

Lorne feels the queasiness begin. They can't. He gabbles. They just can't. "T Joe, come on, be reasonable." They haven't done the preparations. And it will be a pattern, won't it? Too close to Calgary. And what about the escape roads? They haven't driven over them yet. Anyway there can't be more than two or three ways out of this town. But Tommy Joe's face hardens. He smiles blackly, humming, not singing. His lips purse tightly. He might be poising to spit.

"I've got my eye on the Bank of Commerce. It looks right easy, ol' buddy. And I seen that newsstand and drugstore on the corner downtown. I just bet we can knock them all off real quick like and then head back down the road to Calgary. I reckon we're on a roll. We've found that brand-new recipe. I'm the true hoodoo, sweet buddy, wearin' black like the mountains or the wind in the high plains. Just don't you punk out on me, ol' buddy."

Lorne strokes the side of Tommy Joe's face. Grazing downwards affectionately, his hand brushes sharply against the cactus. He jerks it back, gasping roughly, breaking continuously into urgent expostulation. "No, T Joe. No." They should just travel on to Edmonton. They don't want to miss that big one in Vancouver. They shouldn't take chances now. They should find that bank in Vancouver that he has been telling him about, case it like they should, and knock it over. All clean and proper, like Tommy Joe has always told him things should be. When they get back to Toronto, he can sell some stocks and buy them a Camaro, or maybe a Firebird.

Tommy Joe bends across towards Lorne and gives him a quick little kiss on his left cheek. A condescending kiss that doesn't mean anything romantic, and Lorne understands that. "You're a right sweet li'l scaredy-cat, Lorne boy." Tommy Joe chuckles. He steps down slightly on the accelerator and the Mustang leaps forward purposively along the river road. "I'll make you a deal, boy. You just sign over that Firebird to me once we're back in Toronto again. You do that an' maybe I'll drive us up that hill and on to Edmonton." A graveyard slides into view on their left. Then they reach the intersection and there are lights and cars. Grain elevators bulk up on the right. "You do that, boy, an' maybe we'll give them banks and newsstands a miss. You gotta understand, Lorne boy, that a lonesome whippoorwill like myself don't rightly need to share things. I reckon it would be a mistake to share that Firebird."

They have raced back into Drumheller almost before Lorne has realized it. He watches Tommy Joe follow the railway tracks to the centre of town. As they turn off towards the newsstand, he feels himself grow tight and small. Once again his sweat trickles coldly. "Sure, T Joe, sure, you can have the Firebird. You can have whatever I have. Let's keep going back across the river." Tommy Joe laughs like a big crow, like something wild, as he drives fast through downtown Drumheller towards the river. Lorne leans his head over and presses his lips against Tommy Joe's shoulder. Twisting in the seat, he works his right hand through the open collar and holds it against the breast. He moves his hand in a pressing, circular motion inside the plaid shirt. Softly he strokes Tommy Joe's pectorals. The nipples, in their tiny nests of hair, are hard and stiff. He can feel the heart's thudding.

Lorne's voice trembles with relief. "Oh, god, T Joe, I do love you so."

The Queensland Mundungus

The Mundungus was first remarked upon by Captain James Cook's shipboard naturalist, Joseph Banks. Banks described it as a large green bird, common to northern Australia's monsoonal coast lands and some of the islands of the Barrier Reef, characterized by its distinctive stench. The early explorers and settlers in the Capricornia region of Queensland claimed that the Mundungus was flightless and inhabited the dense eucalyptus forests of the coast. Many explorers reported seeing its bright-green feathers flashing through the bush. Although they often tried to track it, following its sharp, feculent pong, the Mundungus always evaded capture. It proved to be a wary, elusive creature that allowed no one closer than its gut-churning effluvium.

In the 1820s, members of the Royal Society in London successfully identified the Mundungus with the Munchausen Giant Green Crane. It was held that it normally flew too high to be seen. The many reports of having glimpsed it flee through the bush were ascribed to imperfect sightings of the Cassowary. Nonetheless, settlers in the ever more populated northern regions of Queensland continued to report having caught glimpses of the Mundungus, scuttling swiftly through the bush, leaving behind only the nose-piercing stench of corpse rot and fresh feces. Since the Mundungus was never actually seen, but only smelt, many diverse accounts of its appearance burgeoned and spread. It was held to be long and slimy, but also squat and putrescent. Later reports claimed that it was dark and lustreless. Those same accounts also suggested that it might be mottled as if spattered with undigested chyme. It was said to host repulsive vermin that crawled through its feathers and swam in its eyes. Grubs, maggots, and pinkly blood-swollen worms slithered in and out of its anus and beak. Many settlers argued that it must be too small to be seen, and that it produced its abundant and nauseous stench in order to drive away predators. In the late nineteenth century one explorer captured a Mundungus, but, it is said, he became so nauseated that, violently vomiting the entire contents of his stomach through both his nose and mouth, he let it escape. Since that time no one has actually seen a Mundungus, but the inhabitants of Queensland speak of it with horrified affection as a characteristic bush-dweller.

Paracursions

> ...perhaps surprised to find how bitterly cold it seems. They would surely die of exposure, were the experience not merely a dream. Near them is a rectangular opening through which they can vaguely see the real world.
>
> —*Call of Cthulhu*

The rain drizzled down outside the porch. It was so cold you might as well have been inside, feeling the damp and mould. And there was this little German Shepherd bitch that kept barking like mad, scratching at the door to the front of the house, knowing something big was going on. I could smell old shoes, boots, wraps, dank paper, staleness in everything. Right where we stood there was a bookcase filled with decaying paper, *Reader's Digest* condensed versions, piles of old magazines, *Sports Illustrated* and what-have-you, textbooks that looked like Old Time religion, paper mould, and rot. And Eric was picking through the piles of games, boxes tied with string, boxes of counters and markers, noisy titles announcing battles to be refought (let the losing side win for a change, I thought), fantasies to be lived through. There were all kinds of mind-traps like that, for kids with intelligence but too little life. That's what it amounts to.

A game is like many trajectories shooting out from a central knot. Each one leads through little knots and back to the central knot again. Or a game is like a cool slab. You can hold it against yourself. Touch it when you feel empty. It stretches away from you and it holds you close. You can follow it as it recedes, if you know how, or you can rest inside it. A game stretches away from you, so many definite lines unfolding towards infinity, and it swallows you at the same time. If you understand it, there is nothing to be afraid of. But you have to understand it. I used to wonder how far it is to a star, to the farthest star even. A game is like that, only you can follow along the lines it throws out until you reach the star. When you understand a game, when you have played it through, it is just like getting to a star. You can follow the trajectories, though lots of players lose their direction. Some games (all of the good ones, really) are tough to play: there are surprises, things don't turn out the way you suppose they will. There are always subordinate trajectories, little knots, knots within knots, intersections, alternatives, choices, chances, probabilities, improbabilities, things you can't predict, not every time anyway. And there is always luck, even when you follow the main lines. Games have adventures in them, even for the skilled player, that's why they are like travelling to the stars. When you play with skill you are a kind of astronaut, flying in a space that the game creates. But you learn to control the surprises. There never are any that are beyond reason.

We spent hours together in arcades. He would play any game there. *Quake* wasn't any better than *Tetris*, really. The arcade was like another world and he just belonged to it, like a citizen, kind of. He would talk funny about games, too. His face would be laughing, like he had just conquered the world or something. Then he would start talking about how games were their own space, how their rules generated the space in which they played. Things that sounded kind of crazy, like that. He would carry on that way no matter how many guys would be staring at him. Most of the time he didn't even seem to hear guys make fun of him.

A game doesn't come at you angry, doesn't try to force things, doesn't contort its face, doesn't fill with howling. You can master a game. I mean, it isn't easy but you can master that kind of skill, become an astronaut in gamespace. Outside games nothing is under control. People hate you and you don't know why. You can maybe love someone, but she will think you're a wimp, or gross for some reason you don't know, can't learn. No one explains. Teachers are sarcastic and you can't see why. They act like you should know. But how can you know anything without explanations, without the documentation? Even mothers are mean sometimes. Inside games there is a cool clarity: the unfolded space that the rules project.

He grew very fast that last summer. He was well over six feet when he died. Before he had to change schools in his final year he had always enjoyed life. His friends used to come over to the house on Friday afternoons to play games. Board games mostly, games like *Risk* and *Iron Dragon* if I remember rightly. He didn't do all that well in school but he liked it. He liked English quite a bit and sometimes he said that he would like to be a sports writer. He subscribed to all kinds of sports magazines. He liked to read about baseball players especially. I remember he could rattle off scores and statistics like an almanac, or more like a set of them. He didn't have many girl friends, but I know that he liked a couple of girls quite a bit. That was one of the sad things when we moved across town because he had to go to a new school and he lost contact with his friends. There was one girl in particular that he liked and I do wish he had tried to keep friends with her. And he didn't make new friends easily. The school he had to go to was a lot larger and he was in his final year and everyone already had friends, or groups that they belonged to. It was funny, he was such a handsome boy, so large and tall, and he wasn't dumb even though he didn't get very good marks, and he was always open and kind but hardly anyone ever seemed to like him much. I know that hurt him a lot, too. But he didn't seem to know what to do about it. He would come home and read those sports magazines and play games by himself. He was happiest when some other boys came over and they could play together. He could play games for hours on end.

Games are just like any other structure, to be played, solved, decoded, transcribed. It's just that games are precise. That's why kids, and adults who want to maximize neoteny, like them so much. They can play them and have all the fun of thinking but none of the loose threads and scruffy edges. Mrs. Jensen was there pointing out games as they were unpiled. She seemed to know them all, like she had played them herself. When they came out of the pile they looked more pathetic than anything else, exposed, vulnerable to hard eyes. Games look inert and dumb when there is no one to play them: human fantasies reduced to the coolness of rules. And they certainly looked unplayed there on that cold porch, worn and battered, like the old clothes and the books in the case. No more players and no more readers in that house. I watched her unpile those games, opening them up for Eric, talking about them as if she understood them herself. I thought that it was as if a priest's arcana were being unpacked and fondled by laymen. But Eric knew what the games were, sure enough, how they were played, and who would like to play them. He recognized them all right, like fantasized images, worn by the mind's gaze, in some old *Penthouse*. He must have played all those games, those very ones, all those Fridays when he didn't come home until long after dinner. And that damn bitch barking behind the door. Mrs. Jensen touched him then, as if she hadn't touched anyone for a long time, shy, soft along his shoulder. She said she could remember him and Earnie playing one of them. One of those Fridays, and yes they had played the game, yes they had had fun. And the dog was going mad behind the door and the rain was flooding down, so many tears I thought, while outside the porch the dusk was settling in thick, wet, September gloom. She would have kissed him, too, mother-like, if I hadn't been there.

In a game the future is predictable. I don't mean entirely, down to every detail, though that can happen in some games, like chess. But the future is within the game from the beginning and you can see its shape, the kind of space it will fill. The future is within the boundaries of the game because the rules project, and limit, what can happen. If you master the rules then you can see what will happen, the gamespace that will be possible, within a reasonable margin of error. You can learn the rules that make the game and then, from inside that central core, you can begin to bring the future out from where it is hidden. Learning the rules is like having reality within your power, like being able to construct things the way you would like them to be. A game gives you something you never have outside, if you just master its rules: control, freedom, power, and an open field for your intelligence to play. It doesn't mock you, it is never sarcastic, and it can be learned better if you get it wrong the first time. That's why it is like a cool slab. The rules are rational and clear and the lines of play that they make possible can be followed, to anywhere, to really strange space, to black starbursts. The rules create space that you can live in without feeling like a mistake, like a defender trying to stop a touchdown run, like everything has been a mistake. Inside a game things make sense.

Earnie was kind of weird, I guess. He liked to play games better than anything. And he played them better than anyone else could. He took them seriously and really tried to understand them. I liked role-playing games best. Fantasy games, really, but where you create your own character and play him through quests and adventures. I could play *Advanced Dungeons & Dragons* all night. I was beginning to like war games and strategy games, too. But Earnie would play any game. He didn't seem to have real favourites, except that on one day he would want to play one game most and on another day it would be another game. He liked role-playing games best, I suppose, maybe especially *The Call of Cthulhu* because it's so complex, but *D & D*, too, and he could always be the Keeper or the Dungeon Master since he always knew all the rules, or how to find them. So he would be our God when we played *D & D* and make sure that everything went ahead, within the rules, no disputes. We went over to his house, before he moved I mean, on Friday afternoons and played, but sometimes he tried to get us to play baseball or hockey games and then I would leave early and head for home. I never knew anyone who could play so many games.

After we moved I tried to persuade him to keep up with his old friends, but he seemed content to let things slip. I knew that he missed them quite a lot, and especially that girl he liked, but it didn't actually make him despondent. No, I don't think that was it. I suggested more than once, Why not call her up, Alice or whatever her name is, and take her to a movie. But he always just clammed shut. He never did call her, so far as I know. He seemed to prefer to mope around. He was always playing one of his games. Sometimes he read those sports magazines, but mostly he played those games. When he didn't have friends over, he would lie on the floor in his room or the living room and spread out one of those games and play it for hours on end, just as quiet and silent as a tomb. For sure, I got after him more than once. I thought his work at school was falling off, but in any case I didn't much like the idea of any son of mine just lolling around, moping and never much speaking to anyone, particularly his mother. I didn't mind the games, really, but I did mind him not doing anything else. He had a job packing at a supermarket, and in the summer he had worked downtown at one of the theatres taking tickets, but he just didn't have much ambition. So I kept at him a bit, I suppose, just to get him to take his work at school seriously. And I would remind him that he wanted to be a sports writer and that he should do well in English and pay attention to his assignments. And I told him to study hard at math so that maybe he could do something with computers after he graduated. He seemed to be in love with that Compaq we bought. There were all kinds of games he could play on it, mostly with himself, and he even taught himself to program it for games that he invented. And so it made sense that he might learn to be a computer something or other. But it just didn't seem to matter much to him after we moved.

I watched this strange woman bequeath her son's games to my son. I had never met her before, never even heard her son's name, but there I was, surrounded by damp and cold drizzle, in the midst, dead-centre, of a ritual. Never heard of Earnie before, but kids are usually mum about their friends. Never imagined that I would stand there helping to stretch his memory a bit. Then she called yesterday morning, her voice breaking, telling me about her son, how much he had liked playing games with Eric, how much fun they all had when they got together. No way to tell her how sad it made me feel. That I felt like there was, or ought to be, a bond between us, parents I suppose. That I would see behind the masks we would have to wear, disliking myself for doing so. Earnie would have wanted Eric to have the games. Eric's had been the only name in the address book she found and that was why she called. She was just tracking down some connection that might be real when nothing else seemed so. Earnie would have wanted Eric to have his games. I knew that all she meant was that she wanted it to be that way. And then her voice breaking again there on that stinking porch, the bitch barking behind the door, barely holding it together under all the stress. I thought, well, she is a brave woman, but she is making a statement of grief. It's an old ritual, as old as the species perhaps, to scatter the memory of someone in pieces through the world, like Echo in painful fragments. And then Eric began to pick up the games. I reached down and grabbed a few myself. We made a rush through the rain to the car. A quick good-bye. I don't suppose that I'll see her again. The games, her son's legacy, will be played a few times, passed around, and then be lost, forgotten. Her ritual of fragments will have been just a stalling tactic, a knee-blocked delay, not worth much except to her. It struck me that the dog must have sniffed Earnie on the boxes and known something was going on. Perhaps she thought the boy was back, was out there on the porch with us. All the brutal on-goingness of things, the rain seeming like tears, in the sky, in the heart, in things. I don't suppose I ever felt someone else's sorrow so strongly as then. Nothing so corrosive as this bloody, dark place, the rain, the grief. So I shouted that I would run ahead and open the car door. Many thanks, Mrs. Jensen, so long, goodbye. I couldn't bear it longer. All the sad, unalterable shittiness.

※

I used to get after him about his homework. Well, I was his mother and that's what mothers are supposed to do. He just couldn't get himself interested. It didn't do any good to yell at him either. I used to threaten him, like what would happen to him if he didn't know anything, or couldn't get a job. I was afraid he would grow up ignorant. He'd just shrug and go off to his room to play some game or other, or to mope. But I never thought that it would end the way it did. I really thought he would straighten out, get a job, find a girl, do things like everyone else. I wish I had told him how much I loved him and that I did have faith in him. I'm sure that he could have become a sports writer or maybe an announcer on TV. I wish I had told him how much I needed him. Now he's dead. And I don't understand why. I'll never understand why. But he's dead now.

※

If you take a coin and toss it up and cry heads or tails, that is a game. It is just as much a game as playing chess or spending days and days playing *Advanced Dungeons & Dragons*. I never thought that a game was any more a game because it was long or because it was complex. A game can be as simple as tossing a coin or throwing a ball back and forth or drawing a card from a pack. All you need is one rule to project the lines of play. Then it will be a game, like hanging from a branch to see how long you can hold on rather than just hanging for the fun of it. You can watch little kids on a playground, running, jumping, or maybe twirling around, and you can see that they are doing it for the pure play of it. But it is easy to tell when this fun turns into a game because the play grows tighter, purposeful, more rational as a rule is introduced. I always liked strategy games like *World in Flames* because the rules are elegant and it is wonderful to see them unfold. But it isn't a better game because it is complex and ends up taking so long to play. A single rule can create a space all of its own. It splits off its own space from all other space, from the universe itself. You have to accept the rules, to believe in them, otherwise a game won't make sense. If you don't believe in the rules, a game will be just a silly way to do something you could do better some other way, like putting a ball in a hole or over a fence, or adding up some numbers to make a certain sum. When you play a game correctly, really believing in the rules, then there is a relationship, like love, between yourself and the rules. That's what lets you split the gamespace off from the rest of the universe. A game has its own time, too. Outside, people work, worry about school or about their girlfriends, but inside the time flows only as fast as the rules allow. The rules create the game's time just like its space.

He was really good at video games. There was that time a bunch of us stopped off at the Golden World after school and we were playing *Quake*, but Earnie went over to play *Tetris* and left us all yelling and laughing. I looked over where he was once and there he was moving the joystick like he was flying a plane. I mean, he was that intense. His face was really happy and I knew then, just like it was written down, that he was there inside, I mean like inside. He was the only guy I knew who liked playing those stupid games that come with new computers, like *Minesweeper* or *Hearts*. He felt games as if they were real. But the funny thing was that he could feel that way about almost any game, even those boring baseball games. He even liked to play sports, which none of the other guys in our group really did, and he knew more about baseball and hockey than anybody. He could quote any kind of statistic for baseball. He liked talking about it and he could get kind of lost in those baseball games while they just bored the rest of us. When we went over to his house on Friday afternoons, if he wanted to play that kind of game, then most of us just left finally and went some place else, like down to the Golden World to hang around. But mostly he would play what the other guys wanted. I liked to play *Risk* at his place. He was the only kid who owned a copy of *White Death*, which was lots of fun for such an old game. Fantasy games, like *D & D*, take a long time to play and you need the place for it. Earnie's mother used to start worrying if we spent too long playing. She'd ask us about our mothers, if we weren't supposed to be home for dinner, things like that, so we didn't play fantasy games that much when we went to Earnie's. Sometimes we did, and that was the best.

I have played strategy games that lasted for years and fantasy games in which centuries flowed by. Even the time of chess, like its space, is different: the moves are like events, but the time that holds them together is what the imagination permits and the imagination must cling to the shape of the rules. You come back from a game like an astronaut crossing an event-horizon and the time outside, when you get back, is slow and heavy, unreal. I have seen guys play chess when they didn't understand it very well and the game has gone on for hours and been traversed by difficult positions, paradoxical possibilities, but the players didn't see this and wouldn't have known what to do about it if they had. That made it a long game on the outside but inside it was a short game because nothing much happened, nothing that was interesting, and the events were all hasty and crowded, like a badly written story. Games like that aren't better just because they are long on the outside and seem complicated. A game can be quick and fast on the outside but long and knotted, like a labyrinth, on the inside. A game that you understand borrows nothing from outside. It is a universe all in itself.

After we got into the car and all those boxes were loaded in the back, the rain drenching us and so cold I felt like wood, I asked Eric how his friend had died. The rain was whipping down against the windshield. He looked away, into the rain. I knew he wouldn't want to talk about it. He said, low and growling, that he didn't know. But I wasn't going to be put off like that. Bloody hell you don't, I shot back. How did he die? I kept at him. He was silent staring into the rain. I started talking about that damn dog. She had tried to bite me when we went out on the porch. I suppose she must have known something, that we were going to take the games away, take the boy's smell away, too. She actually got her teeth around my ankle until Mrs. Jensen chased her back into the house. It's funny how much animals can tell. Even a thick-skulled wombat knows when its existence is shutting down. I was taking an oblique approach to loosen Eric up, but I couldn't get him to talk. He just kept peering into the rain, like he expected someone to come running through it, and I got the car moving ahead into the traffic. Then, suddenly, no prompting at all, he said that Earnie had liked war games best of all. It didn't have anything to do with the question, just brought it out quick, what he had been thinking, not what I had wanted him to think about.

You can get inside the core rules, untie the knot, and make the possibilities happen. I like to feel the shape of the gamespace. It's like cutting the world off, just dumping it somewhere, and then creating another world alongside the first, the one that you dumped. You create an alternative world, but a new one each time, and you get caught up completely. The space of a game bends inwards and the time is closed. That's another knot. The second one is bigger and grows out of the first but it is the first that makes the second possible. The second knot surrounds the first. The inside of the game, when you play it, is closed off, tight, always ending, but tighter as it develops, always bending in upon itself. Then new interiors show up in the folds like hollow worlds. I hate it when a good game ends. No, that's not quite right. I like to see the game unfold as it should if everyone plays well, but I still hate to see it end. The best thing is to start up another and keep playing: let the rules build new chunks of gamespace that you haven't seen before, and then explore them, soaring like an astronaut along the different trajectories.

I thought how strange it was that boys, most of them never having worked a day yet, still in school, could sit around on a floor and refight World War One, or Napoleon's Peninsula Campaign, or Rommel's desert battles, *Rommel at Bay* or some such title. Unfinished human beings, not capable of finding their ways, of loving deeply, or of doing meaningful work or even study, yet second-guessing great generals. Confidently handling the complexities of warfare, battling once more through the uncertainties of Salamis, Waterloo, or El Alamein, and changing the course of our civilization, but never giving a glance towards the implications, slipping the consequences as if they were squibbles along the margins. What validity do all those counterfactual situations have if they aren't tested against the consequences? I tried to explain that to Eric once. He laughed and told me that I didn't understand how games are played. I didn't have a go at him then, but I would like to know, and I felt like making him answer then, what good these gaming kids would be if you put an actual texture on those historical situations? Wouldn't they be back to taws pretty quick? Take the texture away and they run laughing into labyrinths and emerge victorious, nearly as pure concept as the Minotaur's head they flaunt, neither bone nor flesh. Triumphant, but nothing like the men they will have to become.

The last time I heard from Earnie he called me one night about eleven. It must have been a couple of days before he did it. He wanted to design a character for *Advanced D & D* and I asked him why he wanted to play that again. It just isn't as interesting as some other fantasy games and he knew it so well that it couldn't have all that many surprises left. I wanted to talk about *The Call of Cthulhu*, which is a great game and a lot more sophisticated, really, but he was dead-set on *D & D*. That was kind of strange because there are lots of fantasy games and Earnie knew them all. He really loved role-playing but I don't think as much as he loved war games, not really. He was the only guy I ever knew who liked *World in Flames*. That's a game which isn't very playable, just interesting. He liked to talk about it, too. He liked to discuss all kinds of games but that evening he was only interested in *D & D*. He wanted to design a character and the crazy thing was that he only cared about how to get lots of XPs. He wanted to design a Cleric and I kept saying that a Fighter or a Magic-User would be more interesting and that anyway just surviving wasn't much fun. But he wanted a Cleric because with good spells and an advanced level of wisdom and the right kind of outfit a Cleric would have the best chance to survive on a quest. All he cared about was gaining experience points.

I kept at him. I wanted to know what that boy had died of, so I wouldn't let him off easily, just looking into the rain, not talking. I could hardly see, the way the rain had begun to pour down. Even the lights from other cars, and those from the shop windows, seemed to frizzle, as if they were flooded out. He said he didn't know, which I didn't believe for a moment, but then he said that there had been rumours at school though, because Earnie hadn't gone there anymore, no one knew anything for sure. I kept pressing him, asking if it had been a disease, had he died of cancer? His mother had looked so sad beneath her public smiles, and he must have been dead now eight or nine months, that I felt it had to have been something horrible. Probably it was cancer, I thought, something quick, pointless, and sorrowful. And Eric kept looking away, through the rain as if messages might be inscribed in the broken, refracted lights. Not that he would decode them if there had been.

There is nothing messy or angry inside a game. No one is yelling. And when you look into the future you can see what is going to happen, you can even make it happen, but if it doesn't, you can still see why things had to turn out the way they did. Sometimes I can see a game all folded inwards making its own space. I can see it from a distance and I fly towards it across all the emptiness outside. It hangs there, like a drop, shining, tight and closed, and I fly towards it, like an astronaut. I can travel around it even if it is very big and stretched out in time. Gamespaces are all solid, spheres, cubes, and cones, and they are all different. But you can understand them all, fly towards them and enter them, circle by circle, fold by fold, and eventually reach the centre where things are most compact, where the knot is tautest. There the rules are clearest and everything makes sense. If there is a God of the universe, I wonder why he couldn't have made things with a set of rules so you would know what it is you are playing and how to play. If only there had been rules to live by, a framework.

There were rumours. The boy's girlfriend, someone he used to take out anyway, knew but she wouldn't tell, not to Eric. For God's sake, I thought, all this sly dancing, putting distance between things and ourselves. I asked him point-blank if it had been something unexpected, like a brain cancer. I wouldn't let him off, but I don't know why it mattered so much. I think that I was just overwhelmed by the sadness, by the situation, the wrecked boxes, that damn bitch growling, the boy's mother putting on a brave face, the bloody rain, and then carrying off those games like a bequest, scattering the boy to the world. And Eric kept staring into the rain as if he read a message in the wet lights. How? I kept pressing him. How did he die? Then he gave in finally. Earnie had killed himself, that's what the rumours had whispered. How? I asked. But he didn't know, and I believed him. I should have told him right then that there were no messages in the lights, only an empty metonymy of winks.

He was so big and tall. When I opened the door to the rec room at first I thought that he was standing there fixing the pipe. Then I saw that his feet were in the air. I heard this awful noise coming from somewhere outside, like the end of the world, everyone alive screaming all at once. There were thousands of voices, all howling together. It frightened me it was so loud, but it was just my own voice howling like the earth splitting, like a lot of other voices all crushed together but freeing themselves to make one awful noise. It frightened me it was so loud and it was outside me, that's the way I heard it, but it was my own voice screaming. He had hanged himself with the extension cord from that computer wrapped around the pipe. He stood on a pile of boxes and slipped a noose around his neck, drew it up tight, put his hands behind his back into another noose, drew the knot tight, and then kicked the boxes out from under him. He had been very careful and he knew what he was doing. There were games scattered all over the place and I had to pick them up later and try to put them back in the right boxes. The funny thing was that when I threw my arms around him, screaming all the time like my head would break, and began yelling for help, I smelled something I knew but I couldn't recognize it right away. I knew there was something familiar all the time the noise was coming in at me and tearing my head apart. Then I realized that he had lost control of his bowels and that I smelled excrement. It smelled like his diapers when he was a baby and I started crooning, stinkies, stinky poo-poos. And then I talked to him like I was going to change him. And then I started screaming again and it was that terrible noise coming from outside all over again. After a while someone came from next door and cut him down and called the police. He stank just like he did when he was a baby. I kept crooning, stinky poos, stinkies. I was crying so hard then. Like I was crazy, O God. On the floor beneath him, there were two of those funny dice with all the different sides which he must have clutched tight in his fists, like his last secret.

UNDERSTANDINGS

The Sly Man is walking down a street with a friend who is an engineer. They turn a corner and discover, parked in a vacant lot, a saucer-shaped UFO. "What is that?" he asks. His friend, smug in her specialized knowledge, replies that it would be impossible to explain to someone who is not an engineer. "Study engineering," she says, "and then maybe I can explain it." The Sly Man goes away, determined to understand the UFO, to study the whole history of engineering. He learns about levers, wheels, axles, valves, internal combustion, servo-mechanisms, printed circuits, logic boards, and so forth. Unhappily, all his studies do not lead to understanding. The UFO that had been parked on the vacant lot remains inexplicable. Then one day, walking once more, he encounters the same UFO. (His friend, off building a bridge somewhere, is no longer with him.) This time the door is open and an intelligent-looking creature invites him aboard. It explains to him how the vehicle works. Suddenly, the entire development of engineering is clear. He understands its history and even where it may go next. But its history, before he had leapt beyond it, had not prepared him for what was yet to come.

Making Do

In the tropical starlight, the dash glowing dimly, it was possible, though barely, to make out the driver's actions. Tyler leaned over the back of the seat, straining to see. It was black beneath the wheel and the man's back was in the way, but it seemed unmistakable that he was pulling up the floorboards. "He seems to be lifting the floor," Tyler said simply.

Withdrawn into a corner of the back seat, Lynn-Marie stirred. "What for?" she asked.

Tyler didn't know, but he said, rather doubtfully, that the driver must be looking for something. Perhaps he had dropped some change when he had given the boy money for the pop. It seemed like a damned awful spot to park a car in any case. It clung to the edge of the highway, still at least halfway on it. They were on a curve, angling both upwards following the ascent into the mountains and sideways towards the black space where the road seemed to drop away into nothingness. He could make out, obscurely, some grotesque peaks of the *cerro*.

The driver's sidekick, his *socio*, a little boy of about ten, came walking quickly back down the track from the lights at the end that, Tyler guessed, indicated a farm house. He carried a large bottle of Fanta orange. The driver took the bottle and knocked the cap off on the edge of the door. He gave it a single sharp, flat blow with the heel of his right hand. There was a noisy fizzing of warm pop for a moment. ¡*Pum*! the boy exclaimed happily ¡*Pum*! Then the driver bent down under the wheel once more, still holding the foaming bottle.

"What the hell is he doing?" Lynn-Marie asked. "Is he drinking that soda while we dangle here over eternity?"

"You should pay attention," Tyler said, primly. "As far as I can make out, Javier is pouring the pop into the car's hydraulic brake cylinder. That's quite amazing."

"What for? Why would he suspend us above death and then waste a soda that way?"

"He's not wasting it. That's the point. As far as I can make out he is using it for brake fluid. Probably he can't afford the real stuff. It would be an expensive import down here. But the pop will work. It lacks viscosity, but it will work for a while. Until we reach Choluteca anyway. Let's hope. Don't you see how great this is? This is *bricolage*!"

Lynn-Marie barely leaned forward, and stared into the driver's back. The boy had seated himself in the seat next to the driver's. They exchanged a few words that did not seem to point anywhere. Tyler heard the word *fuerte* and he supposed that they meant the pop fizzed a good deal. He would have used, as he had learned Spanish, the word *espumoso*, but he recognized the substitution. But it was a joke, he thought, for while one liquid might take the place of another, fizz could not replace viscosity. Yet clearly it must work for they seemed familiar with the routine. There would be a risk, but they were willing to run it. Lynn-Marie settled back again into the dark corner of the car. "I don't care what they do," she said, "but I do hope they get us where we're going. I have plans for September."

I hope we make it. Cross this space, putting Fanta in the brake cylinder if we have to, and then the next space when we reach it, and maybe we'll make it all right. In the dark car, ascending once more the narrow mountain road, feeling the clamorous silence between them, Tyler gloomily recalled another romantic adventure.

The sky had darkened suddenly. Waves had erupted from nowhere and had begun spilling against the dinghy with rising strength. They broke over the gunwale in a cold foaming spray. The icy salt spray fizzed in his eyes and crusted his lips. Through the darkened air, thick now with the ragged crests of broken waves, the swells building always higher, he could still make out the chalk cliffs at Höjerup and Axel's tiny boathouse. The distance had become a gulf. We may not make it, he had thought, and fear had raked savagely through his guts, like frozen fingers. Then Birgitte had yelled from the stern. She stood staring into the following swells holding only the rudder bar itself, as useless now as a baton. The dinghy began to turn broadside into the racing line of the swells as they poured towards the high, white cliffs. Without the rudder, Birgitte stood unmoving in the stern, unable to keep the bow pointed to the shore. An oar, she had called, give me an oar. He had passed one of the oars lengthwise and she thrust it into the rudder lock, trying to hold it in place with one foot. It had bounced out almost immediately and she yelled for him to come. He scuttled his way in two or three crab-like lurches. Birgitte ordered him to hold the oar in place while she tried to steer. His hands were repeatedly pinched between the oar and the lock, but he grabbed Birgitte's heavy wool scarf from under the thwart, bundling it over the pounding, leaping oar to muffle the pain. His face had been thrust, nearly suffocating, into the wet corduroy of her thighs as she pressed over him, straining on the oar-rudder, and the thick wales stuffed his wet mouth like furred flesh. Hold it in, she called to him, hold the oar in place. Tightly, tightly, she screamed.

It had seemed like forever, but Birgitte steered them in under the cliffs onto a narrow, pebbly beach. They were down the coast from Höjerup when they came ashore, nearer to Rödvig. Struggling in the swirling surf, they hauled the dinghy high onto the wet shingle. In a cleft along the chalk face, Birgitte pulled some waterproof matches from inside her cords and made a fire from bits of brush and sea-wrack, a splintered, paint-stained plank and a broken orange crate. They stripped off their soaked clothing and Birgitte rubbed him with the scarf, hard so that his blood tingled quickly. He looked at her white body against the chalk, legs long as a water-bird's, thighs like sea-spume, red pubic hair burning like the bloom of a flame tree, and he wanted to make love. She let him kiss her, and then she said, No, someone might see us. Later, she said, later when we are back at Axel's house, on the farm, safe from the sea, then we will make love. After a bit they dressed again, their clothing still soaked, and they walked the mile or so into Rödvig, called Axel to come for them, and then drank a pilsner in the cafe. He had never loved her more intensely, but he saw the distance between them stretching more vastly than ever. She was so completely at home near the sea, at home in Denmark in a way that he could never be. He felt a tremendous surge of love for her, but in her green eyes he saw no reciprocity, neither hate nor love, but only himself reflected, small and incompetent, against the green, foaming swells of the Faske Bugt.

Now Tyler stared out over the *cerro guanacaure*, its peaks falling sharply towards the Pacific. In the luminescent night, he could make out distinctly their phallic shapes. He stretched his hand towards Lynn-Marie, but she did not acknowledge him. She continued to face the dark window, the shapes of trees fleeting blackly before her. "We should talk," he said. "We can't go on like this much longer. We should try to work something out." He heard her snort under her breath.

"It's only two weeks since Panama," she said. "In a few days we should reach Mexico. It's really a very short time, so don't exaggerate your suffering."

The old car growled as it hit potholes and rocks. In the front seat Javier and his *socio* were chatting in staccato bursts about the condition of the road. It was a crime, the driver said. But no one was responsible for the decay. It was like the war, the boy added, like *La Guerra de fútbol*, no one was to blame. It was only that the Salvadoreños were more stupid than *cerdos*. The driver laughed. It was like a woman's body. It falls into decay but no one is to blame. He laughed. But with a woman there is always a new one. With the road there is only this one. Lynn-Marie did not understand much Spanish, but she had heard the word *mujer*. Tyler sensed her stiffen. "We must talk," he said.

"Why? What is there left for us to say?"

"This should be an adventure." Tyler felt the querulous whine in his voice. "We've come all the way from Panama together. We should love each other."

"You only mean that we should have sex. You mean that you want to make love tonight. That you can't wait until Mexico."

"Yes," he said. "I do mean that. But I also mean that I love you and that this misunderstanding hurts me. It hurts not to be able to reach you."

"I won't have sex with you," she said. "I will not screw anyone without some means of contraception. In Mexico we should be able to buy condoms. Then maybe we can make love again. If we still want to." She added harshly, "Go ahead. Say 'no' to the possible."

What had the possible amounted to? Just a lot of hassle, Tyler thought, and the urge to spit made his mouth wet. Cuddling, she had said. That might mean a hand job. The best he could hope for, he knew, would be a reluctantly given blow job, an intense moment of gratification followed by the humiliation of watching her scurry to the sink. He had not wanted to bear the sexual frustrations that those alternatives would entail. Her diaphragm! That was the worst hassle of all. If a woman made sex depend upon having inserted a piece of latex into herself, then she damn well ought to look after it. She had always been too bossy, but now she had become a sexual tyrant.

"I don't believe that you lost that damn diaphragm," he complained bitterly. "I don't see how a woman could lose something as important as you claim that was. Maybe you threw it away, so as not to have sex with me anymore."

"That's very foolish, to talk that way. I never said that I lost it. Conchita stole it while we were staying in that pension. You know very well that is all I have ever said. She stole it. There was nothing I could do about that. I don't care what you think, Tyler, but I'm going to keep control over my own body. Try jerking yourself off if you don't like it."

Tyler remembered the slight, furtive Conchita. She had struck him as most of the people in Managua had, as repressed, buried, silent. She had busied herself about them, serving the meals that they had taken in the pension, pouring them the berry-flavoured corn beer, making up the room, but she had never answered questions other than in tight-lipped monosyllables. Parataxis had seemed to be the Nicaraguan mode: short replies slid out unwillingly. It must be an adaptation for living under someone like Samoza, he had thought. All those national guardsmen with automatic rifles protecting the white bunker on the hill must stifle long answers. But he found it difficult to believe that the bustling, taciturn Conchita would steal Lynn-Marie's diaphragm. When Lynn-Marie told him about the loss, he had immediately asked, "Would it even fit?"

"Probably not," she had said. "It will be loose over her cervix and sperm will wiggle around it. Then she will have one more reason to hate gringos."

He could withdraw, he had said, easily. He said it again now. It would be easy for him. He was always in control. But Lynn-Marie only nestled farther into her corner, away from him. She didn't trust withdrawing. There was always a risk.

"God, Lynn-Marie," he had moaned in exasperation. "You are no more capable of affection than the blade of a knife."

They seemed to have reached the highpoint of the pass through the *cerro* now. Women were so damn relentless. The dark peaks, stark and unyielding, hid, but suggested even so, the life in the valleys between them. Bananas, sugar cane, coffee: the livelihoods of peasants. He tried to imagine Lynn-Marie, her red hair smouldering beneath a campesina's wide-brimmed hat, bending over a clump of *caña*, her curved knife flickering in the sun, but failed. She was the child of universities, and he could not imagine her otherwise. The other redhead, Birgitte, had been clever about mechanical things. He could imagine her cutting *caña* easily enough. A woman who carried waterproof matches and could make an oar serve as a rudder would be capable of doing all kinds of things. But Birgitte, who would never have lost a diaphragm, had been inflexible, too. The night after they had been swept ashore near Rödvig still vexed his memories.

Tired, but blissfully warm once more, he had slipped early under the duvet in Axel's guestroom. When he had tried to make love, she had held her index finger to her lips and whispered, "Axel is still awake." Then she had squeezed his penis firmly a few times. She had wet her fingertip with spit and begun revolving it slowly and lightly against the glans. "Shh," she had breathed upon him, bending to stop his mouth with a kiss, "shh, Axel will hear." Then she had grasped his penis again, hard this time but with a slight up-and-down motion. She had taken his ejaculate in her fist and then wiped it dry with a cloth that she kept under her pillow. "Tomorrow," she said, "you must leave for København." When he had protested, she had countered, "Because you are a dry stick. You are not so virile as a Scandinavian man." She had turned to sleep, adding magisterially, "The time between us has now passed."

At the Honduran border, they had learned that there was no bus service. Lynn-Marie had refused to hitchhike. Tyler had scouted around the small central plaza trying to locate a driver whom they could hire. "What a great idea," he had said, teasingly. "Let's not waste time in getting to Choluteca. I want to be alone with you." Lynn-Marie had only glared, like a school teacher observing a small boy shape a spitball. The night before in Estelí she had announced that her diaphragm was gone. At first he had thought it was a joke. He had kidded her about the swell babies they could make together, her red hair, his blue eyes. When he had seen how serious she was, he had promised to withdraw in plenty of time. "Don't worry," he had said, "I will be careful with you." She had only insisted that there would be no sex until they got somewhere they could buy condoms. "We can cuddle," she had said. But he had foreseen his frustration, and he had argued against her with obstinate ferocity.

The late afternoon sun glowed over the roofs of the squat buildings edging the plaza of San Marcos de Colón like a split purple fig. The pale gringos, their heads perversely bare, stood next to their stuffed backpacks arguing. Mad people were commonly irregular in their behaviour, an old man said to a younger. In the plaza-turned-theatre, people had begun to notice them more closely. Gringos were a disturbing people. It was well known that they lacked decency. The thin blond man was, amazingly, attempting to nuzzle into the red-haired woman's breasts.

Roughly, she pushed him away. People heard the woman say *no* several times. They were disturbed to imagine what the man might have been asking.

The driver and his *socio* watching as if a circus had been stowing its gear, the couple had loaded their backpacks into the car Tyler had negotiated. He had explained that the car was a 1951 Bel Air. It amazed him that a car twenty years old would still be running, carrying passengers back and forth between the tiny villages near the border. It was a credit to the skills of these uneducated men that they could keep machines working indefinitely. Necessity, he had explained ponderously, is a fruitful master. She had ignored him, commenting only that the car was the same age as herself. Yes, he reflected, she is just twenty, but she is already as unyielding as a steel link.

In Choluteca, Tyler registered them into a small, inexpensive hotel. As he completed the police documents, Lynn-Marie came into the hotel. She had bought bread and papayas for their breakfast. In the room she placed the thick loaf and the ripe, yellowish orange fruit carefully on a scruffy table that stood in one corner opposite an ancient wardrobe. He watched as she peeled off her green plaid shirt, now darkly sweat-stained, the armpits mottled in the unshielded glare of the room's single light. She is so beautiful, Tyler thought, but so fierce. He watched her breasts, pendulous and slightly quivering, as she bent over the sink to splash water under her arms. Their whiteness contrasted sharply to her sun-reddened neck and her burnt, freckled face. As early as Panama, Tyler had already infuriated her when, watching her bend down, he had said, with casual certainty, "Gravity enhances the female body and gives it definition." Now he kept his observation to himself. Redheads, *pelirrojas*, he reflected, they are like fire licking the whiteness of snowfields. *Pelirrojas*, he thought with bitter amusement, my fate.

When she had finished washing, Lynn-Marie turned, smiling and inviting. Her lips pursing upwards, snapping tiny fricatives in mock imitation of the classic vamp manner, she mouthed him a quick burst of noisy kisses, playful and small. "Come on," she said, "let's do it." Tyler didn't understand what had changed so suddenly, but he stepped into her open arms and, kissing, began to touch her. They made love on a string bed under an old United Fruit calendar. A dark young woman, a fleshly pink hibiscus in her black hair, laughingly held out the usual bunch of bananas. The loose bed sagged, but held their weight. A quick pounding, the act of sex was soon completed. He rolled off her with a satisfied grunt. "Don't go to sleep," she warned.

He caressed her affectionately, but slyly, running his fingers perfunctorily along her upper arm. Letting irony warp his voice a little, Tyler observed that the principle she had just given up had not been worth maintaining. She hadn't been able to hold out, to resist him longer, but it had been foolish to try. "I'm glad that you couldn't resist me any longer. Lovers shouldn't try to hold out on one another. It doesn't make sense."

"You don't actually deserve it, but I realized I could solve the contraception problem. I am taking a risk, but you have become so miserable in just two nights that I decided to go ahead and do it. You seem to handle some things poorly. Like deprivation."

"How did you manage it?"

"At the *abarrotes*, I bought a sponge and some vinegar. That's what I have inside me right now. Nothing more."

"Where did you learn that pre-scientific trick?"

"It's just the sort of thing that women know. But in my case I learned it from George Eliot. It was the best mode of contraception in her day, she thought it out for herself, and it worked. So it should work for me too."

"Amazing. That something so primitive could work."

"It's only *bricolage*, Tyler, isn't it?" She kissed him, contemptuously. He could see through her hair the naked bulb on the ceiling. "Like pop that's used as brake fluid. The vinegar's a spermicide and the sponge is a barrier. I guess Eliot understood the reproductive bio-machine the way Javier understands his car. But it's still a risk. That's what we run for men, I suppose." Her weariness under the weight of the sexual revolution that, as a teenager, she had only just lived through made her words leaden. But scorn tightened her voice. "What it seems I have to run even for you."

In the morning they would find a bus to San Salvador. Yes, she said, yes maybe they could go to Copán. If they could find a bus or a car, they could go, but she wouldn't hitchhike. They could visit there since he liked ruins so much. And, yes, they could make love. Yes, more than this once. She would run the risk. And she would stick with him until they reached Chiapas. In Chicomuscelo, once they got there, she planned to catch a bus to Mexico City. Alone. Yes, he had heard her correctly. She would wait that long to see what he could learn. She would stay with him until Chiapas, but she would take the bus from the border alone. The sooner she could catch a train, the better. She wanted to be back in Montreal at least a week before classes began. Oh, yes, they might stay together longer. It might be possible. Perhaps they could even stay together until Mexico City, but he would have to learn a few things. For a man who knew so many things abstractly, there was a lot he didn't understand. He might know about *bricolage*, but he didn't understand it well. Yes. She could explain that. She had already shown him, but she could explain it, too. He would have to learn how to be more flexible. Yes, she had said that. They could make love, if that was such an important thing, but she knew she would have to bear his inflexibility like a rack. He had never truly learned the art of substitutions.

Deliquescence

Imagine a dish of food. Be precise in your imagining: in your mind's-eye, see a heaping dish of Italian sausages, brown, succulent, and smelling strongly of all the right spices. It looks and smells so good that even a vegetarian might want to sneak a taste. You are talking with a friend and drinking Chianti. Perhaps you are even talking about Italy. About the Uffizi, say, and the restoration of Renaissance paintings. Perhaps you are discussing the Neo-Platonic motifs in Botticelli's *La Primavera*. Or you may ask, How much of Michelangelo can still be seen in the ceiling frescos of the Sistine Chapel since their restoration? While you talk, engaged in friendly conversation, drinking the wine, lost to your own appetite, the sausages grow cold. The juices, which are after all largely fat, begin to congeal. Their clarity slowly becomes lost. As the dish cools, the smell also begins to fade. Slowly, a disinterested observer, someone outside of your conversation, might see a cold, greasy fat-congealed plate of dark brown objects take shape. They would still be sausages, but now they strongly resemble dog turds. Anyone who saw them would surely lose his appetite. Your friend will eye the sausages coldly. Perhaps we should move directly to the pasta, he says.

You may extend this exercise: imagine a fly or two buzzing the plate. Imagine that you had to go away and leave it for a few hours and now when you return the sausages are obscured by flies crawling in glittery masses. A few more hours, and they will be swarming with maggots. White, wriggling little grubs, these larvae, hungry as adolescents, constantly moving, like life in excrement, are now devouring the sausages. The sausages will begin to lose their shape and their identity. They are beginning to collapse, becoming a mound, a mere pile, like shit that has been left to decay along a path. Individual sausages have begun to leak into each other. The whole mound has begun to deliquesce. It has turned into slime. At what point did you begin to lose your appetite? It is not actually necessary to extend the imagination this way. Merely in allowing the sausages to cool, you also allowed the dish to slip from one category to another. It sank from a category of desire (the succulent, spicy-smelling Italian dish) to one of disgust (the fat-congealed, turd-like heap of brown worms flowing into slime). A dog, or a hungry person with no Apollonian categories to worry about, would still find the sausages desirable, still as good to eat as ever. Disgust obtrudes when something is seen to have slipped into a disapprobative category: to have fallen within the boundaries of the loathed, the taboo. Outside those boundaries, everything that is approbative, or anything that might claim, if only temporarily, to be so, displays a certain identity, an explicit social position and function. Within those boundaries, all is sliminess, rot, and ruin. Things lack the sturdiness, the categorical definitiveness of what has been approved. They are ambiguous, uncertain, passing through a phase in the dissolution of existence.

Shultz on Discovery

Shultz stood in the doorway to the crew's galley and stared narrowly at the AB who had just come off watch. The AB wouldn't look back. Shultz might not have existed. No one in the crew acknowledged him standing there.

"Don't give me that shit," Shultz said. "It was a rotten job of splicing. Lucky I caught it before the winch had to be used. I've had the entire wire rewound on the drum, but that wouldn't have been necessary if you had done your job correctly."

The AB peered glumly into his plate, cowed but hostile. The other men concentrated on their food. Shultz's mouth was pursed and his eyes were screwed up in an angry look. No one at the table wanted to be included in that look. They were silent, like philosophers reflecting upon the concept of munching. The AB decided not to defend himself and tried to pretend that Shultz wasn't there. Only wind in the door; the howl of the sea, perhaps.

It's not that he didn't do his job, Shultz said later. If that wire had parted, we would have lost some cargo, some time, not all that much perhaps, or there might even have been an accident, a longshoreman crushed under a pallet. But that's not the point. The poor splice makes the wire weak. The poor splicing shows something else. It shows the man could come apart. Give him an emergency someday, like getting the tarps on the hatches in Lake Superior weather, some bitter November morning, say, or rigging a bo'sun chair in a China Sea gale, just to take the classic example. Would you want to trust him to do those tasks?

No one would. The Third Officer said that you could blame it on the lack of education. It was a mistake to let a man make AB on the basis of sea-time alone and few basic skills. We ought to have a training ship, like they did in Norway and most other places. The Old Man said it was the unions. But that's more or less what he always said. Probably the wire itself had never been any good just because some union men made it somewhere. Then he told the story about the S.I.U. rep who creamed off the men's contributions to some charity. But Shultz wouldn't buy into that.

Strengths and weaknesses were like being spliced, inseparable. Walk down the deck some morning, he said, and think about the men, your crew. They smile or frown or ignore you. Perhaps they don't like seeing an officer early in the morning. Perhaps the first mate is like a pus-leaking boil smack on top of an inflammation. They look at you and would like to lance you, run you through, don't you know? Or perhaps it's the other way round. They love you because you are an officer or in spite of it. The point is that nothing on the surface will tell you. Intention lies deeper, in sand and drift, even than the Titanic. Nothing on the surface of the ship will tell you anything that you need to know. When the piece breaks or holds up, then you know.

The Old Man didn't think much of Shultz's idea. During a gale is too late to discover whether a wire has been soundly spliced or whether a man will break or not. The Third said that if things were done right, you could count on them. If the men were properly trained and knew what to do, then things would normally work out. Shultz only smiled, thin-lipped, and said that there weren't any "Conways" here, and never could be most likely. Work with what you have, he said. Make the most of it, but understand it first.

The Third asked him if he could have known that AB would do such a rotten job splicing. Shultz only said that he did know, now. Figure the men out and then ask them to do what they can do best. Don't ask them to do what they couldn't do well, or wouldn't. The crew were materials that you could shape, if you knew what you were doing, like words. Otherwise, they might splinter apart, or unravel, like that damn wire would have.

The Second spoke up and agreed that you couldn't tell until you had seen a man work what he might be good for. Then he started to tell a story about Manila in the 1950s. He had been Third Officer on a MSTS ship during the Korean War. They had disembarked some American troops, headed for Clark Air Base, and laid over for two days. Reasons were unknown even then, and certainly not to be remembered now. Another Third Officer, Gordon Littlejohn, and he had gone ashore that night and headed up McArthur Drive for the Yellow Bar. That was where every merchant seaman in Manila headed in those days. It was a roaring ginmill where you could buy a good-looking Filipina whore fairly cheap, if you didn't worry too much about crabs and clap. Though, thank God, that was all a man had to worry about then. The cabbie had changed money for them, giving them a good blackmarket rate of two-and-a-half pesos to the dollar. He warned them not to change money with the "boys" and to find another cab driver if they wanted to do more business. But in the Yellow Bar, a boy, perhaps thirteen or so, had offered them three pesos to the American dollar and Littlejohn had bought twenty dollars' worth.

"Central Bank of Manila!" Shultz laughed. "I remember that scam." Sure, the Second nodded, when Littlejohn had tried to pay for the next round, the waiter tossed the money back and told him that the Philippines were an independent country now. Then they learned that the real money was issued by the National Bank of the Philippines. The Central Bank of Manila stuff was just left over from the post-war colonial period, worthless as tits on a hog. What the Second really wanted to tell was how Littlejohn got his own back.

"Passed the phoney stuff, didn't he?" Shultz laughed. "Bought shoeshines from some blind cripple until they were all used up and he had the change in real notes?" Better than that, the Second said, miffed to have his story pinched from him. Much better: Littlejohn had left the Yellow Bar and got into a cab. "Now that was Manila at four in the morning, mind you, a place where it would have been safer to swim the Bay to Sangley Point, or paddle up the Pasig to god-knows-where. He would show the cabbie a good twenty peso note and ask for change, and then he would palm it and give the cabbie one of the notes from the Central Bank of Manila. In the dark it worked. That's how I learned what a brave man Littlejohn was. I would have trusted him to chart a course around the Horn in a pickle barrel."

Maybe he had just been a fool, Shultz suggested. At four in the morning a cabbie wouldn't expect to be tricked by a sailor going back to his ship. He had caught them out three times running, but they hadn't been looking to be caught. Not the dark so much as one fool being suckered by another. But different kinds of fool. Shultz wouldn't have trusted Littlejohn to chart a course up the Detroit River with all the channels marked. What happened to him after that, the Old Man asked. The Second didn't know. Another MSTS ship most likely, and then who could say?

Shultz argued that the Second had simply misinterpreted the facts. He hadn't discovered much about Littlejohn, certainly nothing trustworthy, nothing to build upon. What he had meant about discovering strengths in weaknesses was quite different. He would tell us what he meant. There had been an AB on the Milo about five years before, sailing as Dayman. He had just paid off a Red Capstan Line ship in New York, on the swing back from Africa. Shultz remembered him talking excitedly about the women in Mombassa. He liked colour and movement. Shultz figured he must have spent all his shore time chasing poontang. He would have spent a lot of time in chop houses. He would have eaten the local food, too.

Shultz stood up and hopped on one foot. He mimicked a man, feeling pain, or in agitation, clutching at his arse. "He stood in front of me while I was down on my knees checking some painting he had done in the chain locker. He hopped on one leg, just as I am doing now, to show me what he had found that very morning. He was showing me how he found it after a bowel movement. He had noticed some kind of dingle, that was what he called it, protruding from his anus. So he had got up from the can and pulled on the thing. That's why he was hopping so, holding one leg up so he could grab at his arse." He had looked like a Scotsman doing a fling. That morning he had found a tapeworm. He had hopped around and managed to get a finger around the thing and levered it out from his gut. He had pulled out an unbroken segment of worm that looked like a couple of feet or so. He had kept it in a glass so that he could bring Shultz to see it. Not that Shultz had wanted to see it very much, but it was the sort of thing a First has to take note of. A First had to write it all down for the Company, even shit-smeared tapeworms.

The Third wanted to know what Shultz had discovered in that. It wasn't much of a discovery to find out that your men had poor hygiene. Bad habits weren't anything new. The Old Man thought that it showed how little self-respect the men had. No modesty, he said, no modesty in showing someone else a worm. That hopping around to show how he had found it, the Old Man said, just proved that union men lacked self-respect.

No, Shultz laughed, that wasn't the point. Not what Shultz, but what the Dayman had discovered. That unbroken segment of tapeworm had surprised him the way nothing else had, ever. And he had even seen the worm before. In his stool once, a broken bit of it had waved at him. But the stool had been outside his body, beyond an invisible boundary, and that little boogying bit of worm hadn't meant anything. It had been different when he confronted the raw fact of a tapeworm dangling from his arse and twined around his finger.

"He hopped like that to show me how it had been. That was my job, to look and to pay attention. I was the First. I wrote the reports. I would be part of the evidence. And that was the point, don't you see? He discovered, probably for the first time in his life, that he had been violated, could be violated. So he took action to set things right. I don't mean that he went to a doctor, which he did of course. No, he went to court and sued the Red Capstan Line. No one could prove that he had picked up the worm in a Mombassa chop house; after all the ship must have bought food in African ports, maybe even hired a local cook at dockside. Showing me how he found the tapeworm, and then the beast itself snugged into a glass, were just the first steps. He had discovered violation and it made him smart."

The Third wanted to know what happened after that. The Old Man said that when he had been a young man, sailing on Norwegian and German ships to Australia, a man like that would have been thrown overboard, keelhauled at the very least. The other steamship lines would have blackballed him. Shultz didn't think that he would have been treated like that. There wouldn't have been courts for him to turn to, so he probably wouldn't have made a big fuss. The steamship lines, even then, always paternalistic, would have paid his bills at least. He could have hoped for that anyway. But there had been legal redress on the Milo and on the Red Capstan ships too. He found a New York lawyer who practised maritime law and sued. Any seaman who had wanted redress for an injury could seek it. The tapeworm had been one of those surprises that wrench the guts around and make the spine turn wet, but it had taught him to use the system. That's why we have unions, he told the Old Man, even if you and I don't like them.

The Second asked him what he himself had discovered then. Had he learned anything beyond the fact that a shitty worm in a glass will turn the stomach? The Old Man asked why he hadn't tossed the glass, worm and all, overboard so that there wouldn't have been any evidence. Just hearsay, Shultz's word against the Dayman's. He would have protected the Company that way. Shultz thought this was funny. The Old Man was always like that.

"I learned that a man who discovers his weakness can be strong. Trust a man who will look after himself, I learned. A strong man who discovers he can't splice a wire properly, or put things together so they fit, would set about to learn how. Don't trust a man who glowers. Who stays silent. He lacks an explorer's mind."

On Intolerance

Shultz told me this once. It hangs normally forgotten, but sometimes the exploding sun, when it is glaring and wild, gives it new life. The morning sun urges memories. Then I remember the ship's slight, uneven roll, the swish of water along the hull, and the queer scentlessness of the Great Lakes' air. I remember the compartment in the Mates' Hall, forward in the fo'c'sle with only the anchor windlass before us, in the hours towards midnight as we waited for the change in watch. His voice low and probing. That was Shultz.

"Sure," he said with brilliant indifference, "sure I'm an intolerant bastard. Just as you say." The few wrinkles in his forehead worked themselves downwards into a frown. "Aren't we all. You included." And then, with the manner of a man who has caught a hard point about to be made too easily and is bound that he won't allow it: "Sure, I suppose I am, as you say. It'd be stupid to deny it—at least altogether. That's what folks mean by 'our nature,' isn't it? The capacity for bigotry, I mean. Liking some things, and disliking what we can't like, the devil knows why, no reasons ever given. What sets us apart isn't that, the mere capacity, that's common property enough, but the particular tastes and aversions, the habits themselves. We are the habits we have acquired. That's the true structure of action."

About his mouth would flare the smile of a man who is talking down to someone but doesn't want to be caught at it: the smile of someone who understands facing someone who does not. And I listened. On the black formica shelf that folded down from the bulkhead to serve whatever functions of civilization might be required from a table, our glasses eddied in half-emptiness. Seized by them in blunt reflection, the unsteady glimmer from the overhead fluorescent light threw back the roll of the fixtures. The sough of water working against the bow reached the Hall from the windlass room.

Shultz's smile and frown grew. "O.K. I'm a bigot. No, don't say anything. I'm not insulted. That's what I've been trying to tell you." I took this co-presence of smile and frown to reveal an inner dilemma or perhaps some elegant paradox that Shultz had only just discovered. "Just remember that there's no easy meaning to the word, certainly no single one. And so when I agree that I am intolerant—or at least I grant that you have reasons now to call me that—I mean only of certain things done in certain ways." Shultz paused to drag at his tepid bourbon, fitting words together tightly. "Above all, I claim the right to change my likes and dislikes as my habits change."

A moment lapsed. Shultz began again. "You're pretty much the way I was at your age. I was always pretty damned sure that my opinions were right—a bit more so than I am now. Then my intolerance, as you call it, had more stickiness. It took a lot to make me change my mind. I wasn't entirely unreasonable: I think now and I thought then. It was only that my judgements were quicker than now, and more lasting. I'm most of the things I ever was, but at least I'm slower to judge." I could sense the elegance of paradox forming across Shultz's lips.

"The funny thing is that I changed quite abruptly, on the spot you could say. I mean that I modified an old habit as quickly as it takes to think. Now that's not easy, but it can happen." Shultz had one of his characteristic paradoxes framed: habits are difficult to change, but they do so very quickly. If changing a habit were easy, then educators might succeed with human nature. Shultz would give no comfort for social constructionists either. "If we do get shaped in certain rigid ways, then we also change like quicksilver. Here's what happened. It was the first year that I shipped AB on one of these Lake scows. Deckwatch I was, and the same year that I began to smoke a pipe." He stopped talking, smiling into the bowl of his pipe, circled in circling smoke, and gathered himself for the effort to recapture something grown obscure.

"You know there're lots of rebels working up here, always have been, I guess. But they were thick as dogwood in the '50s. Poor crackers, you know, rednecks mostly, who never had much in the South, brought up here by the steamship companies to offset the unions. Those drawling clodhoppers didn't have any use for unions. I suppose they'd never seen so much money at any one time, never had shoes on before, a lot of them. Those folks stayed up here on the Lakes, many of them—floated around and even did become union men now and again. Anyway, in this story I'm telling you, you have to imagine one: swag-bellied, bad breath, dirt all over him. The sheets on his bunk would have streaks of shit on them. He was shipping as a wiper on the *Durstan* when I was going as wheelsman. The old *Durstan* was a S.I.U. ship at a time when there couldn't have been more than forty or so on all the Lakes from Buffalo to Duluth. The First Engineer told me that this cracker would put all his dirty clothes into an old Navy seabag and then pull them out again when he needed something new to wear. No one in the black gang ever saw him wash things. And those brown streaks on his sheets? They said they showed where he wiped himself in the mornings. He was beyond belief. I thought that it was just his rotten nature, his god-awful nature, always filthy, foul-mouthed, incapable of cleanliness. Or so I thought. He'd sit there at meals with the rest of the black gang, telling dumb, squalid jokes, like some moronic ten-year-old, and sometimes, if I wasn't lucky, he'd be right there across from me, his mouth full of half-chewed food, dribbling slobber down his chin and laughing to himself in a kind of idiot laugh from the top of his throat. Christ! I honestly did despise him. I can still hear him twanging on about all kinds of dirty rot in a cornpone dialect so broad it'd choke you."

Shultz smiled his way into a grin. He was happy in stories. "But you know what?" Shultz pointed his pipe directly into my face as if he might have thought that my attention had slipped or that he had lost me. "I changed my mind about him one day at supper. It was as quick as that. So you see I modified a habit right on the spot—the very spot, mind you, where I most hated to see him. We'd all been talking about a green fellow who'd been paid off at Detroit. Tried to ship as a wheelsman, but not a prayer for it. Steered the old *Durstan* all over Lake Superior, like a drunk on both sides of the white line at once. Well, the skipper couldn't trust him in the channels, of course, so he paid him off, and quick too, like heaving a dead marine. In any event, this self-styled wheelsman had said that he was an artist, a painter—which didn't make the skipper trust him any more than he did, I suspect, but it gave us all a great story to play with. Then this cracker got up to leave and he said, standing there by the table, in his slow cornpone way, that he 'sho envied them artists fellas,' and wished he could be one. I must've looked incredulous, anyway he seemed to pick up on my interest because he immediately said that he thought nothing in the good Lord's creation could beat being able to put down all the pretty things, like colours, a man could see in the sky. Once, during World War Two, when he had been a soldier on a troopship being sent to Australia, he had seen a sunset where every colour he knew, and then some more, had stretched in bands above the horizon, bright and clear, but shifting all the time as if they'd been alive. It had stayed that way for around twenty minutes, he reckoned, and he had watched it all the time. He didn't know if an artist fella could really paint colours that bright, but he wished he could be one and put down all he had seen."

Shultz stared into, and far beyond, the soot-coloured bulkhead, dark as grit just as, it might be, he had stared into (and beyond) his plate. I remember that his stories were like stones chiselled out from past moments, polished to a shadowy glow. And they do return, those stories, when the already-done, in its false afterlight, seems too clear.

On Sexual Disgust

Shultz had a laugh like a camel's sneer. When he was talking, he liked to sit looking over or up at companions, but never down. He would sit on the edge of a railing or on a capstan as comfortably as on a chair or a barstool. His face folding into a frown, his nose pulling up in furrows, his mouth would purse like a man about to spit. He would be laughing though, not spitting. That frown, which no one ever forgot, was actually a smile, quizzical and ironic. He didn't tell a story so much as he probed it. Listening to Shultz, you understood that each sentence, every word, engaged him even if he had told the story many times before, even if he had felt it viscerally each time. A story for Shultz was never like finding the kernel inside of a nut, something definite that he had been looking for or else had found long ago. Telling a tale was more like peeling back the leaves of a pod or unpacking a tightly folded bundle: it would always be a delicate operation and the significance of what was found lay in each leaf, in every fold.

We had been sitting crowded around a small table in a gloomy bar not far from the pier's end. Outside a few vestiges of late summer still showed. There had been a work stoppage and the cargo which we had been loading was now held up. The second mate had remained on deck in charge while we had gone to the bar for a couple of hurried beers. We had hardly begun to drink when a man at the next table reached far down into his throat and hawked up an opalescent gob of spit. It lay on the dirty lino only a few centimetres from the skipper's feet, shimmering like a husked oyster. The Old Man looked at the gob and said that it was disgusting when a man could not control his waste products. The third mate observed that spit was not as disgusting to see as excrement. The Old Man said that he had once seen a young woman shitting alongside a path in Denmark. He knew that she had been caught short and couldn't help herself, but it had still been disgusting to see. Both men and women should control their bodily functions, but a woman must especially do so. It is more disgusting to see a woman shit than a man.

Shultz thought that it was more what you were used to. Anyone who has been a sailor for as many years as the Old Man must have seen many men in such intimate moments, but probably never a woman. But the Old Man stuck to his point, as he always did. Women could be more disgusting than men and their wastes were horrible to see. Shultz responded that many things could be disgusting, actions as well as things, but it all turned upon your capacity to be shocked. What shocked was whatever you had not been raised to see. The young are easily shocked just as they are easily surprised. We knew that a tale was taking shape. One of Shultz's stories would brew up slowly, a few indications like spurts of rain the moments before a squall hits, and then engulf you.

He remembered a young man who had encountered disgust where he had least expected to find it. The young man Shultz evoked for us was nineteen years old. For the past year, he had been working as an ordinary seaman, sailing Mateson Line ships out of San Francisco. He was green in mind even though he had read many different books. He knew a bit about literature, history, and political theory. Callow, depthless, he nonetheless thought that he must be sophisticated. "He had only a few scanty reasons for thinking so," Shultz said, "but that's what he thought. Above all, he believed that he was an accomplished lover. No doubt, he had been misled into this fantasy by the narrowness and simplicity of his previous experience." Shultz looked steadily into the Old Man's eyes as he said this. "You can imagine well enough, his sexual experiences had all been quite raw, happenings like sudden explosions in a quiet world. He had an inadequate understanding of many little things."

Shultz wanted us to understand that greenness, the shallowness of experience or the mind's untried reach, was not the same as ignorance. The young man in his tale had been intelligent, skilful in solving the in-the-world problems he had met so far. But he had been green, just as in a way the Old Man had been green when he had seen that Danish woman squatting to defecate. If the Old Man had been born in India, he would have seen such sights every day, every time he walked in a public park or along a country road. He would have grown up expecting to see misshapen coils of human excrement under the wild pepper and jackfruit trees. They would not have been horrible, nor even ugly, but merely part of commonplace reality. Greenness was only a condition of experience, and it made disgust possible.

One night in San Francisco, Shultz's young man met a woman. He had been drinking with two shipmates in an up-scale lounge off Lombard street west of Van Ness. She smiled at him as he swanked back from the washroom. And, as swiftly as an eyelid winking, he had responded. He told her that she was beautiful, the most beautiful woman he had seen since he got back from Japan. (Saying that, ever so deliberately, he brought his false-romantic life into perspective.) She was certainly pretty. Years later he would remember her red hair, greenish eyes, and lithe body as he would a childhood triumph or his first kiss. She had a long, intelligent face and large, smoky-green eyes. Later, he would always evoke her just as she had charmed his fantasy: with the illusion of superior, intelligent beauty. A few minutes after they had begun to talk, he asked her to leave with him. Lubriciously, he waved goodbye to his friends who leered enviously at his good luck. She whispered to her girlfriend who studied him quizzically.

"Where would you go in that situation? Imagine. You are nineteen and you have just persuaded an older, and beautiful, woman to come with you. Where would you take her?" Shultz was very precise that the young man's greenness made everything doubtful. And that condition of life had begun to assert itself as soon as they were on the street together.

When he actually had her out in the street, hand in hand, heading somewhere, the boy realized abruptly how little he knew about San Francisco. And so of course he let her make a suggestion. "What would you do? Imagine." When Shultz told one of his Hydra-headed tales, he wanted his audience to use their imagination. "See it," he would command. "You must see it." He knew how to impose imagination as a task.

They ended up going to Chinatown. "She takes the task of ordering from him. They eat won ton, spicy shrimp, squid in black beans and garlic, chicken in nuts of some kind. They were cashews, of course, but he doesn't know that. The meal will lodge in his memory like an Australian sunset. He talks endlessly about being a seaman, about literature, about himself. You know how that is. It is important to establish yourself. He wants to display an image that he wants others to see him by. I would bet that we were like that at nineteen." Shultz spoke to the Old Man, but included us all in his glance. "After all, we must all have thought that the merchant marine is romantic, still a bit of the old adventure even with bulk cargos and containers, or we wouldn't have gone to sea. Well, of course you were an apprentice deck boy at twelve, but that was Norway and quite a few years ago to boot. The rest of us didn't begin until we were nineteen or twenty. I was eighteen, not knowing much more about ships than what I had learned in the Sea Scouts. Not much, really."

The beautiful woman said little, but she played with the young man's feet and rubbed his knees under the table. She asked him if he liked women? did he like to love women? did he want to love her? He kept saying that yes, of course, he loved love. Sure. Did he have limits? she asked, her haze-clouded green eyes shimmering. He was limitless. His passion was boundless, his drives unquenchable. Limits, he explained pedantically, were only the pathetic fears of the bourgeoisie made evident. "How would you have answered her questions? At that moment how would you have even guessed your limits? Those questions almost call for lies, don't they? Remember that this young man is only nineteen. It was part of his greenness not to know how to answer direct questions. Neither honestly nor dishonestly."

Eating a good Chinese meal on Jackson, talking about love and sexual possibilities, the boy actually thought very little about her. Her name was Georgie. Afterwards he thinks that this must have been a nickname for Georgia Lee. But he remembers this rather uncertainly. His first "real" girlfriend had been named Georgia Lee and so perhaps he had only confused the two names. Georgie was an artist, but she also had a job either in an art shop or as a teacher. Much later, he could recall some patch of conversation when they talked about frames and framing prints. Did he understand how important frames were? she had asked. Shultz was nearly as obsessed by memory as he was by imagination. For him stories lived in the mind's eye. So it was sad that the details of Georgie's life would mostly slip the boy's memory.

"Georgie's apartment is down the north slope of Nob Hill, on Green street. You know the area. You start walking towards Fisherman's Wharf from the Fairmount Hotel and you cross it on your way. Her apartment looks very lived-in, vivid, an expression of an individual human life." That was the pure Shultz touch. Everyone had an individual life, even radically individual. That was why stories were worth telling, worth hearing.

Reproductions of paintings hung on all the walls. Casually, she pointed out some paintings that were her own. "He learns that she is twenty-five, six years older than himself, and that she had been born in Vancouver just as he had. Their paths have crossed momentarily, never to intersect again, having unfolded quite differently from the same physical birthplace." Their memories were quite unlike, of course: Georgie recalled the city, shops and museums, the university. All he could remember were water and evergreen trees, ferry boats and bridges, islands, harbours, and lakes. "Still, they may both carry tatters of fog in their hair, or wet sunsets in their hearts."

The Old Man was listening, the way he always did when Shultz was talking, his mouth slightly parted, his eyes fixed in total attention. "You know how that is," Shultz said. "You have never forgotten the fjord at Trondheim nor the mountains backing the sea. You are like every other Norwegian I have ever sailed with, stiff and dour, like the rocky landscapes of your home. I am not saying that is bad, of course. It isn't bad that I remember the softer seascapes by which I grew up. It is just that our memories stick with us and keep on revealing themselves in all the things we do. You were raised in a place where women's bodies were hidden from men and so you find them disturbing. You honestly think that a woman's excrement is more disgusting than a man's. The truth, as I see it, is that neither is disgusting in itself. It was only that you were green. The woman in Denmark shocked you because she surprised you."

Years afterwards, whenever the boy saw a modern painting, he would feel Georgie flood back, her apartment off Hyde springing up around him, pervading his mind. She had books, too, mostly museum editions, art histories, surveys, and the like. Once they were inside, she made him a drink, a sticky concoction of pink gin called a Singapore Sling. They sat talking uncertainly about art.

The Third said that a Singapore Sling was a terrible drink, too sweet to enjoy. It wasn't a drink for a man. The Old Man could imagine drinking beer or even wine, but not pink gin. Who would drink that? Shultz said only that they had to imagine how inexperienced this young man was. Every story has a point or two, and that was one.

"You have to see the scene clearly. He moves through Georgie's apartment in a little cloud of bravado, trying to make her believe that he is smooth and hip, sophisticated enough to appreciate all that she has to show." Was he sophisticated enough to recognize the paintings? the Third asked. Both yes and no. "He keeps interjecting comments about novels he has read. Well, that's rather crude. But he understands her when she points something out to him in one of the paintings. That is, he understands a bit, in fragments."

They began the exploratory process of having sex together, or "making love" as he would have said. "Of course, that 'making love' puts his character dead-to-rights, doesn't it? It shows the typical false consciousness of his time." The Old Man thought that the young were always hypocritical in that way. The Third knew what Shultz had meant. We had to imagine a time before communes and love-ins, before Crumb and alternative everything, before women would initiate sex. The Old Man looked startled at that, but Shultz laughed. "That's right," he said, "before then, though not by much. Imagine James Dean, if you can, or *The Wild Ones*. If you can imagine Brando's Triumph 500, you can see the man I am describing."

He and Georgie had settled down together on a dark green calico couch, kissing and touching tentatively, but she delayed his urgency, keeping her legs crossed at the ankles, knees pressed closely together. These stalling tactics were quite familiar to him since they had been standard moves within the ambit of his narrow sexual experience. He had not yet succeeded in even touching her panties when he felt the sudden compulsion to urinate. Shultz drew a comic picture. "He gets up, saying something disingenuous, something absurdly flat, like 'I'm going to miss you' or 'Wait for me, darling, I shall return with infinite desire'. But Georgie follows him to the bathroom. He is surprised, but he is also reasonably familiar with the sexual associations of urination. You may know what I mean, but perhaps not." Shultz had included Old Man in his smile once again. "The 'place of excrement,' at least insofar as that means urination, has been exciting for him. Watching girls pee, as he has grown up understanding sex, has been a fairly commonplace waystop on the way to active intercourse. I bet that even in Norway when you were growing up, boys liked to sneak behind bushes to watch girls urinate." The Old Man looked away from his glass of beer towards the lino floor and his eyes seemed to catch that gob of spit once more.

He was not ashamed to have Georgie watch him urinate and he would have enjoyed watching her, if that had become part of the situation. When he had seen other women urinate, he had always found the experience, though not necessary to arousal, definitely exciting. Five years before, when he was fourteen, he had peeked through some bushes in a local park to watch the first Georgia Lee urinate. "You see, he finds the female squatting position to be charming, endearing even, and delicately thrilling. That, too, is a measure of his greenness as well as of his sophistication. No doubt, he might not be so compliant, or so excited, if it ever became a matter of defecation."

Shultz again spoke directly to the Old Man. "He would be a bit like yourself in that respect. But he would not have been shocked because he could hardly have been surprised. He would not have wanted to see it done, but that it is done, he knew; and what it might look like, he could easily guess. After all, he grew up in a less rockfast place than you. When you saw that woman along the path in Denmark, you didn't turn your head away. You observed her closely because, even though surprised and shocked, you wanted to have that new experience. Unlike ignorance, greenness is a condition that always tries to correct itself."

Urine didn't shock him. "It is always closer to sex than its more robust comrade, and he even likes to hear and see it, even sometimes to smell it, though he would not drink it willingly. All the splotch and splatter doesn't really bother him." In Georgie's bathroom, he expected her to stand beside him watching him urinate and then perhaps to sit on the toilet while, kneeling excitedly, he peered between her legs to watch her. But that was where he did find himself surprised. Not shocked, only surprised. "Can you see the difference? It is just a small surprise, a question of margins really, like seeing an able seaman slip carelessly on a wet deck or fumble a running line."

She reached down and took his penis in the fingers of her right hand and pinched the tip. "Not yet," she whispered. "Don't pee yet." Then, still holding his penis, she had begun wriggling out of her slip and panties while with her left hand she reached behind and unhooked her bra. "Is the scene clear? Does it make sense? His penis has now grown stiff as a marlin spike as she grasps the tip between her thumb and forefinger, leading him. She edges over to the bathtub, moving slowly, even languidly. Anyway, that's how he will remember the moment. There is nothing you can do about the confusions of memory. He can never remember her voice exactly, though he will often try to do so. Was it soft? Inviting? Sultry? Perhaps it was only uncertain."

She had slid down into the tub, opening her legs for the first time, and said, "Do it on me." He had heard of golden showers, but he had never believed in them. They were rather like the very different, but somehow similar, act of eating excrement: he had heard about it, but it was altogether outside his personal experience. He had never explored the intimate relationship between sex and disgust, never even thought about it. This was what Shultz meant by green. "Pee on me," Georgie murmured roughly, her voice darkening. He gaped and felt queasy. He said stupid things like "You don't *really* want me to, do you?" or "You won't like that, I better not."

But Georgie knew what she wanted. She wanted a man to urinate upon her. She insisted. And the situation, afterwards corrosively inscribed upon his memory, did actually seem to demand that he do just that. "Can't you imagine it? What would you do? Run? Leap from the bathroom window? There are many times, which we as seamen should recognize, when one just has to keep on going. There will be no space to move except forward. And leaping from the ship, or from a window, would solve nothing."

He looked down on her. She had small, unexciting breasts, no longer seeming as pert as they once had, and a straggly clump of red hair around her vagina. He stood over her for a moment trying to force his urine to flow through his erection, but then he felt the stiffness fade, ebbing swiftly out of his penis. He aimed at her flaming tuft, as if it were a target, and began to urinate directly onto it. Immediately, Georgie commanded him to widen his range. "Don't do it all there. Pee on me everywhere." He shifted the direction of his stream up to her belly-button, her breasts and along her neck and shoulders. He could not bring himself to urinate upon her face. He watched narrow puddles form alongside her hips and between her thighs. As his stream weakened, he brought it back down to her vagina, the final drops falling upon her knees and feet. Georgie seemed very happy. Could she pee on him? "That's not necessary," he said.

"Well, he sounds foolish. None of you would say anything as absurd as that. But then you are not nineteen any longer." Shultz could smile as grimly as a condemned man's scoff. "He leads her by the hand, naked and wet, back to the green couch. Taking her back to the couch, wet but drying, is simply a ridiculous thing to do, as ill-mannered as insensitive. None of us would do things that way. Not now, anyway. But he can't think clearly at that moment. Much later he understands that he should have let her urinate on him and then taken another shower, with soap and water, with her. That would have been the right way to incorporate excrement into the pleasures of sexuality. But, you can see, the sex between them has been dual, not mutual. There is no true connection in their extreme duality. So now he is easily upset by the actual-life experience of a golden shower. He feels a deep disgust over the act which he might not have felt if he had permitted a bit of mutuality, a bit of sexual sharing. All he experiences is just the kind of raw disgust when the nose crinkles and you can sense a tight gagging in the throat." That would happen when you felt shocked by the sight of something that should not be or doesn't seem right. It comes when something has struck you as dirt. "Dirt where it should not be, like a pubic hair in your salad or on the tip of your tongue, is disgusting, or at least it is until you learn better."

At the door to the bathroom, he had begun to gag and controlled his vomit only with difficulty. His participation in Georgie's desire had deeply disturbed him. Perhaps he even felt lessened by it. Back on the couch, he discovered that he had lost all sexual desire. Georgie's vagina was too wet (from his urine) and everything about her depressed him. He very much wanted to leave and make his way back to the ship. At nineteen, he was completely impotent. Georgie must have realized that her desire for a golden shower had disgusted him. When he lied that he had to get back to the ship for the four a.m. watch, she did nothing to keep him.

"He slinks out of her apartment. You have to imagine that clearly," Shultz said. "'Slink' is exactly the right word. He is ashamed of having urinated upon another person. He has participated in a golden shower and that makes him, he thinks, as guilty as if he had pissed on someone in anger or in violence. He has also stepped over a boundary of sorts into mythology." The concept of a golden shower had become real. And so, slinking, he felt both shame and guilt. He was not thinking about Georgie at all, except to sense a vague disgust at her desire.

"You will understand that, but it may be harder to grasp that she must also feel something. And not the lineaments of satisfied desire." We could see now the twist Shultz's tale would take. The nineteen-year-old man would not be its undisputed hero. Georgie's perfunctory, embarrassed farewell should have told him that she, too, felt shame, and perhaps even guilt for having led him where he was not ready to go. But at that moment his mind had blanked her into the dimmest trace. "Imagine him slinking, like an animal perhaps or more like a man terrified even by himself." It had been a sexual adventure that had gone coldly wrong.

"No romance at all, no romantic archetypes in play, but only a wintry misadventure in human absurdity. One day, he will learn that sexual pleasure takes many shapes and grows out of any number of practices, not all of which receive bourgeois sanction. Right now, at this moment, there are no lessons." Eventually, he would learn an even more important lesson: that shame and disgust, both slippery and nearly uncontrollable affects, were twins, linked in a bawdy dance. He felt shame, but only after he had felt disgust. When he had begun to gag leaving the bathroom, he had not yet felt shame. That came a few moments later, when they were sitting once again on the green calico couch.

Shultz wanted us to understand that the enormity of the boy's act lay in his experience of it alone. This emphasis was mostly for the Old Man's benefit, who often seemed to confuse his upbringing in Norway with nature itself. "He has done something, an act that would have made his bourgeoisie mother physically ill even to hear about, that, in the terms of his childhood training, the strict middle-class order of things within which he has been raised, was unclean, improper, dirty." It might even have been that, upon recognizing his hesitation, even before the surprise of his impotence, Georgie had felt shame first. Then she might have experienced self-disgust, the worming sense of having been made abject. Shultz made an enclosing gesture with his arm, as if to include us all with Georgie's shame. The Old Man stretched one foot out, touching the gob of spit. "I have always supposed that she must feel shame. His hesitancy, his lack of wholehearted participation, his momentary gagging, his impotency, all would work together, as a harsh judgement upon her, sufficient to create self-disgust." Shultz looked steadily at his favourite target. "She might feel as if a stranger has caught her out squatting along a pathway to void excrement, or engaging in a private act of something universally taboo, like necrophilia or infantile cannibalism."

A bit later, after he had time to reflect upon his secret *pas de deux* with Georgia Lee and had tried to make sense out of it, the young man had experienced another kind of shame and even some more self-disgust. In his extravagant creation of a romantic self-image, he had certainly told her that he had no reservations about sex. Sitting in the Chinese restaurant, pushing against her feet and having his knees squeezed between hers, he had let her believe that he was a sophisticated, accomplished lover who recognized no sexual boundaries. He had bragged without knowing what he was bragging about, and without understanding the consequences of speaking to another human being with a lying tongue. "Neither honesty nor actual sophistication in *that* persona: no undisclosed shard of his character is being fashioned now, no ideal conception in evidence, but only a confident falsity for the single purpose of screwing Georgia Lee. He leads her to believe that whatever she desires he will be, because mutually excited, happy to perform."

The next morning, when his shipmates asked about her, he claimed that she had been great, a terrific lay. "His dishonest tongue drips falsehoods. Mostly what he remembers is her sparse red pubic hair slick from his own urine. He hates that memory, but it is stuck fast in his mind, a personal burden that he must carry forward. But it will grow upon him."

Looking back, the young man would romanticize Georgie. He would imagine her as an artist who found her creativity in transgressing the boundaries of sexual experience. She was, Shultz had come to believe, an artist trying to live her life without measure, without limitations. "Sometimes in perverse experience, the rotting domain of the disgusting, you can find creativity." Look for it, Shultz urged us. "Forget your upbringing. Forget your mother's wishes and hopes. Break the boundaries, even if they have been seared into the unconscious with pain. Look how the fingers, the mouth, the whole body, will explode into flames."

The Old Man, who seemed fascinated by that gob of spit, didn't look up from the floor. He spoke up, however. "That is terrible, Mr. Shultz. You are saying that we men should love monsters. Maybe that we should all become monsters."

"Yes. In a way." Shultz laughed. Perhaps it was the story he had been telling, or the Old Man's rocky obduracy, or simply his own audacity, but his laughter was like a warrior's. It splashed over us, triumphantly. "Overcome your horror, nuzzle Medusa's hair, and hear the many little tongues whisper the possibilities of creation. The young man will fantasize that, had he been different, had he not broken her creative dance, Georgia Lee might have painted, later that night or the next day, a picture that never found life: a tongue of fire."

The Old Man wanted to know how Shultz had learned so much about that young man. Had he sailed with him again? The Third was certain that there had to be more to the story than Shultz had revealed.

Shultz laughed once more. "Oh, I knew him well. I still do, though better perhaps. I am living out my life with him aboard."

The Falcon's Tears

The mythographers of QueAng-QueAng claim that once, in the early ages of their civilization, the falcon was forbidden to fly. He was forced to hug the ground like a lesser rhea. Scurrying through the bush, from thicket to thicket, hiding, always on the alert for foxes and snakes, he ate worms, grubs, and beetles. His wings atrophied and grew heavy, his feathers runty and gaunt. Lice and ticks crawled over his skin beneath the remnants of his plumage. From the corners of his eyes, tiny blue tears, as cold as slivers of lapis lazuli, gathered and fell.

The religious leaders of QueAng-QueAng assert that the fable of the falcon shows how dangerous it is to soar above the earth. Punishment, they say, deservedly awaits everyone who attempts to see above the earth's misery. The young revolutionaries of QueAng-QueAng argue that the falcon's suffering tells a different tale. It demonstrates, they say, the sorrows of having failed to soar above earthly suppressions. From the falcon's tears swell the histories of fanaticism and grief.

Processes

They were all so goddamn alike. So aggressive. They're all bullies. Americans. She didn't think she could stand them any more. She couldn't stand him. That was for sure. (Blackie had nearly spat at him.) Kiss my royal Canadian ass, Tyler. You gross American shit. (Angrily, she had sprinkled his hands and face.) Concrescence. Prehension. Shit, Tyler. The way he talked sometimes was really gross. Tyler Haynes, you bully. You *American* bully.

He is standing on the second level at the north end of Eaton Centre. Before him unfold the galleria, the stairways, the innumerable design features reflected in the glass surfaces. Tyler loves, always, from first sight even, the play of mimic planes. Eaton's glass catches, and holds briefly (for nanoseconds), the movements, densely full, intricately atomistic, of an always-changing, already-stable world. The creative advance of that world flows everywhere. Now, walking south, he looks upwards to the flock of snow geese, flying out of their natural system through a design system and into the commercial system, and feels immensely happy. Tyler loves the way Eaton's surfaces, like quicksilver into mist, rush, merge, and dissolve. The exterior space of Yonge Street pours continuously into the space of the galleria, amplifying itself, while shaping an autonomous interior space crowded with the gigapulses of human motion. Along the interfaces between architectural design and commercial activity, the edges of mental and physical structure, there is continuous theatre (watching, being watched) that the sheer vertical surfaces endlessly reflect: theatre in whirling bursts, carnival in routine eruptions. Within the controlled boundaries of design, everything intricately flows. Tyler surges with exhilaration at the realization that he, perhaps only he among all the thronging shoppers who are passing thoughtlessly beneath the high-flying geese, can actually penetrate to the multiple systems that make the processes possible.

(You Americans are so goddamn alike. You're all power crazy. You beat up on the world. That's what you do, Tyler. You beat up on me. You talk about things I don't understand. All the time.)

He remembers Blackie's rage the night before. Her incomprehension had been that of someone irremediably captured within the play of surfaces. (Category mistake: confusing a philosopher's with an American mind.) Blackie caroms happily through the puzzles of experience, through infinite networks of entities, without once thinking that systematic frameworks permeate these entities, make them possible, bring them to actuality, and create the world's play that she enjoys. Beautifully and happily, she is lost in that play. Tyler stops at the Zoom'n Zip to buy some software journals. Then, his heart soaring, goose-like at the thought, he will walk down Yonge to Queen's Quay where Lake Ontario will dance (though brutally inarticulate) in the June sunglaze.

Tyler walks slowly south on Yonge. He is actually strolling, an archaic activity. Blackie's screeching anger the evening before still disturbs him, and he can think of no rational way to account for it. Her feelings about Americans seem extreme: any assumption of centricity or pre-eminence can set her off. She dislikes, but doesn't understand, the mere notion of a system, and she certainly doesn't accept dominance or control, from any direction. Tyler can never be quite certain that what he says will not spark her fury.

As he walks, he thinks of the overlapping lines of force that his path leads him to cross and of the extended objects into whose momentary uniqueness he breaks, like a swimmer knifing through an endless succession of waves which will steadily reconfigure. Purposefully, he breathes the air of a summer evening. Along Yonge, a sputtering flume of traffic flows south with him, and beneath his feet (he knows) subway trains pulse. Signs from numerous buildings seem to call out invitations: style your hair, buy CDs, eat food, shop, save, acquire, shop, buy, own, consume, shop. The signs are impersonal but Tyler listens to their messages as intently as if they have been spoken to him alone. They tell him about his own marginality. His pleasures, normally in his mind, are chilly but labyrinthine. Inescapably an exile, Tyler feels foreign in Toronto; as ever, an outsider, an onlooker. He possesses no symbols to weep upon.

Wind gusts swirl around him. Now Tyler thinks of the buildings as deflecting surfaces, the streets as tunnels, the city as an aerodynamic structure. He understands how difficult it must be to grasp the principle of immanent subjectivity, to suppose that every actual entity within the world, the aerodynamic city-system of Toronto as an instance, had, or desired to have, consciousness. He recalls Professor Hartshorn. In memory, Hartshorn still drifts away from his seminar, lost in the contemplation of an elm tree or some squirrels outside, passing from the smoky loops of language through the narrow leaded windows of Swift Hall into the decompossible world of physical extension. When they had called him back from his fugue, he had stared at them wildly, like a person suddenly awakened, and had exclaimed,

—. Oof! I often wonder what my bathwater thinks of me when I bathe.

Hartshorn had not seen any problem in supposing either the immanent subjectivity or the potential consciousness of all entities. And he had been able to think the universal prehensiveness of things. His bathwater possessed consciousness.

At first Tyler had planned to complete his Ph.D. and carry on with life very much as he had in Chicago. But the opacity of intellectual life, the absence of any serious philosophical inquiry, the self-satisfied, stubborn slowness of an unadventurous society, had drawn out his quirky solipsism. He had given up his plans for a Ph.D., dropped the few friends he had made, taken a job downtown with Ryerson's technical services. He had shrunk into the role he had inhabited ever since, solitary and reclusive. In all the years he had lived in Toronto he had never spoken with anyone about Alfred North Whitehead's philosophy. No one had read Whitehead or, at most, had read only certain parts of the *Principia*. Even so, Tyler has learned to enjoy the sense, which Toronto gives him, of standing outside (above, if he thinks in the metaphor of a map) and looking south at, and into, the States. He enjoys thinking about Rochester, there beyond the horizon, sometimes glowing against the night sky. An exile's role had immediately appealed to him since that made possible the alterity, the high vantage, he needed for examining his own systems. He loves the clogging, oddly polite in-barging, traffic and the city's clamorous, if impersonal, signs.

He had tried to explain to Blackie how cities, even phlegmatic ones, gave the philosophic observer countless complexities to study. And she had laughed. But it was so, he thought. A city was a vast overlapping system (immeasurable: long labours of analysis), the significance of which was at once stereographic and kaleidoscopic. Whitehead had observed, and Tyler believed, that the function of philosophy was to reach the most general account possible of civilized thinking. You had to find the relevant systems, and that meant the systems beneath the structures, beneath the known codes, the invisible relationships that connected all underneathness. Unregarded by its inhabitants, Toronto was a good place to begin.

In his walks from Ryerson to the lakefront, Tyler passes through the city's heart, through the mazes of buildings and underground malls, edging the abrupt fissures that opened across its opaque surfaces. He rides to the tops of the up-thrusting buildings and strolls lingeringly about the observations floors, the horizon of lake and suburbs fascinating his gaze. Taking intense pleasure in the thought, he knows that, however multiplex the city appears in the public view, the deeper intricacies that lie hidden beneath the play of surfaces, the extended, overlapping societies of actual events (all that underneath stuff from which the illusive visible emerges), are open to him alone.

Being a philosopher, Tyler would reflect, must be analogous to being a conductor or a figure skater. There are a certain number of basic rules (like scales or arpeggios) that have to be learned, relatively few yet essential to performance, but everyone plays them differently. No two conductors are ever alike, though they study the same scales in pretty much the same sequence, any more than are any two skaters or philosophers. I am locked into a dance with the reality, he thinks: both, the reality and the philosopher, are explicable only in terms of the underlying systems (the exercises in logic, the rules, the codes, the paradigms, the laws) that make them possible. Nietzsche had said: the philosopher seeks to hear in himself the echoes of the world-symphony and to reproject them in the form of concepts. Whitehead would have urged him to hear the unheard melodies. A philosopher could dance with reality, swirling in an impenetrable choreography, but only another philosopher (hearing the distant, unhearable music) could follow the steps.

(Americans. They're all such jerks. You're all alike. It just stinks. Yes, Tyler. That's it. You have a common face. You all think alike. That's it. You pricks all think alike. You're all so goddamn aggressive. A nation of bullies.)

Eyes glistening slightly in anger, Blackie had looked straight into him. Tyler had looked back, but more softly, bemused. Ever since that day, almost a year ago now, when she had walked into tech services, carrying a miserable cassette-player she wanted repaired, and then had smiled at him (gawky, balding now, always too smart for his own good), unsettlingly, he had become accustomed to her sudden gusts. She had overwhelmed him with her inexplicable determination to make him love her. Abruptly, at any moment, she would dazzle him with her quirks of affection, a private gesture, a public kiss. Then last night something that he had said, some verbal mannerism or reasoned account, had brought her anger slashing upon him. Fragmentary codes, subjectivity, personality, even nationalism, barked in her voice.

And he had stared back at her black rectangular pin with the green trapezoid which proclaimed "The Cure." He had looked steadily into her long, sharp face, distorted in its emotional intensity, its features sliding away from one another. Moist with her anger, her green eyes had peered suspiciously from within asymmetric clouds of freckles as he tried to reassure her. (I'm not really an American, Blackie. I've lived here for nearly fifteen years. I vote in Canadian elections. I think like a Canadian. I am not what you assert.) She had run a hand up through her thick elfish perm: bristling, fury-arched.

(You are too an American. You try to tell people what they should think. You even try to tell me what I really am but don't know that I am. It just stinks. It's gross. You do, too, Tyler. You do. You say that I act the way I do and that I wear the clothes I do because there are systems. That's what you always say. Systems. Goddamn it. And if I don't know what these systems are, if I say they don't exist, and you keep saying that they do, that even if I say they don't exist they still make me the way I am. So what does that make me? Goddamn it, what? A goddamn robot, that's what. Well, kiss my Royal Canadian ass.)

He had looked closely. She wears just so much eye shadow, so much liner, so much lipstick. Her hair is cut just so, in a way that he has seen before on other women. She lacquers her nails with red polish and in warm weather does the same to her toes. She looks, always already, like a young woman from North America or perhaps, if you knew enough about her clothes, from Toronto. You might, if you understood these matters, see that her fashionable blazers had been bought at Holt's. Her pretty face, her intelligence, evident in her looks, gestures, expressions, all are styled in a certain way. She wears sweaters, turns on exaggerated pantomimes to make a point, opens her face in definite expressions that make her look like Cathy in the American cartoon that runs in the *Globe*. Her music is contemporary, but not quite up-to-date. She plays CDs constantly of David Bowie and Peter Gabriel. Her favourite groups are Echo and the Bunnymen and The Cure. She knows and loves to sing every song that Robert Smith has cut. Trained to enjoy Baroque (or, in pop music, the social commentary of The Clash or, even, The Dead Kennedys), Tyler's mind has begun to resonate, never entirely harmoniously, with New Wave playfulness.

Tyler knows that the range of Blackie's expectations, like that of her perceptions, has been constituted by this society, now, within the narrow channels of her present life. How can she think that she is free of systems? Independent? No one ever is. There are always systems of acts, of behaviour, of fashion, of cultural talismans, of everything, just as there must be of language and for thought. For each process there is, has to be, a corresponding system. Everything about Blackie indicates the varied social systems that underlie Toronto. She is a young North American female, with a few Canadian quirks, and everything about her proclaims this truth. And Tyler knows well enough that everything about him must reveal, perhaps even flaunt, the systems that have made him. Does even the way he asks questions, or the way he shapes problems, display to Canadian ears his distant origins? (Always an *American*, only intermittently, because already an American, a philosopher?) Can she actually hear, in the very forms of his analysis, the systems that Chicago had constructed within him? Can she hear a distinctively American system called Aggression?

(But I do love you. Come on. Come. Let's make love. I love your mouth. I loved it when I first saw you. When you think it purses like a kiss. Come on, Tyler. I love you still. But you're just too brainy for an American. You should've been a Quebecois. But I want you anyway.)

He can open an electronic machine, radios, TVs, VCRs, microprocessors (whatever), and fix it. Other people, like Blackie, would see only their devices, their toys. They can play these machines, but they can never understand them. But he can look inside and accurately map the system. Each wire and node, board and port, would fit together into a compact network of functions which, on the surface, could be experienced as the machine's playing. He can remove a motherboard from a microprocessor, hold it between his eyes and the exposed CPU, snuggled tightly within the eviscerated chassis, and perceive the functional relationships of the chips. He understands, can even sketch in his mind's eye, the complex mirrorplay, the analogue manifestations, that they made possible. He thinks about the intricacies of the chips, their etched architectures, the labyrinths of circuitry beneath the threshold of ordinary perception, and grasps not merely the bursts of information, densely flowing, the snapping digital logic (all the humdrum gates that had been opened and closed throughout the course of human history would not amount to the infinitesimal, but ideal, gateness of a single motherboard), but also the tentacularly diffuse background of design and construction. Like Michael Snow's spacewarping geese, the interthreading systems reach back and stretch forward. Beneath them all, the molecular systems themselves swish and flow. Tyler sees the extended lines of force that intersect, quite beyond all direct perception, to create the momentary uniqueness of events.

(You're all power crazy. Tyler, can't you just *enjoy* the music? You beat up on the world when you set about explaining it. That's what you do, Tyler. You beat up on me when you explain me. I must be crazy to love you.)

He turns the corner of Yonge when he reaches Front Street and looks ahead towards Union Station. Opposite the station, the Royal Bank's gold-windowed tower, cool and ithyphallic, thrusts above the railway tracks. Feeling the gusts from the lake, Tyler reflects upon the immense difference between the external weather of the streets and the controlled climates of the towers. He imagines the chilly currents (like an invisible snowman breathing) that flow evenly from floor to floor. The tracks that thread thickly between downtown Toronto and the lake reflect, like the Royal Bank itself, a commercial system of values. Nature had been regularly shrunk. (The image of Chicago's pure lakeshore flicks into his consciousness, grows and spreads: the railway system diffused, held back from the lake, hardly even carbon flakes in the long blue gem.) Here nature could never have been worth the mercantile advantages that immediate access promised. There is aggression in Canada too, he thinks morosely, and there always has been. Canadians have bullied a great number of things including the shores of Lake Ontario. He has never been able to make Blackie see that smug pretensions of mildness and diplomacy might be just another way to kick ass.

(What do you mean strategies of weakness? Tyler, that's crap. Just crap. Adler? I don't know what you're talking about. People are polite and you say they're weak. That's what I keep telling you, Tyler. You're a bully. It's gross. Saying that about strategies of weakness is just your way to bully me. *Please.*)

Blackie had kicked an empty can of Diet Coke across the floor. It was her first visit to his apartment. Unfamiliar patterns set her off. Storming in the centre of the living room, she kicked halfheartedly at the clutter: the stacked and the spinebent books poised against the floor, the notecards, the open journals, the floppies, pens, empty plates and glasses, the discarded wrappers. The chaos of male narcissism. Her tears had begun to well. Goddamn it, Tyler. Let's get married. This stinking mess you live in. You slob. Bullying everyone else but no discipline for yourself. You need me. Goddamn it. She had taken out a joint for them to smoke. Later, in bed, a lazy buzz of euphoria lingering through him, holding a toke glowing in the darkness between them, listening to Robert Smith singing "The Hanging Garden" at low volume, he had said, Yes. Shapeless in the dark again, Smith had sung. In the dark. Shapeless. O.K.

That had been three months before. Since then she has called him a goddamn American several times. But he feels happy that she loves him even though she probably has no grasp at all of how his thinking proceeds. Blackie would not have understood Professor Hartshorn brooding publicly over the consciousness of his bathwater. She would not be able to understand Whitehead's idea of the structuring occasionality of events beneath the on-flow of appearance. And she could not understand, now or ever, how he can take apart the hidden workings of both concepts and mere machines, nor why he feels compelled to drive analytically at surfaces, nor what pleasures he takes from unpacking concepts (smooth, lovely, unassailable: each looking so distinct) crowded beneath their apparent monadic simplicity. But him she does love and he does respond. The acute edges of his thinking are blunted in her presence, grown shapeless.

Blackie has begun to impose herself upon his apartment. She drives him out to Mississauga and makes him buy a bookcase from Ikea. She clears the floor and places neat strips of paper in the books that he habitually leaves open, or which he has marked using other books or pens. She cleans his narrow galley kitchen, the oven, the fridge full of things the nature of which he has forgotten, and the bathroom. A fresh order gestures from even the corners. She buys containers for cereal, nuts, pitted prunes, and the raw bran that he likes to sprinkle on things, not only on the cereal, so that he will stop leaving packages open on the counter, their contents drying into bark and dust. Pointed by new expectations, his life, like his apartment newly arranged, seems suddenly linear, abnormally external. Now when he goes for walks he sometimes finds himself looking at children.

At their wedding, Blackie wears an off-white dress in a paisley pattern of red and brown swirls that reaches to her ankles. (It is a keepsake of her mother's own young life in the promise-veined sixties.) They are married in a park on the Islands, the minister, who wears a long white robe and chain smokes, talks to Tyler about the Chicago Bears. The wedding party is small, mostly Blackie's friends, and they all cross over on the ferry together. A young woman with stiff, pink hair has brought along a boombox, and they listen to a CD of The Cure. Blackie sings "Charlotte Sometimes" softly, in her purring voice, along with Robert Smith. (Tyler hears the haunting phrase repeated but cannot tell, in its aural obscurity, whether he is hearing a name or an adverb.) After the ceremony they eat a picnic that Blackie and a few friends have prepared. There are sandwiches from All the Best Breads and carrot cakes from Carole's Cheesecake Company. A young man wearing an oversize black suit with a green-highlighted Mohawk dances moodily around them like an encircling scroll. Within his solitary bracketing, they dance, the blue-glazed lake behind them, while strolling Torontonians look on in subdued amazement. Tyler hugs Blackie close to him. Sometimes I dream, she whispers. Tyler hugs her to his chest, but recalls, in the soft smoke of her words, the moment when he had said good-bye to Swift Hall. An instant of renunciation that he will never be able, nor ever try, to undo.

She bites, laughing, gently upwards at his ear. Tyler looks over her shoulder. He can see the phallic office buildings crowding the close horizon. For a brief moment, he thinks wildly that they are laughing at him for having, just this once, neglected to think. All the underforming systems, if any, have now dissolved, zapped by a massive global deletion, into zero access. Only the concrete shafts, brutally inexplicable, hulk irrationally in their arbitrary placings, like monstrous outgrowths. For this moment at least, the primordial nature of God has disappeared. Staring futilely back, his vision blocked by the buildings' unyielding blankness, still tightly clasping his bride, he thinks sorrowfully.

—. Forgive me, Whitehead. Forgive me, *magister labyrinthorum*, forgive me for having become a fool.

TRACES

The Sly Man sits in one of the single seats at the front of the bus, facing backwards. Across from him, knee rubbing knee, a young woman, obviously a student, sits reading Merleau-Ponty's angular *Le Visible et l'invisible*. Her short black duffle coat, open to the bus's heat, reveals a beige wool sweater. The Sly Man studies her. Her breasts are pointed and high, but not large. Her face is pretty, though not beautiful, with sharp features, almost a definite *museau*. When she has grown older, her face will rupture into plagihedral surfaces, the distinct planes thickening and angling away from each other. She will begin to look like one of Cézanne's women. The 1890s paintings of Mme. Cézanne, *Woman with a Coffeepot*, or *Mme. Cézanne with her Hair Let Down*, suggest how the girl's face may one day appear: clotted, precipitous, disparate. Perhaps, the Sly Man thinks, the 1895 *Nude*, with its shadowed scalene head, the dark, adze-like nose reiterating the pubic delta, best anticipates her dissolution.

When the young woman leaves the bus at the Luxembourg Gardens, the Sly Man slides across into her vacated seat, seeking the forward view. Settling into the thick plastic seat, he feels the vestigial warmth of her body. Had he felt this warmth on a toilet seat, one of the two-Franc cylinders along St-Germain-des-Près, for example, his imagination would not be so ardent. Then, he might have felt only disgust rising through his throat like a thick coil of burning sludge. Now, the plastic seat feels like fleshy buttocks. Excitedly, he understands that the warmth he now experiences has seeped from the woman's anal and vaginal cavities. It is a trace of her living body, now gone into the Gardens or down the Boul' Mich. If she knew that he, the perfect stranger with the analytic glance, was feeling her body's warmth, even evoking in his mind's eye the corporeal spaces from which it has leaked, would she feel shame? Could it mean anything at all? How would she respond to the knowledge that she, a student at the Sorbonne, a reader of Merleau-Ponty, a woman with a rich and complex personal life, had invisibly metamorphosed into a trace? That even now a tiny, unobserved particle of her being, left behind and unremarked, was being transmuted into the fuel of a stranger's imagination?

What is the reality of a trace? How much being does it possess? The Sly Man recalls Derrida's argument that the etymology of a word contains the spectrum of its previous common meanings, a history of traces, the reality of which is always present even if ignored. The traces of opposed meanings contaminate each concept, permeating its membrane of significance, cluttering the wishful clarity of its intention. Nothing is clean, sharp, and isolated; everything, murky, fuzzy, and collective. Yet the trace is a powerful advocate for lost presence. Whole fictional worlds explode into being from traces no more expansive than epithets, no more substantial than a handful of qualifications. From a trace as insignificant as fading bodily warmth on a plastic seat, the imagination can construct an entire person, exposing her in secret moments of vulnerability. From the tiniest shard, a fragment of sense or an obscure memory, vast structures, intricate architectures, and expansive cities take shape. The Sly Man wonders at this cognitive force. Then he remembers how a dog seems able to sniff a whole other dog into existence. By a mechanism that the Sly Man does not fully grasp, a dog selectively sniffs urinous traces. From these fading remnants of canine being, the dog seems to imagine distinct dogs, no longer present. It responds with excitement or uninterest as if to a representation, to a re-presented presence. The trace, the Sly Man thinks happily, constitutes the irreducible building-block of significance. Meaning seeps from within a multitudinous constellation of ephemeral, endlessly permutable bits.

Rethinking Ludopolis

French Deck. Solitary stoker of cards. He dealt himself a hand. Turn stills of the past in unending permutations, shuffle and begin. Sort the images again. And sort them again. This game reveals germs of truth, and death.

The world becomes an apparently infinite, yet possibly finite, card game. Image combinations, permutations, comprise the world game.

—*Jim Morrison*

If likelihoods always bore fruit, then Ainslie Wellfleet would have become the Prime Minister of Canada. He came from the right family, an extended, rentier-dominated conglomerate of the kind that rules central Canada, and thus the nation. He had the right education. He graduated from Upper Canada College, then from the University of Toronto with a first-class honours degree in Economics and Political

Science. After that he took an M.A. in Philosophy before reading Law. He lacked only one ingredient for success in Canadian political life: a fluent command of French. His family had paid lip-service to the principle of bilingualism, but no one in his family actually spoke French and most were notorious Francophobes. Duncan, his older brother, whom I have long known from brokerage circles, never misses an opportunity to pour contempt on Francophonism. I remember once sitting with Duncan and some commodity brokers in a small restaurant in Montréal when he called the waiter over to our table just as we were getting up to leave. A short, squarely trimmed old man with thick grey hair, a bristling moustache of an out-moded type, he might easily have been a *poilu* of 1918. The old man came up and stood beside Duncan. "Here," Duncan said, quite warmly and smiling, "this is for you." The old man put out his hand discreetly and Duncan slipped him a lighted firecracker. As he ran from the restaurant laughing, his friends hooting and yammering, I stayed to apologize. I left a tip with the old man, but the damage was irreparable, both to his self-esteem and to a tiny corner of French/English relations in Canada. With such attitudes widely spread in his family, it is no wonder that Ainslie did not learn to speak French.

Yet during the long command of Prime Minister Pierre Trudeau, it had more and more come to seem that only a man with genuine pretension to fluency in both official languages could hope to lead a major party and, eventually, the government. Canada's status as a bilingual nation had solidified into official myth just in time to consign Ainslie, and anyone like him, to the sidelines of public life. More than twenty years of his family's indoctrination appeared to have been wasted. It was for this reason, as an act of self-preservation, a desperate move to enable him to cling to the illusory promises of power, that Ainslie decided to apply for a government scholarship to study philosophy at the Sorbonne. It was true that he certainly did not need public funds to pursue an education. He might have studied anything in comfort anywhere in the world. Yet he perceived, correctly, that the cachet of having had such a scholarship would contribute to his aura. He had always bitterly resented the fact that he had been passed over for a Rhodes Scholarship. Hence he seemed disproportionately overjoyed when he received the award. A glowing letter from Ottawa informed him that it was young people like himself in whom the future of Canada resided. He withdrew from the study of Law and left for Paris late in August of 1983.

I think that it is clear that Ainslie Wellfleet did not seriously intend to study philosophy at the Sorbonne. He discussed his plans with me on two occasions during that summer, and I had few doubts that his only purpose was to prepare himself for public life, either in politics or, failing that, in the mandarinate of the public service. As a secondary benefit, he did hope to learn enough French not only to achieve his political goals but also to enjoy dining in the better restaurants in Montréal. He did look ahead to the possibility of a stint as Minister of External Affairs or as an Ambassador. These are roles that would have required him to possess a working bilingualism, to be sure, but nonetheless he consistently viewed learning French as a matter of appearances, a necessary but inessential acquisition. I remember distinctly how he laughed at the thought that the government of Canada had given him the scholarship when there were probably hundreds of studious Francophile students in the universities across Canada, anyone of whom deserved official support more than he did and would have gained more fruitful knowledge from it. That, he said, smiling in the chill, flinty manner that all the members of his family possess, was merely the chief rule of Canadian life: to support the establishment of Central Canada, to which he belonged by birth, habit, and intent. I once heard Duncan's smile compared unfavourably to a hangman's and, when issues arose such as the scholarship, Ainslie made his family resemblance evident. I am sure that when he left for Paris his dominant sentiments were Francophobic. At the party that was given for him by friends from the University and Osgoode Hall, he made a jocular speech in which he treated his departure as a painful exile to a land of poor hygiene, extravagant mores, and cerebral obfuscation.

Hence it was something of a surprise when I received a short note from Ainslie in February of 1984 indicating that he was having a wonderful time and enjoying his lectures at the Sorbonne. He had taken a marvellous flat on the rue de Babylone in the seventh arrondissement with three rooms and a view looking over the Hôtel des Invalides. He walked along the Boul' St-Germain each day, stopping in bookshops on his way to lectures, and then later having coffee with friends from the University. It certainly did not sound like the Ainslie Wellfleet whom I knew, nor like the one who had made the comic speech the night before his departure. The Ainslie I knew had no intention of studying philosophy, and indeed, despite his M.A., had no deep interest in the subject at all. His note baffled me. I realized that something must have happened and that a change so basic, and so contrary to his long-standing dispositions, could not have taken place without sufficient cause. I supposed at first that he must have met a beautiful Parisienne whose presence had lured him to lectures that otherwise he would not have attended. In any event, I was alerted to an inexplicable change.

During the subsequent two years, Ainslie wrote to a number of friends as well as to members of his family. I knew his sister, Rowena, and occasionally spoke to her when our paths crossed. From her I gathered a great deal of corroborating evidence. Ainslie had become a serious student of French Philosophy, loved Paris, and had flatly declined to pay any visits home for the first two years of his scholarship. He spoke glowingly of the distinguished French intellectuals with whom he had met and conversed. The latter comment, which was reported from several sources, particularly astounded me, for it implied that Ainslie had already learned how to speak French well enough to hold discussions with the leading figures of French intellectual life. In a rather snarling manner, Duncan remarked that Ainslie's brain must have turned soft from eating too much French cheese. Ainslie wrote Rowena that he now intended to remain in Paris until he had completed a book on contemporary philosophical issues. His father was thought to be considering ordering him to resume the Law or to manage family property in Saskatoon or Edmonton. However, nothing came of this and Ainslie remained in Paris. His presence there gradually became an established mystery. At dinners, or meeting casually at the Royal Yacht Club, people would inquire after him, exchange witticisms at his expense, laugh, and go on to more interesting matters. However, I never lost my sense of astonishment at Ainslie's change of intention and I began collecting the comments, suppositions, and theories that his friends and family put forward to explain his absence.

After Ainslie abruptly vanished in early 1987, I attempted to discover everything that reflected upon his paradoxical immersion in French intellectual life. I asked to see letters that he had written, begged anecdotes, and turned every conversation away from the tragedy itself to the question of the unexpected fascination that Paris had exerted upon his mind. At the time I did not surmise that my investigations into the mystery of his intellectual metamorphosis might eventually provide an explanation for his sudden and distressing disappearance.

Quite rapidly I began to put together a picture of life in Paris that was wholly unexpected. Repeatedly, Ainslie had written of his Parisian existence in words that must have, as I felt then, described the margins, the fringes, the accidents, but not the essence, of intellectual life. Nearly everyone to whom he had written reported that Ainslie had stressed the odd, the bizarre, the eccentric. He had consistently given accounts of intractable yet trivial problems that he had heard discussed, problems that seemed rooted in the most ordinary experience, or in the pratfalls of ordinary language, but, once isolated in analysis, wore the masks of clowns: distorted, grotesquely funny, but disturbing. Ainslie had been attracted to the experience of play and paradox. This conclusion did not actually emerge from any individual letter but once I had begun to collate all of his comments upon life in Paris a larger obsession became evident. He seldom mentioned restaurants, museums only when they led him on to a paradoxical commentary, and the ordinary aspects of social existence in a great city never appeared at all.

From Ainslie's letters I was able to cull a number of significant anecdotes. They are all linked by his obsession with play and paradox, but they go beyond abstract games. Taken together they present a conceptually coherent narrative in which a limited number of highly colourful issues recur and in which a cast of *dramatis personae*, as bizarrely colourful as the ideas they discuss, create the stage they walk upon. The problems that recur have in common that they are intractable, open to endless discussion but closed to definitive solutions, while being always peripheral to human life as people live it. I have been told that these problems constitute the common playground of certain philosophers and many literary critics. I can only say that they were entirely new to me: I read Ainslie's letters with an increasing sense of amazement and bewilderment.

In his letters Ainslie reports discussions in which leading French intellectuals discuss such problems as signification, play, games, carnival, masks, codes, absence, presence, and the nature of systems or, as Ainslie once put it, systemness. Some of these, at least, would strike almost anyone as legitimate difficulties that intelligent men and women might discuss. In Ainslie's accounts they invariably take on such odd shapes, follow such outrageous twists, that the context of the discussion seems almost to destroy the validity of the problem itself. Certain names assume an immense presence in Ainslie's anecdotes: Roland Barthes, who died a few years before Ainslie arrived in Paris but whose ghost, as it were, continues to haunt all discussion, Jacques Derrida, Gérard Genette, Tzvetvan Todorov, and Michael Bakhtin. The latter appears to have been a dead Russian who, though always absent, makes himself present. Furthermore, there seems to be a secondary group of people, followers and disciples, who participate in the discussions but do so on the level of punctuation. The names of Red Gallagher, Bernard Galazzo, Lysiana Medine, Marie-Hélène Cahuzac, Michel Tasd'homme, Colette Tourbillon, Georgina Hiboux, and Yves Zagli give a sense of narrative depth to Ainslie's anecdotes. I came to know them as his familiars, as students dedicated to the contemplation of essentially opaque problems, if not to their clarification. They are the devoted admirers of the great *maîtres de penser* themselves.

Having made these preliminary remarks I wish now to record some of Ainslie's philosophical anecdotes. I believe that the narrative coherence that binds them will become evident. They do present, to be sure, a distorted, and perhaps unappealing, view of intellectual life in Paris, but it may be a perspective that carries a measure of truth. Significantly, Ainslie's anecdotes, taken together, sketch a scene that, in its intense intellectualism and discursive combat, stands for the all the debates that distinguished the various torments of theory during the 1980s, even in our phlegmatic, steady-as-she-goes Toronto. These anecdotes reveal Ainslie in a way that makes plain the gulf separating himself in Paris from himself in Toronto. I think that they may also suggest why he crossed this gulf so soon after arriving in Paris and why he stubbornly refused to cross back over. It may prove to be a more difficult point to make, but I also believe that these anecdotes, culled from his letters, will cast light upon his disappearance. They may even contain the seeds of an acceptable hypothesis to explain it.

[I have established the following anecdote from collated versions of letters that Ainslie wrote to Elizabeth Scott, Rowena, and his mother between August and the end of November 1984. The first, and perhaps most authentic, version appears in his letter to Rowena dated August 16, 1984. I have been struck by how often Ainslie's *contes philosophiques* take place in museums and galleries. One must suppose that the Parisian *maîtres* spend an inordinate amount of time in visiting museums. Although this would seem odd by North American standards, where philosophers normally appear to do nothing at all, it may not be odd by the standards of Paris. I should think that a museum would be a very stimulating place to carry on intellectual argument. My friend Macdonald Throckmorten, once the curator of a small museum in Nova Scotia, likes to say that a museum is a memorial or celebratory repository. His first cousin, Basingborn, who is more inclined towards the conceptual side of things, argues that a museum is a kind of ocular syllabus of human knowledge.]

One Sunday at the Beaubourg, Genette and Derrida paused in front of Picasso's *La femme en bleu*. "Read this," Derrida exclaimed, and thrust the plastic card with annotations into Genette's hands. The museum's annotations claimed, he observed, that the creation before them, with one breast, no hands, a neck like a pyramid, one eyebrow, two dissimilar eyes, and a face decomposed into six planes, was *un personnage*, a character. (When Lysiana Medine told me this story I at once secretly recalled the painting by Henri Hayden in the Art Gallery of Ontario, which is provocatively called *Personnage* and of which similar questions might be raised.) Genette replied that *La femme en bleu* was an explicable consequence of the artist having employed certain necessary conventions for the formation of character in painting.

Marie-Hélène Cahuzac, who had come to the Beaubourg with them, then asked if it was not the case that a character was simply a proper name. If so, then *La femme en bleu* could not be a character since she did not have a proper name. "Unhappily, no," Derrida answered, "if only it were so simple. That is a falsification of Formalist doctrine for which we are, I believe, indebted to Roland Barthes." He went on to point out that the proper name united the semes, as Barthes liked to call them, and invested them with an identity. Nonetheless, the character was composed of the semes, was constituted by their recurrence, and the name merely capped the heap. The name marked a momentary (that is, illusory) solidification.

"Do you then accept the Formalist doctrine concerning characterization?" Genette asked. "Is a character, for you, merely the inventory of its semes, as Barthes seemed to hold in certain moments, or the totality of its traits as Tomashevsky and the other Russians maintained? That is a surprisingly weak position for you to hold. A character is more ungraspable than that, more incoherent than that doctrine will allow: a character is always a creature in flight." Derrida laughed and responded that if such were the case, then *La femme en bleu* could be a character as much as Odette de Crecy or M. de Charlus, for certainly they are all equally in flight and ungraspable. He then added that an American Neo-Formalist had asserted that literary characters were mostly empty canvas (which, no doubt, applies as well to painted characters) and that was, perhaps, the furtherest position into which Formalism could advance.

Red Gallagher, who was also along, then asked what could constitute a character, in literature or in any other art that was capable of generating characters, beyond the semes, recurring or otherwise. Genette replied that three linguistic functions constituted a character in literature (and their equivalents, if there were any, in painting): the conventions that brought it forth, the idiolectic properties of its discourse, and the focalization in which it appeared, either through the narrator's voice or through that of some other character. He went on to claim that the idiolectic properties of the character's discourse were, in themselves, varieties of semes so that, in the end, it was the combination of semes and conventions. To this Derrida smirked rather insultingly and replied that if M. Genette were correct, if that were a sufficient account of the problem, then *La femmme en bleu* could easily appear in a narrative since the physical aspects of her body, which the museum's plastic card partially enumerated, could be easily transcoded into linguistic signifiers and incorporated into the discourse of narrative. And conventions, he added, are notoriously polymorphic, open (like Cartesian wax) to metamorphosis. Red Gallagher and Marie-Hélène

Cahuzac agreed that this seemed so. However, Red Gallagher reminded everyone that Barthes had said that discourse itself was a character and he wondered how, in a reverse process of transcoding semes, one would paint discourse. Everyone then turned to observe Genette phrase his reply.

"Yes, that may be so," Genette responded, ignoring Red Gallagher's final question. "With a knowledge of narrative conventions, one could, indeed, create a discourse in which *La femme en bleu* could be constituted as a character." Derrida laughed at this, having already placed his secret response in readiness. But before Derrida could intervene, Red Gallagher challenged Genette to write such a narrative. To everyone's surprise, he agreed to do this and it was decided that in two weeks they would all meet at L'Auberge Basque to hear Genette read his narrative. Before they went on to another painting and different problems, Marie-Hélène Cahuzac asked Derrida what he actually thought might pass for a sufficient definition of character. Derrida laughed once again and replied that M. Genette had fallen into a trap, a typical trap of Formalism, perhaps an inevitable trap. "There are no characters," he exclaimed, with the vivacity of a player exposing a hidden check in chess. "There is only characterization." He went on to explain that a character, if constituted by anything, must be made from signifiers, but these, to make sense, depended upon a principle of structuration, a hidden artifice which was, no doubt, what M. Genette had in mind when he spoke of conventions. The hidden artifice could only be known through the signifiers and hence, paradoxically, it must change as the play of signification shifts (as it will inevitably) with each reading. Change invariably becomes exchange. A character is no more stable than the discourse which constitutes it and that, he concluded triumphantly, is indefinitely unstable.

Two weeks later, at L'Auberge Basque, Genette read his narrative. In it a man becomes obsessed by a beautiful woman with long black hair and classic features. Whenever he sees her, she wears blue. In his obsession, the man begins to dream about the woman. The dream continues and each night he dreams once again about the beloved. However, in each dream the woman is subtly different. Features shift, change their location minutely, in an endless play of mutability. Some night, in some dream, Genette proclaimed victoriously, the man will dream *La femme en bleu*, for at some point that particular combination of traits must be reached.

Derrida admitted that Genette had solved the conundrum brilliantly. There is only characterization, he observed, and never character, only the play of difference between the semes. "M. Genette has hit upon the solution to the problem of character: in the free play of characterization, which is no more than an aspect of that which constitutes the text, its shadow, and its synecdoche, it is not necessary to have been played, to be played, or to become played. It is only necessary that the play be open." Marie-Hélène Cahuzac giggled and remarked that she believed that Picasso had known this before Derrida's claim that Genette had learned it (if he truly had).

[I have collated the following anecdote from several versions written between February and March 1985. The most important version appears in a letter written, within a context of affectionate reminiscences, to Elizabeth Scott. Duncan has informed me that, in a letter to him, Ainslie once referred to the Beaubourg as the omphalos of Paris.]

Another afternoon at the Beaubourg, Derrida stood with Genette looking down from the acrylic tubeway on the fifth level. The Place Georges Pompidou was, as always, crowded with hawkers, buskers, spielers, acrobats, artisans, confidence men, and (one must suppose) every variety of human *escamotage*. Both Genette and Derrida were drawn to the efforts of a Houdini-type escape artist who was struggling to free himself from a series of ropes and knots that his audience had loaded upon him. The escape artist had been tightly bound and his efforts to break loose seemed to be in vain. There, Genette exclaimed, is the struggling icon of this museum! Art fights against immense odds to free itself from its official enterrement. Even in its failure to break free, it mocks the mighty success of its captors, its bounds, its official status.

Michel Tasd'homme, who usually makes a point of accompanying the philosophers when they visit museums, then asked if art did not on occasion, as every Houdini, succeed in struggling free. Genette suggested that the unsuccessful Houdini could only be an icon for art captured within the walls of a museum, as the modern art collection was bound, on moveable walls and plastic cards with simplistic annotations, like Beauty in the castle of the Beast, there within the Beaubourg. Derrida laughed at this. (I have been repeatedly struck since I arrived in Paris by how often Derrida is reported to have laughed. Many of the stories about him begin with him laughing. He seems to be, in this respect, the incarnation of Democritus. Perhaps philosophers who believe in the Void must laugh. Certainly a concept of void, not to say voiding and voidance, seems to put things into perspective.) Abruptly, he flung an outstretched hand towards the Gothic shape of St-Eustache in the middle distance, his fingers sketching it against the acrylic walls of the tubeway. There, once the Revolutionary Temple of Agriculture, named so fittingly in honour of a Roman general, stands a more authoritative icon of aesthetic constraint. And it, too, he added, is constructed from the emptied contents of hourglasses. He then remarked to Michael Tasd'homme that, as usual, M. Genette had played a losing hand.

Anything may be twisted into an icon of anything else, but it gains, from this honour, no more than the bare illusion of substance. The audience has bound the escape artist in order to see him free himself: that is similar to the way readers bind the text, with conventions of order, priority, and expectations, in order to fix the meaning that they wish to know. The ropes are like the text itself, binding, holding, but always capable of being slipped, of giving way, of slipping free, of being free, of freeing. The man, who reminds us so forcefully of Houdini, is significance: bound, struggling, but infinitely resilient. He doubles textuality.

Georgina Hiboux recalled that Julia Kristeva has once observed that the process of semiosis, the mind's unconscious *chora*, resembled a circus. The acts were like the spontaneous out-pourings of signification. Kristeva has once seen Martine Gruss at the Cirque à l'Ancienne leaping the garters in a voltige act and it had reminded her of the mind's, the unconscious language's, spontaneous domination of form. The slippered feet high above a horse's back indicated, Georgina Hiboux argued, that art can slip free much as unconscious semiosis does despite the bounds of syntax and usage. But Michel Tasd'homme saw in the Kristevan anecdote only the illustration of binding, not freeing. Gruss' feet had been trained, he pointed out, bound in a way nearly Chinese. It might have been that her feet, before binding, had been spontaneous, capable of spontaneous play before play loses itself in the specious salvation of games.

Then Derrida invited Michel Tasd'homme to drink a beer with him. The only icon, he observed, is the movement itself. But M. Genette, like every other binder and unbinder, wishes to freeze this movement at some congenial point. In reality, if there is a true literary Absolute, it is movement itself, the irreducible play of signification. Genette writes as he does in order not to become bound himself and thus, in unbinding, becomes bound. He is always a bound binder of the unbindable unbound.

[Of all the philosophers who play the dominant roles in Ainslie's anecdotes, none is more appealing than Todorov. He appears to possess a genuine humanity. Ainslie records him quite lovingly, which is unlike the way he describes Derrida or Genette. Derrida seldom appears physically in the anecdotes other than as a laughing holder of the last word. Of course, he is said to wear a leather jacket and to have, like a fugitive character from a Malraux novel, the cold glance of a terrorist. Todorov, however, is often described as thin or angular, and as having a lion's-mane of unkempt hair. Ainslie several times records his odd habit of speaking with his hand inside his trousers, as if he were unaware of his own body when he spoke and needed to remind himself of its essentiality. The following anecdote is mentioned a number of times in letters written between the end of 1984 and June 1985. The events it recounts must have occurred some time earlier.]

Todorov led a group of the young followers of the *maîtres* to the Place Denfert-Rochereau to visit the catacombs. Whispering giddily, almost like children, they descended the one hundred stone steps into, Red Gallagher exultantly observed, *l'Empire de la Mort*. (Although he was only reading aloud the inscription over the lintel, the mere whiff of Rhetoric caused several to snicker.) Todorov, his sense of social formation and purpose always acute, attempted to provide some relevant history, pointing out the official origin of the catacombs shortly prior to the Revolution, but several philosophers protested that he made himself sound like M. Foucault. Everyone knows that the Enlightenment promoted system, Colette Tourbillon remarked, and an ossuary for storing bones is analogous to a system for storing knowledge. Are these catacombs, then, similar to the Encyclopedia, Georgina Hiboux asked her. Red Gallagher observed that the Encyclopedia, whatever its systemic faults, could never have smelled of dampness and mud in quite this way. The smell is that of death, Yves Zagli asserted, in his dour Maghreb way. Colette Tourbillon asked, rather slightingly it seemed, if he spoke in personification or only in an abstract noun. With these pleasantries out of the way, Todorov led his friends down the long corridor of bones.

At the Tibias Rotunda, Todorov, still smarting from the correction of his historical intervention, quickly reminded everyone that orchestras have played funeral marches in this spot. Chopin? someone inquired. Saint-Saens most certainly, Todorov replied, flinging his arms wide in a flamboyant pantomime. It would be appropriate for a Dance of Death to be enacted here, in grim counterpoint to the excited flow of traffic on the surface, like a spectral Paris of cerebral pustules. My countryman, Fred Radford, who had joined the philosophers for this visit, but who owes his primary devotion to the sewers, interjected that the more than two thousand kilometres of sewer tunnels constitute a reverse image of Paris, a negative or shadow city beneath the luminous City that we all know so well. They form an intricate rhizome that mirrors the leafy foliage of the crowded streets and inexhaustible traffic. His comment precipitated an intense conversation concerning *Les Misérables* and in particular Hugo's didactic description of the sewers, their fetid streams of slime carrying away the richness of life above ground. Todorov insisted that Jean Valjean should be remembered for his cartographic sinuosity, a hero perhaps, a protagonist certainly, but actually a drawing-pencil that maps Paris like a cursor tracing the outlines of a structure. Or an argument? Red Gallagher wanted to know. Before Todorov could reply, no doubt an incisive disconnection intended, Lysiana Medine reminded him of his recent accident with a bicycle.

Todorov loves to ride bicycles. He can often be observed riding along the streets and boulevards of the fifth and sixth arrondissements. He rides to and from his home in the eleventh arrondissement over the Pont de Sully sometimes more than once a day. One morning, riding with an insouciance that has become legendary, he fell from his bicycle in the midst of traffic at the intersection of rue Jacob and rue Bonaparte, causing a minor traffic jam. He was fortunate that he had not been immediately run over. As the traffic piled up, increasingly jammed, knotted and corked, he had begun to reflect upon the consistency of traffic. He had fallen in front of it, almost under it, and had impeded it, turned it back, blocked, jammed, corked, knotted, and perplexed it. (He had bent, Michel Tasd'homme had claimed, a straight line in upon itself and created both a knot and a labyrinth: each a perplexity of straightness.) What then was his relationship to this traffic? Was he a jester? A revolutionary? If the traffic flow was official (legitimized by the laws of France, the conventions of driving, a community of shared intention), then merely in falling he must have become unofficial.

Lysiana Medine, who had joined a waiter from the restaurant on the corner in helping Todorov from the centre of the intersection, remembers that he asked her as soon as she reached him whether he had become carnivalesque simply by falling. Had he inadvertently mocked the official flow of traffic from Montparnasse to the Seine? If only momentarily, he had become what the unofficial always is: disruptive, mocking, parodic, an unwelcome travesty. Later, Derrida reminded him that, taking the uncertain Romance etymology of "traffic" into account, a term from exchange, negotiation, commerce, and trade, he might just as well wonder whether he had become a pirate. Yves Zagli is reported to have suggested that Todorov describe himself as a *filibustero*.

In the catacombs, nothing seems official and nothing, other than drops of water, actually flows. The ossuary freezes life and it is, immutably still and laid-out, as official as a rule or code of laws. Nonetheless, the dead, Red Gallagher asserted, are officially carnivalesque. Necessarily so, he added. The catacombs, simply in being, mock the traffic above in the Place Denfert-Rochereau. On the other hand, the sewers, which flow constantly and emit, even in the public space along the Gallery Belgrand, a perceptible feculence that inspires visitors with an almost literary *frisson*, are inescapably proper. No one could look more official than an *égoutier* in spotless blue uniform, Fred Radford added, and they are officially charged with the maintenance of *les égouts*. Bernard Galazzo, who had kept his silence until this moment, abruptly framed the paradox that had now emerged, scarcely observed. With considerable glee, he pointed out that the catacombs look official in their coldness and immutability but are carnivalesque in function, while the sewers, although they might seem unofficial, mocking, and parodic of the life above, are actually, as M. Radford understood so clearly, systematically official. Todorov obviously took pleasure in this paradox. Paris has two reverse images, he exclaimed joyfully.

Michel Tasd'homme, who attempts to speak for Derrida when he is absent, observed that the surface of Paris is, like all others, a permeable membrane, a false boundary (although highly evident) across which flow traces of either region. The unofficial makes the official possible and each is defined in terms of the other. He had begun to explain the relationship between the catacombs and the sewers when Colette Tourbillon grasped his point in advance and excitedly observed that there must be a permeable boundary, a membrane of sorts, between the two underground domains. There is earth and rock, even, it must be, numerous tunnels and ducts between the two, Red Gallagher remarked. Colette Tourbillon rewarded his intervention with a look of scorn. The true membrane, the conceptual boundary, permits the traces of each region to flow freely in ideational exchange. Human waste, the abject of surface life, is sent underground, shunned and exiled, either as a ceremonial ossuary or as cascading effluvia. On the surface, there could not be an abject unless there were a place to which it could be banished. Beneath the surface, the abject could be neither frozen pageantry nor fluid expulsion unless both were possible and each summoned, while excluding, the other. Delighted to have seen so much in such a crowded space, the philosophers, whispering together in giggling inconsequentiality, climbed back up the stone stairs to the Place Denfert-Rochereau, blustering as always with its noisy, circling traffic.

[In first culling, and then in editing, these anecdotes, I have been struck by the central position that the dead Russian thinker, M.M. Bakhtin, occupies in Parisian intellectual life. The philosophers, normally so arrogant and xenophobic, appear to have opened their mind to this most unParisian, one-legged Russian linguist. The following anecdote can be found most fully expressed in a letter that Ainslie wrote, on October

14th, 1986, to his old friend from Varsity days, Dr. Woods Drumm, now a professor of linguistics at the University of Lethbridge. I have modified it slightly by reference to fragmentary versions of the anecdote in other letters.]

After Todorov, following Kristeva's lead in her *Semiotikè*, had published his study of Bakhtin, certain dialogic concepts became widely discussed. Both Red Gallagher and Abel Trigo-Cabral have been loud in their appreciation of Bakhtin's insistence upon the concept of dialogue, of duality in human utterance. Structuralism, Red Gallagher likes to argue, is essentially (he draws that word out, underlining it with his lips) monological. It has always been an act of theoretical terrorism. Lévi-Strauss, Greimas, or Bremond might be seen to have the same relationship to human thought as terrorists to human society. In another incarnation, Red Gallagher would say, they might have been thugs, slipping up behind unwary victims: practising the sudden garrotte with an elegant waxed cord.

Todorov has always insisted upon viewing Bakhtin whole. He dismisses discussion of dialogue or carnival outside of their place within the onion- (and domed) layered edifice of Bakhtin's global strategy for linguistic analysis. However, even after Todorov had published his book on Bakhtin, Parisians discussed the notion of carnival or of dialogism but not much else. (One did, occasionally hear, even before Todorov, if I can believe Abel Trigo-Cabral, about polyphonic discourse and even heteroglossia, but these were distinctly minor chords in the labyrinthine fugue of Parisian discourse.) In particular, "carnival" (a charismatic word if there ever was one!) tends to be assimilated to play or to game (*jeu*, of course, so one can never be quite certain) which transforms the Bakhtinian term into a net of wide applicability (having large holes) ideally suited for seining. Hence carnival, as it is commonly used, becomes a mere synonym (though quite picturesque) for *ludisme*, the playful transgression of official rules.

After Todorov fell from his bicycle, one heard the question of official as against unofficial discourse occur more frequently. He had been struck by his own suddenly unofficial role and continued his meditations out loud even after he had regained his official status as semiotician and intellectual. Followers of Todorov in the matter of Bakhtin began (adopting the masks of urban ethnologists) to observe the authentic expressions of carnivalesque spirit in Paris. They actively sought out instances of collective play, spontaneous or ritualistic (it didn't seem to matter: although Todorov himself thought that it did), in crowds and flowing throngs.

The steps in front of Sacré-Coeur and La Place des Poètes beneath the Montparnasse Tower are cited as fruitful vortices of the carnivalesque. Indeed, most of the well-known squares, places, parvis, and concourses of the city seem normally (or can become) carnivalesque. On the other hand, such crowded places as the Boul' St-Germain-des-Près or the rue Saint André des Arts do not seem genuinely carnivalesque since they are thronged by tourists, by semiological outsiders. (They are also linear and this makes a difference with respect to carnival: authentic carnival is both spontaneous and synchronic, an exploration of the available paradigms for action, and hence metaphoric, but tourism is planned and diachronic, a run-through of the possibilities for combination, and hence metonymic. As the Bakhtinians define it, carnival is a metaphor, but tourism is just another metonymy.) It is impossible to have carnival at the Opera, even if they are singing *La Bohème*, Red Gallagher likes to say, but one can always have a bit of carnival in the concourse of the Metro at *l'Etoile*. How can you have ludic transgressions of rules where the rules are not understood? Wherever one can observe readers of tarot cards, shell games, singers of folksongs, fire-eaters, mimes, buskers, clowns, African strongmen, Houdinis, or what-have-you, there is a good chance to observe authentic carnival.

The place in front of the Beaubourg (the spot where Derrida and Genette had remarked an escape artist fail, and, from this *échec*, drew both semiological and aesthetic conclusions) has become the favourite vantage from which to observe the unflowing of carnival. And in one sense it would be difficult to find a more spontaneously carnivalesque spot in Paris (being every day what the steps in front of Sacré-Coeur are on the night of July 14th). Derrida has been heard to remark that the kaleidoscope of acts (all extremities of human prowess, hence "acts") mocked the glacial congealing of modern art that takes place within the Beaubourg. He is said to have looked down once from the fifth level pedestrian tubeway and watched a Cameroon strongman press his chest against the tines of a pitchfork as three men attempted to drive him from within a circle he had drawn on the concrete. There stands, Derrida laughed, modern art resisting the official impulses of French government to humiliate it, to defeat it, to push it away out of its spontaneous signification.

Todorov, the lessons of his bicycle fall always fresh in his mind, refuses to allow the assimilation of carnival to a concept as generalized as *ludisme*. Carnival is essentially unofficial, he likes to say, but it cannot exist other than in a dialogue with the official. The mocker must always borrow (or steal) the utterance he intends to mock. To parody one must speak in the voice of the parodied: together, locked in a discursive embrace, mocker and mocked (screwer and screwee) perform a semiotic dance. Todorov often cites Propp that "theft cannot take place before the door is forced." Abel Trigo-Cabral, his admiring follower, declares that Paris is a city engaged in a carnival that fills the space between the exuberance of the people and the inflexible constraint of the official rules. The one cannot exist without the other. Their co-duration constitutes human existence.

[In editing Ainslie Wellfleet's anecdotes, I have been repeatedly struck by how central a role is played by the concept of play. In all my studies at the University of Toronto, I do not remember that play was ever discussed. I should have thought, prior to reading through Ainslie's letters, that play was something that children did until they grew up and that there was little more to be said about it. However, it appears that earnest philosophers can take play seriously and that it can pervade the most astringent arguments. I suppose that I should confess that I had never taken "carnival" to be an important concept and yet, within the milieu in which Ainslie lived, it was clearly important. In Canada we have many winter carnivals, of which we are justly proud, but I doubt that anyone has thought about the word itself or attempted to define it. Duncan surprised me when he reported that Ainslie had called the Beaubourg the omphalos of Paris by adding that Ainslie must have lost his dictionary since, clearly he should have called it the *aisselle*. Now that is a good example of Torontonian wordplay, if rather unusually bilingual. Our play is dry and precise. Hence I think it is evident that Ainslie's interest in play indicates, more than any other single factor, the distance that he had crossed over. The following anecdote comes from a letter written to me in November 1986.]

Paris is a city at play. The unofficial voices are heard in all the gardens, on all the parvis, in every place. I attempted this definition (and its poor English pun) the other night in conversation. Yves Zagli thought that it was improper for me, who have lived a bare three years here, to offer definitions of a city so many-levelled, so labyrinthine, as Paris. Bernard Galazzo was more encouraging. He suggested the first act of a mind confronting a phenomenon it cannot understand is to define it. There then arose a dispute as to whether I had offered a definition or a classification (some cities are at work; others, like Paris, at play), an analogy or only an impression. Yves Zagli reminded everyone that Walter Benjamin had called Paris the "capital of the nineteenth century" but this rubric (whether definition or impression) would have made sense neither to the Parisians of the last century (obsessed by Baron Haussmann's urban renewals, the consequences of revolution, and the implications of alien ideologies) nor to those of this century. I might call Paris a city at play, if I chose, but it would only reflect my outside-not-yet-inside condition. Such an account could only be an interpretive, not a genuinely hermeneutic, move.

Then Bernard Galazzo remembered that Derrida had once suggested that Paris should be considered a Ludopolis (certainly not, as Maurice Roche had claimed, a Mnemopolis) in recognition of the levels, the varieties, and the conceptually distinct modes of play that can be observed here. A philosopher's paradise (he said) and hence a Ludopolis. Genette had replied that M. Derrida must not mean that Paris can be defined in terms of its freeplay (*jeu libre*) since that, as everyone who had ever tried to read M. Derrida's writing knew, was simply the condition of signification, of everything, *tout court*. No doubt he must mean that Paris can be defined by its modes of transgressive play, its mere *ludisme*. Like any text, Paris is constructed upon diverse codes. To play, one must understand these codes (just as in playing a game one must understand the rules: if one didn't understand the rules of chess, he might play with the pieces and board, he might make them into playthings, but he could not play chess): codes are the matrix of transgression. Hence the play of Paris (Genette had continued) is full of knowledge. It is like M. Derrida's writing, like *Glas*, say, but not like his concept of play. The play of Paris is a game of initiates, of code users and code violators. It invaginates an external system of repression into an internal ludic space. Parisian play is not (as M. Derrida appears to believe) merely a random mutability. It is not something so prior in necessity that it must be ontologically unbound.

Bernard Galazzo further remembered that Todorov, who had been listening intently but silently up to that point, interjected to remark (in his Bakhtinian mode) that Paris was an infinite utterance (*un énoncé infini*) in which the unofficial voices speak to the official, undercutting but also enhancing them. Derrida, who (for obvious reasons) does not highly regard the Bakhtinian concepts that have attracted so much attention, then proclaimed that *if* Paris were a text, then it would contain its opposite, its *obversus*, hidden within its shadows. One must then read it (if M. Todorov's assertion were correct) according to the conventions of semiological construction, and one must expect to encounter all the semiological bogeys that, like a Spanish *sacamantecas*, lurk along the dark interstices of signification. For that reason, he added, laughing, the play of Paris is perhaps most evident at night. But it is, in any case, the condition of all its meanings and not simply (as M. Genette has claimed) the ludic acts of transgression, however many of these there are.

Todorov then interjected (inconsequentially, Bernard Galazzo thought) that, as Bakhtin had remarked, realism is only one of the possibilities of reality. Derrida responded (in the high spirit of philosophical laughter) that if this were so then one must maintain that reality is merely a possibility of realism. It is then no more than one possibility of its own textuality. A single street, a single action, a word lost in passing, become immediately (even as, and only because, they exist) another, touch upon some other, separately constructing intentionless networks. There the semiological bogey lurks, the one (a true *sacamantecas*) who drains the fat from healthy constructions: there is where the playful find their play. The infinite text of Paris might best be renamed a kaleidoscopolis.

[The following anecdote appears in its most complete form in a letter written to Rowena on January 10, 1987. Some time not long afterwards, Ainslie Wellfleet disappeared. Fragmentary versions of this anecdote occur in letters written as early as September 1984. The meal to which Ainslie refers must, then, have taken place during the summer of that year. I have collated all the available versions of the anecdote. Oddly, the only significant discrepancy regards the exhibition of paintings by Vlaminck to which Ainslie refers only in a letter to Elizabeth Scott.]

Colette Tourbillon likes to cite Barthes to the effect that "we live in a sleeve (*une manche?*) of semes" or, as she occasionally remembers the phrase, in a semiotic envelope. Once sitting with Georgina Hiboux and Michel Tasd'homme in a restaurant across from l'Ecole Militaire (avenue Duquesne), she was asked when (since it appears nowhere in his writings) Barthes had used this phrase. Michel Tasd'homme broke in immediately to deny its authenticity. Barthes could not have used such a phrase since he believed that we, humankind, generate and construct signification in our cognitive activities. To live in a sleeve of semes would make one too passive for authentic Barthesque analysis. Then, just before Colette Tourbillon could make an angry rejoinder, Lysiana Medine remembered the amazement Barthes had experienced when he discovered that there was a science known as "moulinologie." Shortly before his fatal accident, Barthes had travelled to Chartres in the company of Genette, Red Gallagher, and Marie-Hélène Cahuzac. Their intention had been to study clownage in the stained glass (that is, faces, gestures, and costumes that indicated clownage). Barthes had always enjoyed reiterating the fourteenth-century monk who had observed that "images are the literature of the layman." During the afternoon they had made a brief visit to the small museum behind the cathedral particularly to see an exhibition of Vlaminck's paintings. However, while they were in the museum they stumbled upon a display dedicated to windmills: their purposes, history, construction, and distribution. Barthes was delighted to hear that there were Frenchmen who chased windmills, worked (like amateur archaeologists) to discover the sites of vanished windmills, collected parts and surviving bits, and generally spent all their disposable time studying and collecting information (and bits) about windmills. A large *affiche* under a wooden model announced that the study of windmills was known as "moulinologie." Barthes was especially happy in this wonderful neologism since Jean Moulin had once lived in Chartres and had, indeed, been the prefect of Eure-et-Loir. Moulinologie would be the scientific study both of windmills and of Jean Moulin.

It thus appeared, Barthes noted, that moulinologie is a subdivision of hagiography. It is the archaeology not only of a certain type of edifice but also of a certain type of human spirit. It will carry its students (even if they decline to travel together) from the fields of Normandy to the Pantheon. Then Red Gallagher reminded Barthes that the study of windmills must also be a subdivision of literary history since one of the seminal narratives concerned, at least in one striking passage, the shapes, movements, and significance of windmills. Genette evidently liked this codicil to Barthes' discourse since he then began to argue that *Don Quichotte* had been the central (the inescapable) narrative in the history of narrative. Red Gallagher then quoted Marthe Robert to the effect that *Don Quichotte* had given the modern novel the work it had to do (*sa tâche*): everything that later had come to seem so massively significant, was, like a germ (a sprouting seminary, I thought), already contained in that novel. Genette liked that idea and expanded it, in returning to his initial proposition, to claim that the significance of *Don Quichotte*, as a narrative, as semiotic system, as a text to be read, and as a manifestation of textuality itself, was already contained, encoded, within the early encounter with the windmills. For this reason "moulinologie" could be seen as the prototype of literary archaeology.

Barthes was even more delighted by this proposition. Moulinologie became not an obscure and aberrant pursuit (akin to stalking mare's-nests or tilting up *faux-fuyants*), but an essential exploration of the human spirit. It was at once the disciplined study of Jean Moulin, of Don Quichotte, the character, and of *Don Quichotte*, the text. By an obvious expansion, it must also be the study of literature itself. Perhaps all semiotic investigation should be renamed moulinologie, Barthes suggested. Would it then be the case, Genette inquired, that they had all become, by the inadvertency of discovery, moulinologists? Or perhaps if we believe Julia Kristeva (and he nodded, smiling precisely, towards Georgina Hiboux), they must all, in the full flowing of semiosis, ride unendingly the mill's sails, like Don Quichotte at the exact moment when his lance catches the illusive fabric.

Lysiana Medine reported that they all had returned to Paris in good spirits and ate a meal of goat cheese to honour their arcadian discovery and to invoke the memory of the archetypal subject of moulinologie, Don Quichotte, who had once eaten goat cheese and, in so doing, had himself been reminded of the Golden Age. We all enjoyed a good laugh at this anecdote. The hostility between Michel Tasd'homme and Colette Tourbillon that had been brewing over Barthes' imputed use of the term "sleeve" (*un manchon?*) now calmed. In a spirit of empathetic reiteration we all called for baguettes and goat cheese. And laughing, perhaps just slightly carnivalesque (though if Todorov had been there he would surely have denied it), we bent our minds to the furthering of moulinological analysis.

[Ainslie's final anecdote indicates that he had adjusted fully to the life of a philosophical disciple. He appears to be at ease, confident, and fluent in French. I infer that last point from his careless use of the English word "sleeve." It makes quite a difference in French whether one says *une manche* or *un manchon* but in English there is, of course, only the single word. I believe that someone less than fluent in French would have attempted to translate the term exactly as, for example, a "shirt-sleeve" or a "cylinder-sleeve". Although there is some comic potential in saying that we live in a shirt-sleeve, there is, I think more philosophical sense in saying that we live in a surrounding cover of semiotic signification and in which, like pistons, we slide to and fro. Anecdotes such as this one make Ainslie's disappearance all the more unbearable for we can see clearly what intellectual riches he might have, in time, contributed.]

After I had several times read through Ainslie Wellfleet's letters to his friends and family, I culled from them a number of anecdotes that suggest the style of life he had elected after arriving in Paris. These that I have published here are typical, but they are not exhaustive. I soon realized that Ainslie had done little else in Paris than listen to talk. He had been fortunate, it seemed, though perhaps it had been natural enough for a young man who had always known the most important people in

Toronto, in making the acquaintance of certain important *maîtres de penser* and their followers. If one's purpose is to learn French and study philosophy, then what better way could be found? To that extent, it seemed self-evident that Ainslie had simply followed his usual intent, purposeful, highly efficient way of going about things.

After a time, it became apparent that Ainslie had derived more than a casual pleasure from these conversations. His French must have improved rapidly, for it did not seem likely that his new friends would have admitted him into their company if he had continued to *balbutier* as he had always done in the past. What began to emerge was a picture of a young man who had taken himself in hand, so to speak, and changed himself in very significant ways. He had undergone a massive transformation of character. Ainslie Wellfleet had allowed himself to become Frenchified with a will. He must have set himself the goal, with the true determination of the Ontario Establishment, of becoming a full member of the circles he attended. Perhaps he even longed to become an insider or, as he quotes Roland Barthes, of becoming an inside-outsider. Considerations such as these tend to explain why he steadfastly refused to return to Toronto. It would not have been like him to run against the wishes of his father and older brother except for something extremely important. I submit that the attraction that kept him in Paris was not a Parisienne but Paris itself or, to speak more exactly, the scintillations of its intellectual life.

Of course, this does not explain his tragic disappearance. His family assumes that he has been murdered. Perhaps, indeed, he was robbed and then dumped in the Seine or down a convenient sewer. Those of us who knew Ainslie can only feel deep sorrow and chagrin at the thought. Canada's loss, if this is true, has been great. However, my close reading of his letters has suggested another explanation. One not less stunning but one that is, at least, less appalling to contemplate.

Several cognitive attitudes are evident in Ainslie's letters. If one reads them casually, or reads them in the context of an emotional involvement, as gossip or familial reportage, say, then it might be easy to miss these qualities. Needless to say, I read his papers with an eye to discovering how his mind worked and I tended to blot out mere family gossip and to concentrate upon the anecdotes that indicate Ainslie's relationship to the intellectual life of Paris. Looking with such narrow eyes, I could see that all his accounts of life in Paris reflected intense pleasure, even joy, in the discussion that took place and a deep commitment to making himself a part of the milieu. It is not difficult to surmise that Ainslie found his life in Paris so enchanting that he had no wish to return to the wintry greyness of Toronto. In itself, this does not provide a hypothesis to explain his disappearance.

In rereading the anecdotes that I had culled from Ainslie's letters, I observed a striking fact. In all of his accounts Ainslie assigns names to the participants in the conversations. The great philosophers are indicated by their last names alone and their disciples are designated invariably by the combination of their first and last names. Thus we encounter Derrida and Genette but also Red Gallagher and Lysiana Medine. Ainslie's practice in reporting the discussions in which he participated or, in some cases, heard about after they had occurred is to give a precise indication of who said what in order to characterize explicitly the transsubjective dynamics. He needed no supernumeraries in his accounts. Nor, given what seem clearly to be his methods of writing, should one expect there to be any. Yet there is one.

Throughout Ainslie's reportage there is one supernumerical character. He is never said to speak. He makes no comments. He does not participate. He seems only to observe. Significantly, the longer Ainslie remained in Paris and the more detailed his reporting became, the more commonly this silent, observing character appears. Thus one reads such notations as the following: "Farkhondé Sabi was present" or "Farkhondé Sabi sat in a chair near the window." or "Among the group Farkhondé Sabi took his usual place." Ainslie gives this character a bare notation, simply acknowledging that he was present, that he sat, or ate, or stood. He alone of the characterizations that Ainslie works so hard to develop remains always silent. It is my hypothesis that Farkhondé Sabi is, in reality, Ainslie Wellfleet himself. Why else would Ainslie make a point of noting his minimally discursive presence?

If, for the sake of the hypothesis, we assume that I am right, that Ainslie Wellfleet referred to himself as Farkhondé Sabi, we have then both to answer the question why and to show how this explains his disappearance. The first problem is, I think, dealt with easily enough. Ainslie was shy. Initially his French must have been shockingly weak. Yet he was accustomed to being at the centre of discussion, to being taken seriously at all times. It would have rubbed deeply against his grain to record that he had remained silent, cut out of the dialectical passion that inhabits discursiveness. By adopting the mask of Farkhondé Sabi, he could record the conversation that he witnessed, and which so fascinated him, without calling attention to his own silence. Farkhondé Sabi was silent, not Ainslie Wellfleet.

I believe that Ainslie first adopted the mask of Farkhondé Sabi and then dissolved into this assumed identity. It became his war name. It would have been easy to accomplish. Easy at any time, perhaps, but superbly easy in that ludopolis, that city of play, of carnival and masks. It may even be that some of his friends in Paris knew of his metamorphosis but have kept their silence about it. That would explain why Ainslie's father and his brother, Duncan, were unable to locate him, or even to find anyone who remembered having seen him in the recent past. These same people might well have known where to find Farkhondé Sabi. Thus Ainslie may have found the means by which he could make himself, more readily at least, an insider to the circles he admired and by which, furthermore, he could break completely those ties to Ontario that he had come to find irksome, if not odious. Farkhondé Sabi would not need to leave Paris. Neither imperious father nor condescending brother could ever make claims upon his obligations.

This much I think that we may confidently assume. Ainslie Wellfleet has disappeared, but only as one identity flows into another. His disappearance has been that of metamorphosis, not extinction. I also suspect, though I admit this is neither easy to support nor to believe, that Ainslie may have chosen this metamorphosis in order to undertake certain acts of anonymous terrorism. French intellectual life is, after all, terroristic in its deep grain. Its spirit is that of thuggee: determination, laughter, and a waxed cord. It destroys all cognitive stability. The soundest models are twisted and hurled, askew and broken, into the dustheaps. It is something to be feared as well as admired. My own very personal conviction is that Derrida chose Ainslie for acts of terrorism outside of France and that his *nom de guerre* is, precisely, a warrior's name, a war cry to be shouted and to spread terror in the minds of traditionalist thinkers.

In my mind's eye, I can see Farkhondé Sabi walking the streets of Vancouver, Melbourne, Dublin, or Atlanta, wherever contemporary French philosophy is unregarded. He walks, his face suffused by an oblique leer, wearing a cap with a rakish tilt, in the pursuit of intellectual combat, seeking conversations to enter, arguments to explode. He masters discussions: a raking finger jab, a quick mind trained to grasp analogies, an opaque but glistening lexicon, all bringing intimidation, breeding fear. In each gathering, each pub, tavern, or café, he drives the disputants to surrender, to admit defeat, or to give up thinking. People who have been confident in their assumptions, who have never needed to examine the bases of their discourse, are driven, perhaps in tears, certainly in anger, to concede the doubleness and undecidability of their arguments, the pluripotency of his own. Perhaps even today Farkhondé Sabi is driving a taxi in Vancouver. Perhaps he has enrolled as a student at the University of Melbourne: pulling the cloak of rationality over his tutors like a sheepskin hood.

Crossing Boundaries

The Sly Man has set out to walk across QueAng-QueAng. He is looking for the frontier. He carries a small knapsack packed with conceptual resources. Among these intellectual fictions there is a map to help him plan his journey. The map shows the frontier of QueAng-QueAng. It is ahead of him a certain number of kilometres, running from one point to another, dividing QueAng-QueAng from another place, a neighbouring land. This next place will be very different, the Sly Man believes, and more open to argument. He has found QueAng-QueAng stifling since everyone there reasons as he does, top to bottom, but begins from different principles and reaches, with an ease that he must admire, conclusions he rejects.

On a mountain path, the Sly Man meets an old professor of history who tells him that his map will never lead him to the boundaries of QueAng-QueAng since these are in the past. Once the land had been ruled by a succession of wise kings. They had held to the principle that the freedom to explore, to play with the possibilities of the imagination, was indispensable to human life. Then the people of QueAng-QueAng had grown weary of freedom, lethargic in the exploration of difference, slothful in the play of imagination. At that point they adopted the grim principles by which they now live. The frontiers of QueAng-QueAng are in the past, the professor exclaims, and you cannot leave it until you have learned where it has come from and why it has changed. Later, following a narrow trail through a forest, the Sly Man encounters a group of revolutionaries. The leader tells him that the only frontier that matters will be in the future. Then QueAng-QueAng will be transformed into a free society in which the only collective obligation will be to respect the freedom of others. Still later, a hermit sitting on a rock in a forest glade hails him. There are, he tells the Sly Man, many QueAng-QueAngs, as many as there are different minds to think them. Some of these are, as the old professor had said, in the past, but others, as the revolutionary leader had declared, are in the future. A map can show only the horizontal, physical boundaries, but the ones that count most are vertical and conceptual. There are frontiers of hope and others of dream. In their best dreams, people may imagine a possible country, perfect in all respects according to their lights other than in its non-existence. The true boundaries of QueAng-QueAng are everywhere but, always invisible and hermetic, impossible to reach. QueAng-QueAng is like a vertical shaft, a horizontal path at every point along its height, in which coloured strings, like sequences of possibilities, float up and down pausing only briefly at each imaginary crossway. Even within QueAng-QueAng, there are many who disguise their disaffection and alienation. They pretend to accept the collective principles, but actually imagine different lands, other fundamental principles. Their QueAng-QueAng exists only across the boundaries of their dreaming.

Mapping Toronto by Darkness

Blackie tools their 1987, still jaunty, RX-7 east on the Danforth. She whips south on Woodbine Avenue.

—. She didn't ever actually puke, did she?

No, Tyler doesn't think so. He had watched the whole time and he is sure that she had not vomited. She had never bent her head down, as Ross had stuck his muzzle into the mud, and heaved.

—. Putting on a display?

How did it seem? It was evident that she was strutting her stuff, rattling the people eating, frightening them even, but not actually sick: a too discontinuous performance. When people heave, like dogs, they just keep going. In the gleam-fragmenting Caravaggio night, Blackie turns east again along Queen and then slows through the Beaches.

Tyler remembers the dogs vomiting at home. Every once in a while, a dog would blast its stomach with something rotten or poisonous. Sick, it would eat grass. Stretch its legs forward, spread wide, and heave. He remembers his retriever, Ross, his front legs stretched apart, his throat and back muscles rippling beneath the short, white hair, like an old man spewing his booze.

(The noise, rasping, repetitive and deep in the throat hacks, continuously. With each spasm of muscles, the hacking rises. Finally some white, thick vomit rushes downwards. A couple of more heaves, more deep shudders, then only some elastic strings of slaver hang along the lower jaw, bridging the teeth. On the farm the dogs would often be sick. Usually you didn't hear them, but he remembers clearly how, when he was eleven or twelve, Ross vomited in the yard. Mama, he had called, Aunt Bessie, Ross is sick.)

Tonight has been different.

A muggy July night, noise from the Danforth grinds behind them. They are sitting on the brick terrace at Pappas. Tyler sits with his back to the traffic, looking over the other diners. Wearing her hunter-green linen blazer from Holt's, Blackie faces him. She could see the traffic but doesn't look. She is eating lamb souvlaki with okra. There are roast potatoes, but she won't eat them. Tyler is eating a Greek salad with extra feta and black olives. He plans to spear a couple of Blackie's potatoes later. They are drinking Kourtaki retsina to ready themselves for an intense conversation. That is why Blackie has worn her special-occasion blazer which, she thinks, makes her freckles look exciting. They are eating out to talk domestic relations. Blackie would like to reorganize the front room and move the bookcase into the second bedroom that Tyler uses for a study. Tyler would like to reorganize everything, including Toronto's streetcars and the Metro Council, but he likes the bookcase in the front room, just where it is. That way he can browse without leaving the stereo behind.

The first noise is harsh and continuing. Diners start into silence, staring. Unnerved, Blackie asks Tyler with her eyes, What is it? At first it sounds like a two-stroke engine getting going. Low and wet, the noise natters in the distance, but ahead and to his left. It is in the street, or across at the other Greek restaurant: the deep resonance of someone vomiting. Dry heaves, Tyler thinks. But then he can hear the wet struggle for release, a steady irregular retching. He imagines the straining, convulsive passage between chyme and lips. It's a woman barfing, Blackie exclaims thinly. A dark-skinned woman in a gold jacket stands behind Blackie in the centre of the street, hawking deep in her throat. She is holding her arms apart from her body, bent towards them as if in supplication, staring. The strangling noise rises and falls, breaks off and restarts. Tyler, fascinated, wonders if he should offer to help. Blackie turns back to him.

—. She's horking. Barf-a-roni.

It grossed her out, like, to the max.

Blackie finds many things repulsive. She draws her hands back quickly or slides sideways. A tomato gone soft and deliquescent, a cucumber turned liquid, its white flesh darkening to yellow, makes her squirm away. Tyler knows that he can be disgusting himself. The space between them fills with messages: slob, intellectual egotist, pig. Once Tyler might have reached out to comfort her, to touch her arm or hand. Now he just withdraws a bit, waiting for the spasm to pass, her feelings of revulsion to ebb. When they first began living together, Blackie tolerated, but despised, his favourite hobby: Tyler makes games.

Now she actively shows her disgust that a grown man can spend so much time in making games, not even games that he expects to sell. If you could buy them at the Games Emporium or at Games-A-Lot, that would be different. But Tyler only plays them alone or sometimes with friends from Ryerson. He used to program computer games to play versions of SimCity, Life, or maze games, scavenger hunts and interactive who-done-its, all in cyberspace. He has played, still plays, the Glass Bead Game. These days, taking a real-space path, he has been making board games. He transforms novels into games that are played with dice, using his Ventura graphics program to design the boards. The dice actualize matrices of possibilities. But Blackie hates to see fiction that she has liked, or might have liked if she had read it, turned into games. It is too cerebral. She does, truly, find it disgusting.

—. Take *Lord Jim*.

When Tyler explains things his voice moves up a decibel or two, taking on an quivering whine. Blackie's spine crawls and goes stiff.

—. Start with Jim in the lifeboat.

Then it would flow from there like any decision-tree. You would play Jim's forks in the road. The idea was to get him accepted back into the hierarchies of power. He could even command a ship if you played right. You could play solo, like patience, or you could play two-handed against Marlow as the representative of Victorian conformity, evading or pleasing that watchful eye. Before you started to play you would determine the characters by rolling dice for traits, out of the character-matrix, just like any role-simulation game. Tyler's Jim could be either cowardly or indecisive, depending upon the initial throw. He could be as sound as a gold sovereign or possess some infernal alloy in his metal. Marlow could be more or less morally rigid. He might even let a ship sail in the wrong sea-lane on occasion. He would be intellectually curious, more or less, but that was a trait that works differently depending on the moral vision you gave him. Then you would go from there. Blackie had flicked the board, all Tyler's markers and tokens crashing to the floor, wheeled out of the room, going ukk, ukk, vanishing.

The other diners are looking around. The muscular waiter, white apron, black hair, is staring across Arundel Avenue, towards the Omonia. He has plunged his hands into the pockets of his apron.

The hawking noise grows and decreases in intensity. A dark young woman in a bronze shift with an open gold lamé bolero jacket stands about fifty feet away, north on Arundel by the alley. Tyler can see that she is wearing Roman sandals. She moves in a rough circle towards the tables in Pappas' terrace, and then turns away, back up Arundel. Blackie has twisted around on her chair, straining to see where the hawking is coming from. Other diners are also turning and staring. The thick-set waiter with the glossy hair stands in the wide doors leading back into the restaurant, beneath the exaggerated Palladian windows, wiping his hands nervously in his apron. Across the street on the terrace at the Omonia, other diners are also turning, glasses and forks suspended. Conversations are interrupted. No one is eating now, all mute in collective horror. The girl, so very beautiful, has her mouth open, but her lips are too dark to see. Blackie puts her fork down. Pieces of okra, still pierced on its tines, slide back into the lamb juices. Worried and tightened, her eyelids draw up into her skull. Her mouth quirks upwards on the right as her facial muscles tense.

Blackie finds many things that men do disgusting. When she sees a man blowing his nose, a forefinger pressing one nostril closed, a wad of snot snorked into a gutter with the force of a sneeze, she feels like vomiting. She tells Tyler that leaving the toilet lid up grosses her out completely. She doesn't like the way men sometimes bite their fingernails. She hates nostrils clogged with hair and boogers. She doesn't like hairy backs and bellies. Tyler is a comparatively hairless man, but it makes him nervous when Blackie finds other men repulsive merely for having hair. Once she saw an older man with hairy ears walking out of Harry Rosen's on Bloor and, walking just behind him, pretended to barf on the street. Pointing. Tyler finds all these mannerisms off-putting, but he understands that sloppy behaviour can be disgusting. Perhaps, he often thinks, Blackie is right and men should trim their hairy ears and nostrils, just to make other people comfortable, not to draw attention to their hairiness. Hair is primitive. Men with hairy backs remind her of apes. She could never make love to a hairy man. She thinks of them as belonging in cages. She tells Tyler that leaving things scattered about is disgusting. So is not changing his clothes more often. Jockey shorts that stink of piss gross her out maximally, so she won't, on principle, touch men's underwear. And the way he talks about things, so abstractly that other people can't follow him, makes her want to toss her cookies. Games, except to play them, some of them, rank only marginally above stinky undershorts and boogers. Long words make her think of thick, knobby turds.

(Ross stands with his front legs wide apart along the edge of mother's vegetable garden. His paws are half sunk in the spring gumbo. Bowed in concentration, his muzzle points into the mud. His back shudders rhythmically. The rasping reaches wetly through the windows. Tyler runs to the veranda to see. Oh, Mama, it's Ross, he cries. The dog continues shuddering and hacking. His eyes shift sideways, wander skullwards, distractedly, perhaps seeking help. His nose points steadily into the mud. Thick cords of slaver hang from his jaw. Then a final shudder and a flowing noise, a sluice opening, displaces the raw hacking. White pulp pours from his muzzle onto the black mud. Tyler runs forward to hold Ross around the still-quivering shoulders. The high, sharp stench of sour puke clogs his nostrils. Chunks, like cheese, stand out from the chalky pool. Mama, it's all right, Ross is all right. He must have been sick. Aunt Bessie stands on the veranda, her wet hands closed within her apron, laughing.)

A thin, angular man wearing a blue nylon windbreaker and a red tie leans across from the next table, twisting to his left. There is an emblem over the heart that Tyler can't read. His companion across the table, facing like Blackie, is busy ignoring the disruption. He tells Tyler that the girl must be on drugs. It's probably an overdose. Must be a hooker. But Tyler doesn't think that an overdose causes vomiting. You just pass out and don't wake up. Danforth and Arundel isn't a corner where you see hookers anyway. The man insists.

—. She's ODing, you can bet.

Tyler hears the twangy American accent. Border state. Blackie turns back around now, still holding a piece of okra speared on her fork. Her mouth is slightly open, her full lips glistening.

—. Look, she's crossing the street.

The young woman is strutting diagonally across Arundel to reach the terrace at the Omonia. Hands on hips, she bends over, gold jacket falling forwards, like puking into the sidewalk. Everyone there has stopped eating now. Tyler sees the diners in the row along the edge of the terrace covering their glasses and trying to protect their plates. The girl's hawking reaches across the street, but broken and unsteady. Consternation follows her, like a shape-shifting cloud.

—. She's very beautiful.

Blackie looks back at him, amazed.

—. It isn't very beautiful what she's doing now, is it?

Tyler agrees the contrast is shocking. To see a beautiful woman retching in public is fairly intense. Blackie doesn't believe she is really throwing up.

—. She's been going at it too long.

The waiter across the street is talking to her now. She retreats, turning away, back into the street. Blackie swallows the piece of okra.
  The angular American has something to say. Tyler sees the emblem on the man's jacket for the first time. It is a white embossed anchor with two hands clenched across. Beneath are the letters S.I.U.

—. Don't be put off. Everybody spews once in awhile.

You had to take it in stride. Blackie looks as if she could never do that. A man had handed him a shit-covered tapeworm once. Tyler's eyebrows lift. Blackie turns away to watch the girl who has crossed the street again. The man's companion groans softly to herself. He had been a first mate, and it was evidence in a case against the shipping firm.

—. This stiff pulled it from his rectum. Lower than slug slime.

He had handed it over in a glass. He wanted to sue the company. Tyler is curious about details. What had he done with it?

—. I reckoned he got his tapeworms eating in chop houses in Mombassa, some other trip.

But he had covered the glass with Saran Wrap and put it in the cook's freezer. It was evidence. Not very pretty though, a shit-smeared tapeworm.

The young woman is now crossing Arundel directly towards their table. The waiter at the Omonia has come out in the street to urge her on. His hands are expressive, but keep a distance. The angular man says, loudly in a stage whisper,

—. Better cover your plates.

Diners are staring at her as she comes closer, nervously holding their wine glasses, putting arms between the railing and their food. The young woman is now standing only a few feet away, just over Tyler's shoulder. Blackie's eyes, large and fixed, intently follow her. Now Tyler swings around to see her. Under her gold bolero jacket she has spaghetti strings holding up her bronze shift. There is gold embossing across the top of her shift, over her breasts. It looks like a fist. The angular American claims that it is a tongue. Blackie says that it is a narrow face, like a primitive sculpture. Thinking back later, Tyler agrees that it was a tongue, but now it looks like a fist. She has large hoops in her ears and clusters of bangles on her wrists, gold, or perhaps brass. Her toenails are bright red but her lips are not. The bronze shift is strained and tight, unevenly hitched up her muscular thighs. Her face is set and serious. Her black hair reaches her shoulders. The angular American whispers, Look at the dreadlocks. Tyler sees only curls covering the top of her forehead. When they discuss the episode later, Blackie will admit only to having seen ratty bangs. Probably she did have dreadlocks, Tyler supposes, but it had been too black on the street to see well. The serious, closed-in, dark face, partly covered by curls or dreadlocks, shining with hatred, or perhaps only dismay, grows on Tyler. He would have liked to think his way into her mind, but the distance is very great. Without a map, he could only wander.

The girl passes their table. She hawks and pretends to strangle. Now she stands just behind Blackie, arching her breasts. Tyler can see her sharp cheekbones and, down through the railing, the coins in her sandal straps. Her lips are still indistinct. Her teeth are square and bright. She has pushed both hands into her curly black hair, tugging, or twisting her dreadlocks. Blackie covers her wine glass and pushes her plate sideways towards the restaurant. The waiter has gone out into the street, turning the corner at the Danforth end of the terrace. The girl, watching him coming, rumbles loudly, bends over towards a table, a feint, and then skips back to the centre of Arundel. Blackie looks drawn, her freckles like smudges in the unsteady light. Let's go, she whispers. Tyler wants to finish his salad. He wants baklava too.

The waiter at the Omonia seems to put his hand gently upon the young woman's back, pointing west along the Danforth. He may slip her some money. Taxi fare. Tyler can't see clearly as they get up from the table. Once out on the street, he looks for the woman. She has disappeared.

Tonight had been very different.

Blackie has turned east along Queen and they drive slowly through the Beaches. Tyler looks dreamily at the restaurants, still thinking about the dessert he has missed. No, she hadn't been ODing and she hadn't been sick, except in spirit perhaps. Blackie, feeling reflective, becomes loquacious.

—. She must have hated everyone there. Hated them for being white or having too much to eat.

But she was well dressed. Loud, maybe, or brash, but good clothes. Tyler doesn't like the simple answer. White. He would like to find a mental landscape in which rough country, uprolling hills, finally mountains and deep valleys, became a map. The map would show where unexplored declivities, underground streams, ice caves, thermal springs, were located. White would name a certain peak, a sheer escarpment, but not the entire range. You could climb it if you knew the paths, across ridges and crests, that led up to it. Once Tyler has a map, he can discover things that it doesn't fully show. But to make a map, you must have a starting point and a scale. You can draw the lines only from a precise spot and according to a ratio of similitude. He thinks about the beautiful dark-skinned woman. He tries to imagine her intention.

Blackie whips across Victoria Park Avenue and heads off snappily behind the Palm Beach Courts. They walk down towards the lake, turning onto the grounds of the R.C. Harris Filtration Plant. Tyler knows that she has driven here because she wants to be serious. This is one place they came to walk and be romantic with each other before they were married. Down over the huge sloping lawns, the thickset brown-yellow brick building rises like a Florentine palace. The lake is calm, hardly a whitecap. The glow from Rochester behind the horizon glimmers across the darkness. Down the coast, Toronto, dream-city of towers, shines variously. Blackie holds his hand, palm out, tightly against her hip, as they walk. They pause on the projecting foreshore, against an ATLAS dumpster, and hug. Let us be true.

—. Friends?

Blackie raises his hand to her lips and kisses it. She is sorry that she knocked over his games this morning. She apologizes that she gives him such a hard time. She loves him.

—. Like the woman at Pappas. Showing disgust. I can accept that.

The spot begins to take shape. He can see it as an intention. It is the dark woman's desire to spill over, to engulf, drown, what is other. White is a rocky peak then. But the map places it as a remote tableland, the way to it leads across jungles and swamps, deeper than Borneo's. Shit-smeared tapeworms slither from the dense, fume-clogged sludge, huge and implacable. From the edge, where all the paths start, spread burning plains, distance in each hot grain. Blackie squeezes his hand tightly.

Tyler imagines Dante's burning plains, the usurers and sodomites parching in the wind's fiery dryness, nothing onwards but pain. In the map that has begun to unfold within his mind, the burning plains, though surely barren, stretch out towards further dangers through indifference. Featureless people hunch over food, looking nowhere, like pale maggots. He feels the scalding air clutch him, enveloping him sheath-like from scalp to toes. The map shows exclusion, the unending nature of shutness. He feels the burning gorge rise in his throat.

—. Tyler! You aren't listening. I love you. Dearly.

The cool winds from Lake Ontario make them shudder harmoniously together. Blackie thinks, despite everything, she is happy with him. Even though his mind is crammed with games.

Self-Enhancement

In a university whose name I do not choose to remember, though here we may call it the University of Ultima Thule, the English Department advertises for a position in Theory and Postmodern Literature. There are several applicants, but one stands out. His record indicates brilliance and a promising future. As a graduate student, he has already published in the leading journals, and his thesis has been accepted for publication by a distinguished press. His references are wildly enthusiastic and promise the highest levels of professional achievement and success. Yet the selection committee is disturbed that each letter of reference concludes with comments urging them not to make quick judgements or to judge the candidate at first sight. Do not make his physical appearance the basis of your decision, one referee writes. When the selection committee finally meets the candidate, they can see why the referees have cautioned them. The young man has a tattoo of a spider on his forehead. He is cheerfully nonchalant about the uneasiness he inspires in the committee and, while they interview him with averted eyes, he brushes his hair back with his hand, making the spider even more conspicuous. In his interview he is as brilliant, and every bit as promising, as his referees had suggested, but when the committee asks him about his current research, he points to the spider and answers, "carnivalesque emblems." Is he mad? or is he merely brashly imprudent? Does he get the job? Under what conditions would a selection committee hire him? If they will not hire him, why not?

Apprehensions

Hesitantly, Alexandra poured coffee. She bent across the laminated table to kiss Chris on the cheek. He raised his lips bloodlessly, without desire. He reached for a small jug of milk while Alexandra hovered, waiting for him to say thanks or perhaps for a second kiss. The November wind blew small willow branches against the window and Chris, if he paid attention, could hear it howl, distantly and muffled. Outside always seemed so far away, not like the houses at home where the outside crept cheerfully into the rooms and made itself comfortable. Physical boundaries were more like porous membranes there. Now, this very moment, the late spring sun would flood the veranda and kitchen. He might have been sitting in the light-glazed house in Mornington, Port Phillip Bay glimmering like blue glass, slicing fresh peaches or mangos from Queensland. Instead, he sat in this rather chilly kitchen, the cold autumn winds howling their dislike for his bright memories, wrapped in a sweatshirt and a borrowed robe. He would eat toast with pasteurized honey while Alexandra flustered about him. Looking, he supposed, as she always did, for substance in her world of shadows.

"Are you all right?" The coffee pot poised in the air like a question-mark. "Say something, Chris. Don't be so silent." She edged closer, pressing lightly against his shoulder.

He pretended affection. It seemed to come out rather stiffly, unnaturally mannered. But he did want to reassure her. "Sure," he laughed. "Sure, I'm only thinking."

She glanced suspiciously. What about? Her eyes yearned.

"After that business last night. I mean, after you woke me yelling, I got to thinking about an old story. I guess I was writing it in my mind just then." He feigned a playful fellowship between them.

"Tell me, Chris." She was enraptured. She had a passion for anecdotes, but his story, conceived in her bed, would be like a cord, a series of links. Tell me, she whispered, striving for kittenishness. She pushed against him once again and he could feel her breasts.

"Fair go, Sandie, this isn't high art, not your usual deathless masterpiece. Just a story that a walk-about sociologist has dreamt up. So listen. Once there was a little princess who wandered alone across a barren moor. That's what princesses did long ago, before either Feminism or Sociology, but don't ask what she was doing, whom or what she was seeking, that's always part of another story that doesn't get told. You'd understand that. A woman who reads all the time must have come across more stories than an entire department of sociologists."

She was looking into his eyes fixedly, like someone caught too easily by a swinging watch, mesmerized. There was magic in telling stories, whether chanting creation myths in a rock cave, young eyes turned upwards, spellbound, or inventing a kind of pseudo-folktale across a breakfast table for one's unsettling (nightmare-ridden, terrified, terrifying) lover. He saw her fading now, like the receding coastline of a tiny island.

"So: she came to a beautiful palace just as night was falling. She knocked at the gate and the gatewarden, who was an old man with a bushy white moustache, came down and let her in. He took her to the great prince (handsome, of course) who ruled the palace and she begged him for a night's lodgings. The prince, who was every bit as kind as he was good-looking, granted her this, but he secretly doubted that she was truly a princess. And so he decided to test her truthfulness. He knew that a true princess would naturally feel a little bit cold in bed, so he instructed his chamberlain to lead her to a guest chamber and to count the number of blankets that would be necessary to make the little girl warm and cozy in a strange bed. Then the old chamberlain led her to a large room where there was a single bed, a slight draft blowing through, and no fire, not even a few embers glowing. After the little girl had slipped into the bed, the chamberlain laid a blanket upon her. 'Are you warm enough?' he asked. But she was cold and lay shivering beneath the blanket. So he laid another blanket upon her and again asked if she were warm. But she was still cold, trembling sadly beneath the two blankets. This went on and on until the blankets towered above her and the old chamberlain had been forced to climb upon a ladder. Finally, the blankets towered above her and nearly pressed against the high, domed ceiling. The little girl, who was definitely a true princess, said that she believed that she now felt sufficiently warm to sleep. But during the night the palace was startled awake by the princess's screams. 'A basilisk! a basilisk!' she cried. All the inhabitants of the palace (which was really very large indeed) came running down every corridor, from every distant corner. The prince and the old chamberlain clambered up ladders to capture the basilisk upon the blankets, carefully shielding their eyes. But all they found was a single, insignificant moth. The princess, who was truly, truly a princess, had passed the test. But you mustn't ask what happened next."

"That's wonderful, Chris. But it's rather like 'The Princess and The Pea,' isn't it?" She looked at him uncertainly. He saw the horizon of doubt that stretched inwardly from her eyes. "Where did you learn it?"

"I found it where one goes for stories. In the Dreamtime, I suppose."

"Where?" She had moved away from him towards the stove, shuffling her slippers across the lino. The coffee pot had become an ellipsis.

"Oh, that's a saying aborigines have. In the Dreamtime: the time of myth, of the original stories. But I only meant that I had dreamt it up last night when you woke me. It's not aboriginal at all, in any sense. All credit to whoever told it first. Blankets or peas, you know, it's all in the telling. When you study anthropology, you learn that every story can be told countless ways, and the better it is, the more ways there are to tell it. I guess that I couldn't sleep anymore after you had frightened me, so I thought of a way to retell it. Can't even say that I made it up, can I?"

"Did I really scream *that* loud?" She toyed nervously with a half grapefruit: hoping that (perhaps) the night might be remembered differently.

In his sleep, stirring outwards towards Alexandra, his hands grasping emptily for away-floating strands of hair, his little finger had brushed her. Distinctly, he felt once more the faint sensation of her skin as his nail, distantly touching, had slid smoothly over her upper arm. In his broken dream, he had called out yearningly towards the girl in the tower. And, noticing him standing below, she had let down her golden hair, tumbling in two thick braids, a single strand of pearls wound loosely through each, and he had begun to climb. Upwards, hand slowly over hand, he had pulled himself up the girl's massive braids, his eyes fixed longingly upon her blue, laughing eyes. Then the tower had dissolved and the long bright hair had disintegrated. A shrill laugh flooding his ears, he had begun to fall. Slowly, downwards, half tumbling, he had fallen, his hands reaching out, attempting fruitlessly to clutch the broken braids. A single long, golden hair had glided just beyond his outstretched fingers when he had brushed Alexandra. She had begun to scream, increasingly shrill and desperate, while he, now fully awake, had shrivelled from her in terror. Leaping from the bed, she had stood beside it, huddled in the sheet that she had dragged with her, the blankets thrown back into a tangle, and screamed as he imagined a banshee might, her voice rising in a piercing chirr. He had never before heard anything so stridulous, so penetrating. And he had lain there, trying softly to calm her, while he felt his flesh tingle, his skeleton boldly highlighted, distant but clearly discernible, in its floating envelope of now-electrified flesh.

"You bloody well did. Never heard anything like it before."

"I must have been dreaming when you touched me. I think I was dreaming that I was in Akko, where I was last summer. I was lost in a crusader castle there, down in a tunnel. There is a tunnel there that runs to the sea. And an Arab was trying to grab me. That must have been when you touched me. I'm sorry."

She looked towards him beseechingly. Forget the screaming. Try to understand: it was only a dream, and a dream-Arab, not you, touched me.

Chris smiled across at her. Try to be reassuring, he thought. (He remembered how she had clung to him the first time they had gone out together. It had been an early September afternoon, the sky like a pewter bowl up-turned, the clouds scudding blackly, and winter, unbelievably, had seemed fiercely on-rushing. They had walked along park trails, holding hands, talking about university life, where they had been, where they would like to go, comparing their alien disciplines. A thin, chill wind had knifed among the scrawny poplar trees. They had cowered from its knife's-edge together, and Alexandra had held on to his shoulder as they walked, clutching his upper arm as though she might be swept up in an overpowering swirl of the arctic wind. They had stopped behind a thick clump of brush and he had clasped her tightly, kissing her with an unsteady passion more simulated than real. As he had touched her cunt, reaching down inside her Levi's, forcing his index finger, she had begun to moan. She had held clingingly to his arms and chest, her moan ascending unreasonably towards a whistle-pitched shriek. Then under their parkas, sweaters hoisted, they had made love. He had been quick and rough, but she had gripped his arms and back, gasping. The wind blowing nastily about his buttocks, his rectum slashed by its chill blade, his scrotum gripped within its icy glove, and his knees hurting painfully on the hard, frozen earth, he had come even so. Alexandra had gripped even more tightly as she had felt him shudder. Her voice seemed to have become entangled in the wind's currents. And then, hand in hand, they had walked slowly back towards his car, talking softly. It had grown abruptly dark, but they walked easily enough by the trickling starlight. Chris had thought that he could make out the shifting threads of the northern lights, twisting from and back into the night's blackness, just where he had so often been told to look. Alexandra had said that it was only the reflection of the city's lights on the clouds. The poplars had gabbled obscurely.) He thought: try to be reassuring.

What were the roots of her apprehension? (He chuckled privately at the secret wordplay distance had made possible.) With professional clarity, he understood that fear lurks behind bizarre disguises. He must try to calm Alexandra's many fears. Perhaps he could. At least, he could put on a few bright masks of his own. Tell her not to worry. (She's right, Sandie, yer're a bonzer sheila.) Touch her.

She sweated insecurity, frightened by relationship as easily as by its absence. But she must hold secretly within her the roots of fear which (Chris felt certain) could have nothing to do with him, or them together: root-experiences, submerged, buried, probably repressed, that compelled her to hold tightly, to grasp, to shriek out in the night. Dream-Arabs in Akko or foreign lovers, entangled together in her rhizoid emotions, might equally rouse her fears. And they might equally have nothing, or little beyond accidental causality, to do with the matter. She piled blankets upon herself against the cold, clung fiercely against being forsaken, shrieked at night-terrors, but it must all be surface: foam on some deep structure. He would probably never understand that structure, but he could, try to at least, reassure her. At least while he was still her lover, he could try.

Chris himself knew what it was to feel up-borne on waves of terror which he did not fully understand other than to know that it had nothing to do with any precise concreteness in his life. He would feel as if he were floating loose in emptiness, a tiny Leucippian atom spun in void. Or he would dream that he was shunned. A crowd would stamp about him, but always ignoring him. Shunned, an anguished outsider who desired a precluded inside, he might then wake up and call out for (god help him) bloodless images. Lynette. Moira. Shirleen. Help me. Or the image might come close, holding out a hand, puckered lips, eyes inviting, and then, laughing, dissolve. Help me. He would reach out, seeking, helpless in his isolation. And then he might meet Alexandra, running (always terrified) down passageways, down tunnels. When he touched her, she shrieked. The vastness and plasticity of things sluiced through his guts. It is space, he thought, space and its distances. Always the tyranny of double distance: far from here, now far from there. Space is what you bloody well have to endure. Conquering isn't the half of it.

Rohdan Uschenko had stopped him one day as he manoeuvred along the corridor towards his office. Students in thick sweaters and padded nylon jackets plodded obtrusively up and down the narrow passage. Chris could see that farther along two young women were standing in front of the door to his office, evidently reading the notice of his office hours. They looked unfamiliar in their winter garb, but the inference was clear: they were his students. (Once they put on their winter clothing, these northern dwellers seemed much alike: it was unreasonable, he knew, since their parkas, jackets, sweaters, and balaclavas, often handmade, were usually bright and individual, but his perception was, still, inadequately acculturated.) Surfaces of many kinds danced, suspended in their mere phenomenality, before his eyes. The students glowed dully in bright wool and nylon. Before he could reach them, Uschenko had held his heavy hand up in greeting and command. Smiling quizzically, Chris stopped.

"I see that you have a new article out. More of your Australian material, it seems." Uschenko made a faint grimace, as if he had tasted a prawn gone slightly off. He shifted a crammed document-case from his right hand to his left.

"Oh, those were the results of some work I did in Australia two or three years ago. Before I came here." He heard himself sounding wretchedly apologetic, babbling, like a man begging forgiveness for his babyhood.

"It is strange material." Uschenko stood pondering heavily, his hairy right hand stroking his shaven chin. "It does not appear to show a regard for method as we understand that term here on this continent. Do you give much weight to methodological considerations?" His eyes glinted at Chris coldly, inspecting difference. "On this continent we consider a value-free terminology important."

"Of course. I can't very well imagine what you have in mind." But he could. He could visualize Uschenko's cold eye cast slightingly upon his books and articles. The austere theoretician could not like his casualness about the informants' veracity, his evident sympathy with the subjects of his inquiry, his unguarded comments upon the aboriginal policies of successive Australian governments. "I have never before been accused of methodological errors." He had been, though.

"Possibly sociology is a somewhat different discipline where you come from." Down in his throat, Uschenko laughed roughly.

The two young women standing before his door turned towards him as he left Uschenko and continued along the corridor. In the wide, smiling face of one, Chris noticed an inviting gap between her top incisors. They both wore knitted ski caps with long tasselled cones. Tiny red maple leaves swarmed against white fields. They had come for photocopies of the Schütz essay that he had promised his senior course in ethnomethodology. He stepped into his office and returned, smiling, with two copies of the essay. He felt disagreeably like someone dealing in contraband.

Like Uschenko, most of his colleagues seemed to inhabit a positivistic space filled by statistics, correlations, tabulations, distributions, derivations: the graphic expressions of clear solutions to explicit problems. When Chris tried to explain what had been done, historically, to the aborigines in Australia, or tried to evoke the squalor of places such as Melbourne's Fitzroy, the actual lifeworld of most detribalized aborigines, his colleagues would shrug, look away, peering into a realm of quantifiable urban movements, and allow him to drift back into his inescapable marginality. He was always open to attacks upon his biases (his personal proximity to his subjects, his trust in their own accounts of detribalization, his insistence upon the insideness of social phenomena, his activist stance) or upon the supposed slackness of his methods. He would reflect scornfully that all their professional concerns seemed to boil down to spending millions of dollars in grants to locate whores upon elaborate grids of socio-economic factors. (But who gave a bloody damn for the individual whore's heart of gold? or of lead?) Why had these people wanted him? Not, it seemed, for his reputation as a comer. Mobs of intent social scientists, their projects securely locked into attaché cases and Tilley shoulder bags, turned their steps purposefully away from him. Their eyes flashed scorn and opprobrium. Beyond the mob, taking shape within a horizon of mist and smoke, Rapunzel smiled, her long golden hair falling in waves, the braids parting, and beckoned.

Up-clawing madness abraded Alexandra's personality. Chris found it easy to track the symptoms. The clutching, the fear of being left alone, the unshakable chilliness, the night-terrors, the monstrous dreamshapes, and the screaming, all indicated a woman who could never, over the long haul, manage the world. It overwhelmed her, he thought. She would retreat further into her botany, into useless and redundant lab work, and into the slushy, vapid stuff she liked to read. Finally, she would fall into some mad fictional (and not really possible) world that she would construct for herself out of linguistic fragments. The shards of language reassembled to make her life bearable; a fiction that might work for a time, but not for long. He saw the bright constellation of madness into which she fit. He could do nothing for her. She was broken and doomed. (He did not see that the scorned, isolated figure of his own dreams, its hands extended towards dissolving dream-figures, rejected, always yearning, must also reflect the grubs of apprehension beneath life's skittish foam.) He saw the screaming, huddled, terrified woman draped in a sheet, frightened, looking sideways at everyone, judging their reactions, piling blankets upon the bed, struggling to ward off a coldness that could never have come from outside. And every eye a basilisk's. He could not see the compatibilities between them, the courses along which they might have helped each other. He felt only the immeasurable distance between them and his slight desire.

He smiled at her across the breakfast table reassuringly. Don't worry, Sandie, it's all right, we all scream sometimes. Nothing in that to make yourself nervy. She smiled, reaching over to squeeze his hand, gratefully, lovingly. Morosely, he perceived, unfolding towards infinity, the vast blankness that stretched between them. The scruffy plastic table might have been a paradigm for the universe itself. Ever so flatly, like tapping a delete key, Chris resolved never again to touch her.

THE BLACK THONGS

In QueAng-QueAng, there is a deeply held conviction that everyone is guilty. If you were to ask an inhabitant to name the guilt or to identify the guilty, the answer would always be the same. A shrug. A wry grimace. Eyes rolled heavenwards. All acts are guilty acts; all intentions, evil.

Many years ago, the religious thinkers of QueAng-QueAng determined that everyone, being guilty, deserved retribution. Whatever bad happens, they proclaimed, you have deserved it, you have brought it upon yourself simply by your being. Other thinkers were quick to point out that, the premise of universal guilt having been granted, everyone should die quickly and uniformly. Indeed, it seemed as if they should not have existed in the first place. Why, they asked, should retribution seem so arbitrary? Many of the guilty lead long and, evidently, happy lives. Is that just? they would ask. Is that right?

In this manner, the institution of the black thongs arose. Certain young men, having passed all their examinations in religious doctrine, were given the holy task of killing their fellow subjects. The chosen instrument of execution was a black leather thong. The sanctified killers would stain strips of animal hide with their own blood and then wax them to preternatural slipperiness. In the setting sun's red effulgence, the black thongs would glow sullenly like burnished wires. The young religious students stalked out into the country, travelling even to the most remote spots and the smallest villages. With their black thongs they would strangle unsuspecting men and women, none of whom would ever know what had happened, nor why. The spirit of retribution swept through QueAng-QueAng. Subjects believed that they would die suddenly, without warning, and that it was right that they should die so. The men of the black thongs carried out their holy work on streets, in alleys and lanes, in fields, and in mountain passes. They worked in the evenings and in the early mornings, both night and day. Soon the people of QueAng-QueAng began to yearn for their deaths. If retribution was right, and life an unearned gift of which no one was worthy, then death could never come soon enough. People would kneel silently along the streets, in fields and mountain passes, hoping to be strangled quickly. Ancient travellers to QueAng-QueAng compared the black thongs to the thuggee of India, if these had ever existed, but death by sudden strangulation was never celebratory in QueAng-QueAng. It was always a matter of mutual duty.

Today the institution of the black thongs has nearly disappeared in QueAng-QueAng. There are secret communities in the mountains, heretical believers insisting upon the old ways, who still send out young men with black thongs. These are few, their visitations rare and uncertain. In the days when the black thongs flourished, the people of QueAng-QueAng learned that once retribution has become certain, a mode of execution rather than a manifestation of a symbolic order, it transforms existence into a sullen deathwatch. There were, the religious thinkers learned, no reasons to live rather than to die. Gradually, QueAng-QueAng evolved the present-day attitude towards retribution. Everyone is guilty and deserves punishment, but the agency of punishment is the state, and the state only. The state possesses many tentacular arms. These reach out into the cities and the remote corners of QueAng-QueAng in order to select certain people, who must act as scapegoats for the rest, for public killing. Having become theatre, at once arbitrary and symbolic, the idea of retribution lifts the heart and charges the mind with dreams of an unknowable transcendent order.

The Scarlet Crab

A mist curls through the flat, like the vapour that rises when lava strikes the cold sea on Big Island. Nestling down onto a soft cushion, Vladimir sits slouching, his right arm stretched along the back of the rattan chesterfield. Birgitte has snuggled her face into his shoulder. Across the room there is a quick motion along the bottom of a unit of wall shelves. (He understands that the room recalls, but does not exactly replicate, the condo furnishings on Kauai.) The motion takes an abrupt shape. A large frog with a dark-blue back, purple almost, and long, bright-green legs climbs up the shelves, gracefully hauling itself up over the drawer handles. Volodka marvels at how easily it climbs perpendicularly, its dazzling body fully extended. Suddenly from the right a large crab with a brilliant scarlet shell attacks. It leaps from the shelf of the wall unit onto the floor and rushes toward the shelves. The frog scurries around two or three small, plastic bins to reach the edge of the chesterfield, but, scuttling sideways quickly, its two stalk-eyes bent forward, the crab gains ground in full pursuit. The frog cowers just beneath Volodka's left arm stretched along the chesterfield's armrest. When he looks down at it, the cold mist making it appear dim and distant, he can see that the frog oozes fear. Its bulging eyes stare out from the unmistakable consciousness of extinction. Volodka sees it quiver in its death-terror. There is also a small lizard that he has not seen before. Both animals now run under the chesterfield while the crab still pursues. He knows that the crab will eat them, though this is not natural food for crabs. He can see that the crab is a land crab, more like the ones he had seen once in Vanuatu than the crabs he and Birgitte had actually seen in the water, or washed up on the beaches, on Kauai. Crunching and snuffling noises spill from under the chesterfield. They know that the crab is eating the animals. Birgitte holds him more tightly, incoherently moaning her empathy. "Birgitte!" Volodka snaps awake, calling out.

"Birgitte!" "Birgitte!" Calling her name, Volodka runs toward her, as she stands under the gold watch, indifferent to kitsch, to Japanese sham. He remembers the green nubuck jacket, the black trim setting off her red hair, the one they had looked at together in Harry Rosen's just a couple of days before she had split, walking west on Bloor, waving over her shoulder as flurries of dry snow danced slantwise. They had looked at it together and now, he guesses, she wears it only to prompt him to think of what he has lost. The people sitting at tables beneath the Shot Tower, momentarily concerned, look up at him sprinting, waving his arms. He hasn't seen Birgitte for more than two years, and his body feels eager, like a long, fiery itch. Hugging, only a few people looking up now from their tables, he keeps kissing her, whispering, "Do you remember?" Then. Those times. They race, skipping almost, up to the Museum entrance, whirling about within their hugs. When they reach Swanston, he tries to kiss her once more, but she has cooled already. Two years have passed, now halting briefly, and time has begun to flow forward again. More calmly, they walk south to Latrobe and head east, up the street to the Lumière. Volodka continues whispering about the past. Then.

At the Lumière, they are screening Krzysztof Kieslowski's 1991 film, *La double vie de Véronique*. Birgitte feels sympathy for the young woman who leads two lives, one Polish, one French, that do not connect. She clutches his arm at her unhappiness. When Véronique dies suddenly in her Polish life, then the camera staring unblinkingly up through a glass lid as dirt is shovelled upon her coffin, Birgitte ducks her head down upon his shoulder, her nails digging. Volodka can feel their hard, cold points through his jacket. In her French life, Véronique is more unhappy, Birgitte's voice weeps, her affairs so wretched, so despairing. But alive, Volodka whispers. She shifts her head away from him. He wants to tell her that he has heard Morten Kyndrup give a lecture on this film (in Danish, he adds, for Birgitte's benefit) in which he spoke about the irreducibility of Kieslowski's narrative to a *fabula*, all so angularly postmodern. After the film, he thinks. After the film, sitting in a Carlton bistro, she asks, Would being two have made me more unhappy? Would it only have made me endure repetitions?

Birgitte has never been out of mind. Almost to every step, Volodka can recall the places they have gone together. Do you remember making love on the stairs of the lighthouse on Samsø? he asks. The fog wisps wafting off the Kattegat made you look like a seamaid, a selky splashing within a wreath of fire.

—. When I was in Hawaii I remembered you being dumped in the surf at Waimea, and then laughing, your eyes still blinded by salt, sand in your mouth, your hair like dark kelp. Or how we walked that one night, hand in hand, along Kalakua toward Diamond Head, the stars like plankton. You were excited, swinging my hand in yours, telling me about the ocean you grew up near, cold, stiff with its boisterous mythology. I remember things like that.

—. Every summer, remember, each June, my family would build fires on the beach, honouring St. John. When I was a little girl, I would ache for the *Sankt Hans* bonfire. Midsummer then, not winter, and the days would slide for me downhill to school and then to Christmas. Volodka, you have always a mind more memory than hope. You remember more than I do. Even about myself.

In the bistro, they laughed and told stories, the way they had always done though it had been even better that night. Volodka had never forgotten the range, the excitement and laughter, of her voice then, walking through starlight along Kalakua.

—. If only you were with me once more, you would help me remember what is slipping.

So much had vanished, leaked, or even skidded from his mind. Volodka imagines that mind as many dark bins. At first he had tried to configure his memory as a honeycomb, the different cells containing distinct larvae, each a kind of experience. But now he pictures rows of bins, like a field neatly ordered in stooks or, more usually, a warehouse. He can sort through them, discovering forgotten bits, shards of past experiences, stored and waiting to be retrieved. He supposes the bins to have names, labels that help him find his way. Go to the first bin on the first right-hand row for sex, the second for love, but seek in the third row on the left for beauty. In that row he stores all images of unusual appearances. In the third bin, he keeps not only images of a few extraordinary women, such as Vikki, but also certain rainbows, sunsets, mountains, and waterfalls. There he can locate green sunsets, such as the one he had seen a distant April evening driving across Gippsland toward Melbourne when the sky erupted briefly in pistachio kernels and guava peel. Vikki, who was in that bin but also in the first and the second on the right, had twisted toward him, reaching across the seat to squeeze his arm, and moaned in the moment's beauty. But often he wanders aimlessly among the bins, casting about in the darkness, looking for surprises. Only yesterday, anxious for his meeting with Birgitte, he had found an evening when they had stood together in the garden just north of the Sultanahmet Camii and looked through the spraying water of the fountain while summer lightning flickered in glaring sheets across the Bosporus, illuminating the Mosque like a gothic peepshow. In those moments of recovery, Volodka feels himself split, conscious but doubled, a castaway from experience beached, no more than drying wrack, on memory's sands. Then he hauls himself up, and begins poking about in the murky bins. If Birgitte would come back to him, she could be the ship that stands above the horizon, coming to the rescue, lifting the castaway from the desolate shore, from tidal pools, anemones and crabs.

—. There is so much rubbish, piling like mountains behind me, mud sucking. You would tell me where the shit comes from and what other people do to manage it.

In his dream, he can hear the scarlet crab devouring the terrified frog. The small lizard makes shrill squeaking noises. The bones crack loudly. Birgitte clutches his arm in fright, but he stands up, trying to see under the chesterfield. The wet, hanging mist is much thicker near the floor. There is a great deal of quick scurry, scrambling, and wild commotion. He knows that the crab will eat both the frog and the lizard, though they are not natural food for crabs. He understands that the crab is a land crab, like the ones he has seen in New Caledonia, and thus it can run quickly, scuttling across roads, through ditches, or over dunes. He continues to hear crunching sounds, swallowed by the piercing shrieks of terror. He knows that the crab is eating both animals.

Birgitte and he might create again those odd little maps, with all those crazy conceptual crosshatchings, poised just over the surface of things. Like then. She would have understood the woman Volodka had seen this winter. A woman with destination on her face, she had walked toward him though blind to him and to everyone else.

Volodka likes the gold-velour bikini, the fuzzy material crinkling and folding inwards at her crotch as her legs cross and recross. Over her shoulder, she carries a silver-grey Fendi bag, the thick black stripes signalling to the world that she has taste, or money, or just difference. The bag may hold her beach gear, if she has any, or it may simply emit those signals to the world. She has a matching Fendi case for her sunglasses hanging over her left hip from the cord of the high-cut bikini. In her right hand, she carries a large white sandwich with a muffin balanced on top. There are four men, soldiers from Fort DeRussy, sitting at the table nearest him. They begin to watch her bear down. Lithe and blonde in her gold bikini and Fendi bag, she catches the eye. He thinks, They can't miss the muscular rippling thighs and the firm bum, signs of care, of athleticism, of narcissism. She is somewhere in her middle thirties and, he supposes based on what she does, from southern Europe. Slinky Eurotrash, Birgitte would say. Tell me about cultural shams, he had once demanded, and she, with Scandinavian pedantry, had replied that, first, there is similarity and second, there is difference. Sisters in the same household, though they do not always like one another, cannot deny the resemblances that link them, but they keep their eyes sharp for falsehood, and for hidden intent.

Volodka quietly observes the soldiers. Not much to watch early in the morning when Waikiki is mostly empty, but he has been sitting vacantly on a concrete bench sipping a coffee from one of the kiosks at the beach-end of the Waikiki Shore, his eyes peering across the low surf toward the ships slowly outlining the horizon. Half a century ago, the beach at Fort DeRussy was engineered out of a tropical swamp that lay between what are now the Waikiki Shore and the Hilton Village. Along the entire length of Waikiki, with its flat surf and sharp stones, it is the best place for swimming. He has been overhearing the soldiers tell stories about Desert Storm and complain about the drill at Fort Drum, or Bragg, or wherever. Abruptly, they stop talking and just watch this woman approaching, gliding along the promenade walk like vapour taking a floating shape.

She draws parallel to Volodka and just a few steps from the four soldiers, then gives an exasperated shake of her head, a grimace almost, and throws the sandwich and muffin onto the tiny square of sand at the foot of a palm tree. He stares, fascinated. Birgitte would remember how clean Waikiki is. Lots of sleaze, but high order. And hardly ever any trash on the promenade or even on the streets. The trash, Volodka knows, walks around in tee-shirts and flip-flops. Official people pick up whatever slough does get left behind. There are bins everywhere, with *Mahalo* written on them, that make it easy to throw dirt out of sight. A person would have to be pathologically self-absorbed to chuck trash thoughtlessly in Honolulu. And here, he thinks, is this woman from Italy, or wherever, slinging her sandwich down onto that neatly groomed square of sand.

There was a bin, *Mahalo*, just to her right, not more than two steps out of her path. Volodka thinks, Eurotrash, self-absorbed, what a cretinous twat. But he doesn't say anything. The four soldiers respond as if they have heard hostile gunfire in the distance. Starting into erect sitting positions, they gape at her like a sudden enemy patrol.

—. Hey, ma'am, what'd you do that for?
—. Ma'am, there's a garbage can just behind you.
—. Lady, that ain't the right thing to do.

The blonde woman looks at them sharply. And then with extravagant leisure in her gesture, she gives them the finger American-style, bending forward and thrusting her right forefinger, the one now freed from the sandwich, into the nearest face like a stiff, vertical tongue. Fuck off, jerk. A thick-faced redhead, flushed by ruptured vessels, starts back, on the edge of diving for cover. Saddam Hussein could never have unnerved him more. That long, slow finger with its pointed red nail registers like a sudden barrage of in-coming shells. It has its effect. The soldiers shut up completely, pivoting slightly on the concrete stumps to watch her pass. She swishes by.

Birgitte would remember the time in Frederiksborg, in front of the royal castle, when they had watched the Danish man watch the Spanish woman throw her cigarette under the tree. By her norms, the woman was behaving well: grinding out the fag-end on the footpath and then kicking it circumspectly onto the dirt under the tree. But this Dane with a Jacques Tati expression had seen her do this and his mouth flapped open in shock. He moved off a few steps, hands clasped behind his back like M. Hulot, and then turned back to stare. Volodka could recall that the Spanish woman had looked rather imperious, dressed in a dark-tan leather pantsuit with boots up to her knees and long hair streaked with grey falling below her shoulders. It was the grey more than the leather that made her seem peremptory. She hadn't even tried to disguise her age, she was that confident. Unsettled, puzzled, the Dane had watched her board the bus again, and then he had circled the crushed fag as if it had been a dangerous insect. Volodka had felt certain that he would pick it up and throw it into a nearby trash bin.

But finally he had simply stared in profound dejection, trying to pick her out through the bus's tinted windows, and then walked on, hands still clinging to each other behind his back, Hulotesque. At that moment, Volodka would have bet that he was thinking, Euro-monsters, and wondering what would happen to Denmark as the South, ever more assured, moved north. Birgitte would remember. They had sat there on the bus watching the whole episode, nudging each other and whispering like kids. The soldiers at Fort DeRussy seem to feel the same kind of culture shock and a similar desire to pick up after a barbarian, to make the world sparkle once more. The sense of civic duty works them hard.

A big dark man, maybe Hawaiian, with black and green tattoos on his legs and arms, rises from the soldiers' table and heads over to the sandwich. He kneels down and picks it up, balancing the muffin on top just the way the woman did. He carries the trash over to the bin, but before dumping it in he has an idea. Holding the muffin squished between his left arm and chest, he opens the sandwich and with one finger scrapes the contents, junk meat or pressed turkey, into the trash. He dumps the lettuce into the bin and rubs hard at the smear of tomato sauce. Then he ambles by Volodka to the lawn behind the tables, breaks the bread into chunks and throws it out for the pigeons.

—. Look kinda hungry.

Dismissively, deprecating his own kindness, he shambles back toward the table. His comrades gave him high-fives and turn away, looking for a surf that never comes that morning. Just at that moment, two Japanese girls, both in their early teens, run over to the bread. They have been sitting at another table closer to the Waikiki Shore and Volodka hasn't noticed them until now. They chase the pigeons away and begin picking up the bread-chunks. Bemused, he experiences a strong surge of unreality. And so must the soldiers, who wheel around, speechless. They stare at the girls like suspicious movements on the periphery of their position. Volodka feels amused that the girls are even more civic-minded than the tattooed soldier. They won't even allow the bread to remain on the grass for as long as the pigeons need to eat it. The girls take the bread in big handfuls over to their table and then (he imagines Birgitte saying, "amazing, simply amazing") something unexpected takes place: they spread the bread out on the table and begin to crumble it into small pieces. He supposes that they are breaking it into rice-sized bits, trying to achieve the optimum magnitude for eating. They gather up the bread once again and start throwing it back to the birds in wide arcs. He sees their purpose: more pigeons can eat and more comfortably. Now they can even pretend that the bread is rice. The girls are also being civic, but in their own twee manner.

He had wanted Birgitte there. He had needed to hear her laugh and say that every culture has ideal solutions but only bizarre practices. Shams are just the reward for seeing in panoramic shots. She would have giggled at the gold bikini, smiled at the soldiers, and told him that every cultural stereotype is, seen from within its use, a form of prayer, but seen from a concrete table at Waikiki it would be more like a curse. He would kiss her then, or nuzzle her hair as if he were sucking licorice, and feel that the world was more straight-forward in its complexities, though these might well be greater, in her company.

When they had swum in the small bay at Lindos, St. Paul's harbour, she had jumped from the rocks while he watched her hair stream out behind her, rising to the surface like coils of tar, and, following her, he dove for the sunlight glinting off her dark hair. They swam into a sea-cave and he had wanted, so passionately then, to make love to her, but she, treading water, touching his cheek, her blunt nails striking down over his lips, said that once St. Paul had visited Lindos. Vikki's grandfather had come from Rhodes, and that was why she knew about Lindos, why she could speak serviceable Italian. Would St. Paul have made love in this cave, unchanged since then, still home to urchins and squid? Oh, Volodneka, probably not, she exclaimed, pursing her lips in her serious, reflective way, but his student did. A handsome young man from a village in the Galilee, from Capernaum perhaps, a tiny spot north of Tiberias, a scholar who spoke Greek in strong Attic formations but with a definite Aramaic accent, he had met a pagan girl with hair like Thetis. He rowed them out to this cave, Pindar's ode evoking Rhodes echoing in his mind, and they made love here in the dark. With only reflected starlight to guide him, he had kissed her unsandalled feet, holding her head above water with the crook of one arm, her legs with the other, nuzzling her toes. Moments later, in his rapture, he had called out, "Thetis! Thetis!" The next morning he walked behind her up the stairs to the acropolis where she would worship Athena Lindia. He stood within the stoa and wondered if it were possible that he could see the one, true God in her hair. Did Thetis have black hair? Volodka asked, and Vikki told him, no, probably not, the gods of ancient mythology are always blond and fair: moon-pale Artemis; flame-capped Apollo. Even sea nymphs? Yes, Vikki had laughed. When he had jumped after her, he imagined that she was a nymph, even Thetis, had he been wrong? Yes (very serious now), you were wrong. The young Jewish scholar was wrong too because he had thought that the girl he loved, who had flowing hair black as obsidian, resembled Thetis, wife of Peleus, mother of Achilles, sadly the lover of Zeus along an earlier pathway in her life.

Volodka walks slowly down an aisle. As he walks, he gently fingers each bin in turn. Today, he is seeking something extraordinary. He wants to find the memory of a palimpsest. He is looking for the archaic mythology of the Aegean, for a cave on Rhodes where St. Paul's follower might once have copulated with a pagan girl, where he and Vikki had made love. He touches one bin cautiously, feeling its density and quick heat. Would Vikki have forgotten Lindos? He, never. In the cave, holding her from behind as she clung to a rock ledge, treading, like a sea-god rutting in surf and dark pools, he had pressed, then slipped, into her, the hot pleasure rising like a film between his body and the cold water. She had called out a mythological splinter, "Poseidon!" twisting backwards to brush his flushed cheeks with her lips, one hand holding to a sharp-edged rock ledge, shrieking. The flat lapping of the water had filled their mouths. Afterwards, pushing through beads into the darkness, they ate yogourt and honey in a small kafeterion near the Panaghia. Vikki said the best honey in all Greece comes from Thessaly. Not from Sicily? Not Hyblaen? No, always from the cool highlands, from Thessaly or Macedonia. Then, the day after, she had left for Nauplion, casting him off for good.

Volodka had walked up the hill behind Ródhos, to the ruins of the temple of Zeus, the ancient columns patched with Italian concrete, and looked across the channel to Taslica. He could imagine Fethiye, further off in the other direction, where they had slept among bedbugs and eaten grilled eggplant for breakfast. Then toward Istanbul. Near the Blue Mosque one day, she had been shocked, startled from her self-absorption, and he had read outrage in her face. She had spun around quickly, looking for the man who had touched her, thrusting his finger between her legs as she had bent forward to read a plaque in German, pressing. He was gone already, even as she turned, vanished into the dark, colourless crowd. It was her hair. He had tried to explain that her red hair flamed, seemed to blaze, a revulsion to women, an attraction to the men, and that she should cover it. But she laughed at deference, at Islam, and continued to let her hair blaze. Respect, Volodka had whinged, is not cowardice, not giving in or accepting. But Birgitte only laughed, brushing her hair briskly until it shown like the glowing red-tile roofs south of the Bosporus, and they had gone out. On Ordu Caddesi, near the covered bazaar, watching the dancing bears, so uneasily wrung from reality, a man touched her and a woman had tried to steal her purse. City of differences that crushes difference, Istanbul had stunk in Birgitte's mind like excrement.

He ran west on Bloor calling her name. "Vikki!" "Vikki!" When he caught up by the door to Longhouse, he saw that it was someone else. The November wind blew east toward the Danforth. His heart felt colder, that moment, than his face. Vikki, he mouthed her name, would she remember how the sun burst each morning from Turkey as they swam? They had walked up the long stone stairway to Palamedes' castle to look across the Gulf of Argolis toward the Peloponnesos. He had peered westwards, across the innermost tip of the Gulf, and tried to imagine the Spartan armies marching northwards, toward Athens, in the year that Pericles was archon. Vikki showed him the islands that she had visited as a girl, her father sailing the Gulf as he might have done his private lake, often as far as Psli. She had dived for octopus among the rocks and, in the early morning twilight, caught timid squid there. She remembered that, once, they had reached Spetses where they sat on black rocks near the beach, eating urchins and drinking retsina from a bag, her father producing lemons he had brought. The shallow surf had licked her feet. Volodka imagined her curled in the bow watching the limestone cliffs grow large or sitting in the stern, next to her father, dipping her hand in the racing currents. Once in a restaurant in Ródhos she had been able to smell the rotten fish through the cooking oil. She had learned that trick sailing the Gulf of Argolis, beneath Palamedes' walls.

Volodka liked to think of the hero building the castle above the Gulf. Was it before Aulis? Before games? Afterwards, after Troy, she said, since when life has always been peering through surfaces, distrusting what is given, discovering hidden rule-matrices. Palamedes taught us to pull codes forward into light, like squid, opalescent but still dark as they writhe above the surface. (Or, Volodka remembers, the black scorpion, hurtling up from under the rock Vikki had overturned, tail arched, while she stumbled back, clutching his arm.) Then the experience of the underneath, that rich hidden life that sham obscures, had not yet been entirely submerged, nor yet needed rediscovery, in the thick growths of Mediterranean civilization. She told him that Palamedes' castle had been rebuilt by the Venetians, doubled and transformed, so that now only an archaeologist could tell what was original, what added two thousand years later in the Renaissance. But he still liked to imagine the hero in Bronze Age armour, directing the building, telling the Trojan slaves what to do, how to lay one ashlar stone upon another, just so, the walls mounting skywards as the gulf began to seem less threatening. Troy rose to music, Volodka said, but Nauplion to play. Vikki snorted, gesturing sharply toward the Gulf of Argolis, people have always worked, fishing or hewing stones. Fierce as Athena's, her face had drawn back.

They saw *La double vie de Véronique* at the Varsity, walking up Yonge Street from Eaton Centre through thick, wet snow. He touched her arm when the dirt is thrown on Véronique's glass-lidded coffin, filled with the sadness of passing, but she snarled under her breath that the film was the silliest she had ever seen. What sense does it make to imagine a single woman as two? You might as well suppose another Vladimir, right now, even now, sitting in a coffee bar in Buenos Aires or dancing a tango, just being himself which is also yourself. Would that Vladimir know about this one, here now in Toronto, who has just seen Kieslowski's senseless film? If the Argentinean Volodneka doesn't know you, if neither of you are conscious of each other, then how could you be one?

—. I might take a photo from a bus window, someday travelling in Argentina, in which the other Vladimir happened to be caught, couldn't I? Then if someone else, back in Toronto, saw the photo and recognized me, the doubling would become obvious.

Her dark eyes glistening, Vikki was fervent, unyielding in her insistence upon rationality, upon lucid consciousness. If the two Vladimirs do not share a consciousness, how can they be one? You are confusing appearance with identity, just as Kieslowski does. Now, Volodneka, she laughed, tell me what do the two Veronicas have to do with each other? Their minds are different, alien in their difference, how can they be the same?

In his dream, Volodka stands up from the chesterfield, feeling a vicarious terror. Then he begins to read an explanation to Vikki, or an account of some kind. It is printed on the back of his blue anorak. He can't make it out, the mist is very thick, and now the message seems only half there. He tries to read it on his fleecy black windcheater, the one that usually has a Weiss Kookaburra soaring up the front. It drapes carelessly over a scruffy bin where he must have thrown it. Now he cannot focus and his eyes fill dimly with confusion. The words dance crazily. He can hear the crab munching beneath the couch. There must be an explanation, there on his windcheater where he feels certain he has already seen it, if only he could make it out. His armpits feel drenched and drops of sweat run chilly down his ribs. He is conscious, hotly aware, that his crotch has begun to stink from fear and that Vikki can smell him. The phone rings. Who would call him on Maui?

Vikki twists away, striding through the flurries along Bloor, passing Harry Rosen's without turning, her charcoal nubuck jacket, the green trim setting off her black hair, fading through the snow. She waves over her shoulder, carelessly, like one saying farewell to a casual shipmate, as slantwise gusts of dry snow prick against her. Volodka follows her through the crowd across Bay Street, beyond Avenue Road, but loses her. Perhaps she has gone down into the St. George subway. Or perhaps she has walked farther on to Spadina. He continues down to the platforms. He takes the first train south to Museum thinking that she may have gone up to the Royal Ontario Museum, where they had once walked, holding hands or letting their fingers link, among the collections, looking at ancient Greek vases and Ottoman tracery. He runs up the Museum exit, taking the escalator steps two at a time, into the Diamaru Centre. On the level above the Shot Tower restaurant, he sees Birgitte standing beneath the gold watch, her hair luminous as a blazing wick above her green jacket. He runs forward, calling her name, "Birgitte!" "Birgitte!"

The scarlet crab emerges from beneath the chesterfield. The noises from the dying animals have ceased. Volodka steps back in terror, but the crab turns slowly toward him, looking. Its two stalk-eyes fasten on him and seem to pause in consideration. He tries to call out for Vikki, but his mouth now feels dry and puffed, his tongue blackly swollen. Vikki has vanished, and he understands that he is alone. He can hear the phone ring, but he doesn't know where to find it. Having deliberated, the crab starts toward him, its two claws scuttling, click-clack, click-clack, over the tile floor. It edges between two small bins, heaving one sideways. Perhaps the crab is only trying to frighten him, but he steps quickly back, holding a chair between himself and the scarlet, now angry, crab. The phone rings insistently. The crab grabs one leg of the chair and shakes it furiously, and he stumbles back once more, this time into a corner where he grovels. The stalk-eyes follow him. He can hear the scuttling noise of the claws once more. Trying to wake up, he screams and then calls out weakly, impotently. He has the ringing phone in his hand now. When he answers, "Hello? Hello?" a distant female voice, muffled and distorted, wishes him a happy birthday. "Happy birthday," the voice repeats. Vladimir's mouth thins and rounds into a piercing shriek, more shrilly as each moment he understands more clearly that he is alone.

EVIDENCE

The Sly Man has been swimming in a pool alone. When he leaves the water, he can see small waves, the ridges and eddies of different currents. That movement in the water is himself. It is his own energy, transferred by ordinary bio-mechanical processes, converted into disturbances on the surface. After he has climbed out of the pool, he may look back at the surface and see himself, or his traces, in a kind of ephemeral signature. However, suppose that when he enters the pool, the surface is already agitated, the small waves and ridges of current are already in play. What can he infer? That someone, not himself, has been swimming? But of course an antisocial neighbour may have been swimming her dog. Children (those on the tenth floor perhaps) may have been playing ducks and drakes with stones to which they have attached elastic cords. The plumpness of the waves may suggest that the fat individual on the third floor has preceded him. Their activity and rapidity of movement may suggest the slender athletic person on the seventh floor. The Sly Man will not be able to infer back from the waves, obvious traces of energy, to what has been their cause. He will be baffled.

Methods

Chris tossed the cube lightly from hand to hand. He had twisted its lateral sections several times but no pattern had emerged. There might be a way to do it, probably there was, but he wouldn't fight for the solution any longer. He wasn't even certain that Eric had solved it. His son had pretended to have done so, but no one, not even Jennifer, had seen him. Chris thought about other puzzles. There had been the old black in Calgoorlie who had claimed to have seen men killed by bone-pointing. And he knew that other aborigines had been sung to death. The bone-pointing was the hard one, though. A knot with no loose ends. People whom he believed about other things claimed to have seen it done. The old man had said "fair dinkum" and then told how the young man had wasted, wasted away, and died. Like the body of a wallaby drying in the sun. Flesh, blood, the sap running one minute, and then only wasting, the thin, atrophied muscles shuddering, drying, death. How did they do it?

—. I just don't know how. He looked at Sylvia and shrugged helplessly. A touch of the mock fool could always cover social failure.

—. Just say it straight on. Don't beat around. Just tell her.

—. I don't know how to begin. I think I know what to say to Eric. Get your head on straight. Believe in your own future. Explore your talents. Develop them. You know. But telling one's daughter about puberty. That's hard. How does a bloke go about it?

—. It's just the same for daughters. Directly is always best. If you have to, get a pamphlet from your doctor. That's all my mother did for me. "Now You Are a Woman" kind of thing. I'll do that for you, if you like. You could even send her to the manufacturers' Web sites. They do exist, you know. Lots of educational content.

Sylvia glanced at him with mocking inquiry. Chris had not known that the makers of sanitary pads maintained Web sites. But, of course, it made sense that they would. He put the Rubik's Cube back on the table. The sequence of coloured squares repudiated pattern. Sylvia continued to smile at him enigmatically. He would like to hold on to her, but she seemed as slippery as hope. A delusion, only a dream of warmth and blue eyes, of fulfilment. Uncertainly, he reached his hand out to hers.

—. Whatever you do, just make sure she doesn't feel like a freak.

—. Have you given much thought to your procedures? Many researchers might suppose that you patronize those aborigines you claim to study.

Boychuk's eyes were hostile, an emissary from an alien realm, a holist scanning the microlife of a doubtful niche. A hollowness rose slowly through Chris' guts, expanding as it moved. He felt himself surrounded by unfolding space. From the window of the faculty lounge he could see the winter-swept city and the legislature building standing, falsely classical and incongruous, on a bluff overlooking the river. Condensation hung low upon the building's dome like a greasy cap. Far away the Pacific broke rhythmically across white sand beaches. He fixed a stare into Boychuk's cold eyes.

—. How's that? I'm objective, as dispassionate as I can be. And my statistics are exact. At least that is my goal.

—. That is the point. You are always outside. Like a god or a father. You are a classical sociological investigator, without empathy. Sociologists such as yourself make reality into an esoteric symphonic system. But reality is always lived.

—. How does one go about showing empathy in sociological research? You aren't suggesting that I should falsify data, are you? I was trained to believe that one should keep one's sympathies, like one's aversions, separate from the problems of research.

Method, properly conceived, was necessarily without affect. When he had been an undergraduate, glorying in his Honours successes, Professor Blacklaws had stressed methodological universality: the clean, gleaming knife that would cut anywhere.

—. You like to call yourself an urban ethnologist, but perhaps you haven't read extensively on ethnological theory. Have you really thought about it? There is no self-consciousness in your published research. There are no meta-discursive moves that might indicate that you are conscious of the problems in your procedures or that you are aware of the difficulties that you seem normally to bury rather than to solve. Above all, you do not see that your informants, those detribalized aborigines in Melbourne whom you study, live in their own environment. It cannot be denied them. It is their *lebanswelt*. In it they not only walk, eat, reproduce, and get drunk but they must also feel, think, believe, speculate, and dream.

Boychuk arched his eyebrows. His eyes were large in their intensity, almost glaring. He rapidly gathered his papers together, snapping shut, like a snare, a tooled black leather briefcase. The emptiness in the coffee room seemed to stretch in space to the hazecast city, to the ocean, to the remote eddies of lotusland. The downsuck of time swirled around Chris' spine. (The bluestone buildings in Fitzroy and North Carlton rose squatly in his mind's eye. Laughingly, he shouted a round for his mates in the Rob Roy, their dark eyes beneath hooded brows fixed distrustfully upon him, but a bond of some kind shaping.) Sneering, Boychuk excused himself to keep an appointment.

From the balcony of Chris' apartment they could look across the university towards the city. Lights made intricate patterns in the highrises along the north side of the river. The city itself shimmered in lights, sharp in the winter air, and looked, Chris thought, larger than it was. It was nearly like a real place, like Melbourne when one came up from the south, from Geelong or driving up the Nepean Highway, its highrises and towers projecting the importance of human transactions. At night the cityscape clad its illusoriness in light. Like the warm chinook wind, he thought, like the climate you can never trust.

The sensation of melted snow, squishing in the carpet that covered the balcony, worked through his shoes. He circled his arm around Sylvia, who had snuggled her head against his shoulder. She raised her head, puckering her lips, so that he could kiss her.

—. What am I doing, Chris?

—. You want me to kiss you, I guess. Or I want to kiss you and you are letting me do it. Or we both want to kiss.

—. You are so damn literal, Chris. I'm holding up the neb to you, to arm you with the boldness of something you probably don't understand. Don't look so worried, I'm just quoting a famous king.

—. I don't understand, but I do want to kiss you.

—. With the inside lip, Chris. You are so literal and so very unliterary. Don't sociologists ever read anything except graphs and tables of statistics? I read those brilliant papers of yours and I always wonder what happened to all the living, the feeling. Something must have lived behind all the data. Once.

He put his arm around her shoulders, pressing (he meant it to seem) lovingly, and kissed her upraised lips. He would have liked to turn this relationship into something more. He yearned for the pale blonde face, the quick intelligence, even the ironic playfulness with which she treated him and his scholarly work. Perhaps he could even love her. But it was unclear what he could do next. He didn't think that Sylvia would move in with him, not with two children already on the scene, and in any case he felt chilling apprehension at the thought of domesticity. If possible, he would have bound her to him in some way without incurring heavy obligations. (The memory of his humiliating liaison with Shirleen hurt like a shameful suppuration. His exercise of his own fatuity had sapped his confidence. Having been both dumped and duped, he now felt himself as insecure, as unstable, as the weather, as the glimmering city itself.) He would like to hold on to Sylvia, snuggle into her breasts each night, anticipate her trout-like thighs before sleep, but how could he make it work? How could he tell her how much he needed her without seeming weak? or predatory? She could intuit male weakness as swiftly as a horse a skittish rider. He might love her even so. In time, he might even learn to love the cold and the snow.

—. With the inside lip, Chris. What's happened to your national character? What happened to the warm days and the Christmas picnics on the beach?

How should he go about it? In the long sweep of random lights along the north bluffs of the river he could discern the harsh brittleness of intellectual discourse. Positions were taken, attacked, defended, modified, given up, finally abandoned. The configurations of lights held shapes that flickered into other shapes, into rationality and argument, into nonsense and incoherence, like paradigms emerging, stiff and friable, from disconnected words, from the lucid implosions of discourse, and then dissolving back into the unshaped matrix of words again. He would have to explore some new methodologies. Perhaps he could work up a project that his colleagues would recognize as valid. He could find a way to go about it that would seem less foreign to their eyes. What had Boychuk said? Meta-discursive. That was it. He could become brilliantly meta-discursive. He could begin again. Learn to love the cold. Take up snowplay. Marry Sylvia. (Marry me, Sylvia, and save me from the fierce struggles of academic discourse.) He looked over Sylvia's shoulder, into the horizon of lights, and saw only a vast network, the order of which was unknowable, everywhere hidden, and yet strongly implicit.

—. Why is it, Chris, that when I want love with you, you become moody? Sex and mind are like hostile roommates. Just love me.

The inner flesh of her lower lip tasted sweet. His mouth became chilled as the night breeze, chinook-warmed but wintry, blew across his lips and tongue. He held her more tightly, feeling her body press dreamfully against his chest.

Eric refused to meet his eyes. He sat on the edge of the chair opposite Chris, eyes slantwise, his fists thrust into the pockets of his ski jacket.

(Long oblique sunlight filled the room. Winter here was like living inside a lightbulb. The sharp low southern rays blazed into rooms mercilessly for the few hours of each day when there was any light at all.) He wished that there was some way he could speak easily. Not even a sociologist could analyze all the barriers between them or fully account for their etiology. No quantitative model could express adequately father/son relations. He knew that there was resentment over the move to Canada. There was the problem of loss, of friends and familiar places denied him. Probably he missed his mother more than he let on.

—. Can you solve this? I can't begin to work it out. Chris held the several-coloured cube between them. The coloured squares were in completely random patterns.

—. Maybe.

Eric squirmed to one side in the chair, looking up only briefly. His heavy downfilled jacket was open at the neck as was his plaid shirt. Chris noted with interest that his son had long straggly hairs growing on his chest. He himself was nearly hairless there. He wondered if his son was sexually repressed or if he was getting it off with girls at school. Or, more likely, with boys. My god, he thought, how bad I am at this kind of thing. He plunged ahead.

—. I realize that you aren't happy here. If we had stayed in Melbourne, I would have enrolled you in Melbourne Grammar. Or perhaps Trinity. They would have made certain that you studied and kept up. Here you have to accept what there is.

Eric slumped more deeply. The flood of brilliant sunlight brought out the details of his skin. Chris studied the irregular pattern of pustules along his chin. Zits, they were called here. Did kids use that word in Melbourne? How do you relate to an adolescent son who is sprouting into manhood? When he had been a boy the joke was that masturbation gave you pimples. And hair on the palm. He had fallen for that trick at least twice and looked. What did Eric do with his secret time? He played games. Chris knew that but he didn't understand how to put it into perspective. He had played chess at one time and when he had been Eric's age he had played card games. A social scientist, he understood game theory and could analyze mini-max situations with professional dexterity. Eric's games were something else. The determination, passion, and obsessiveness were more like addiction than play.

—. You have an excellent mind, Eric. But you must use it. At Melbourne Grammar they would have kept your toes to the mark. Here there seems to be too much room for private fancy. Too much escapism. I can understand the pleasure in playing games, but it is possible to become excessive in anything. You will just have to put your head on straight and get on with the task of living. You have to keep your marks up and try to make sure that you get some training. If you contemplate going to the university and having a profession someday, you will have to cut back on the time you spend in playing games.

Eric slumped farther. He shifted his position. He glanced up at his father with what Chris recognized as contempt, possibly hatred. Chris knew that he hated Father-talk, but he could never discover how else to talk to his son. Eric made an abrupt angry gesture with his right hand. Leave me alone, it said. Leave me alone to be myself.

—. You don't understand about games, Dad. You never played anything except chess. You don't understand *The Call of Cthulhu*. You just don't know what smart kids like to do today. You don't know how boring school is here. You don't know how stupid most of the kids are. I play games because it is the best thing to do. Dad, this conversation is very boring.

Chris felt the familiar muck, tugging his feet, wrapping around his legs, swallowing his guts. It was like trying to talk to Moira. Like trying to reason with dragons. Crouched in their lairs, the membrane over their barely parted eyes, flames in their mouths, they would struggle against him on every point. He experienced a sudden flush of frustration and hopelessness. How does one explain things? How does one even go about talking?

Mobs of students in ski jackets or coarse Salish sweaters with animal designs, the occasional hunting vest, bright red or green, interrupting the pattern, pressed by him. Chris sat at a table in the university mall drinking coffee and trying to finish an article in a past issue of *Mother Jones* on homeless street-dwellers in American cities. The hurrying, noisy students didn't bother him especially. He tried to imagine that he was reading at a table in an Italian coffee shop, along Lygon Street perhaps but somewhere in North Carlton in any event, aware of, but undistracted by, the tumbling shouts and laughter. Coldly, the winter sun drenched the mall through the acrylic bubbles in the high ceiling.

—. Hello, Dr. Mann.

Chris looked up from the magazine to see Frank Stevens, one of Uschenko's graduate students, standing above him, smiling. It was not a smile that he felt he could trust.

—. I read your article on leadership roles among Australian aborigines. I found it interesting, though the subject is remote.

Chris perceived that no joke had been intended. He smiled back. He could not believe that one of Uschenko's students would actually like anything that he had written.

—. Well, urban aborigines at least. In Melbourne specifically. I suppose that at this distance such distinctions tend to become lost.

The young man's smile had metamorphosed into a chill rictus.

—. Have you given much thought to your methodological procedures, Dr. Mann? I find certain aspects of your research puzzling. I am afraid that I don't quite understand how you reach some of the conclusions that you do.

Frank Stevens would put him under the knife, Chris realized. As Uschenko's student, that is where he must spend of most of his own life. Like Uschenko, he was an exponent of quantification, logical analysis, local concentration, and meta-language. Keep it concise, get it straight, make it precise. Deal only with the quantifiable.

—. I follow procedures which I believe to be fairly normal, and I do so with as much rigour and exactitude as I can manage. I was trained in precise methods of quantification.

—. I am puzzled that you seem to assume that questionnaires have a self-evident validity. Wouldn't it be more correct to say that a questionnaire has no more validity than the investigator builds into it and the respondents permit?

—. That is why one builds in cross-referential questions, is it not? And that is why the sample is chosen with care and considerable preparation. I should think that you would know that.

Chris could sense the rage prickle along his neck. He felt certain that his face must be flushed. Drops of icy sweat formed in his armpits.

—. Nonetheless, I find it puzzling that you readily trust what those detribalized aborigines tell you. How do you ascertain their trustworthiness? Professor Uschenko likes to say that the questionnaire merely collectivizes the general ethnological problem of the informant. Your language, so far as I can tell, lacks objectivity. It is a co-optive discourse.

—. My discourse is studied, painstaking, and quite professional enough.

—. Professor Uschenko says that you are causally involved.

Chris felt like screaming. How could he find a place in this competitive environment? Boychuk hammered him at every opportunity because he was too much an old-line sociologist, unconcerned with the phenomenology of living within an individual lifeworld, a person's value-world, but Uschenko mocked him, through his students when he could not do it himself, because he was too involved, too much a participant in his own analyses. He would have to formulate new projects. How could he develop a method flexible enough to disarm hostile attacks in advance? How could he learn to thread his way confidently through this realm of depthless illusions?

He held Sylvia's hand across the jumble of dishes and glasses. The bottle of Jacob's Creek claret stood dismally empty between them. Thin bars of laughter reached them from another table. Directly is probably best. That is how to confront problems. Just meet the problem head-on. He would tell Eric to study more seriously or have his arse kicked. He would tell Jennifer, directly, what was going to happen, or perhaps what had already happened. He would make love to Sylvia tonight and then simply ask her to live with him. He would expand his research and not allow his colleagues to intimidate him. Just tell them directly where to get off. Tell them not to come the raw prawn with him anymore.

—. Tell me about sociology, Chris. Is it a true academic subject? Everybody I know seems to despise it. And I mean really despise it. Probably more than they hate the Dean even, or Central Administration.

—. Sociology, in Garfinkel's immortal words, is only the study of commonsense knowledge. One likes to know how ordinary people, you or me, say, or the hunters and gathers in the Tanami Desert, rationalize their practical dealings with each other. That's the simple view.

—. I'm not trying to be bitchy, Chris, but Professor Jay, one of the readers for my thesis, likes to say that sociology is only the use of a jargon invented for that purpose. It's just a way of making trivial things important. Like a granfaloon.

—. I like to think of it as methodical curiosity. How societies function, the relation of one function to another, the evolution of these functions, the models that will explain them and their development into analytic methods, all strike me as interesting. They damn well are interesting! How do English professors explain the relationship of literary texts to the social structures that make them possible?

—. I don't think that they do. They just try to interpret those texts.

—. And that seems like insufferable nonsense to me. How does anyone meaningfully interpret a text without knowing where it came from, why and how? Or who uses it? Both why and how. How can English professors blithely deny that literary texts, like everything else in culture, are the consequence of human work?

Sheer fault-lines, dividing different ways of thinking about similar things, spread gapingly beneath their entwined fingers. A shallow waterfall flowed easily over rock lips that split and began to crumble. In the falling spray two figures, their bodies grotesquely disfigured by unlike tattoos, danced intricately to dissimilar melodies. Beyond the waterfall, the wind howled.

—. I have one colleague who despises my work because I ask the wrong questions. Wrong questions of my informants, of course, but also wrong questions of myself. I never ask about values and the feelings that go with values. It's almost a literary objection, rather like your own, in fact. Another colleague thinks that I ask the right questions, or some of them anyway, but that I ask them in the wrong way. Perhaps even of the wrong people. Some of them think that I use the wrong models, others that I draw the wrong inferences, others that I construct invalid sociograms. You see, there really is a lot of diversity in my line. How can it be all jargon?

—. I guess the more interesting question is why you, Chris Mann, wanted to be a sociologist. You might have been something else. An anthropologist or even a literary critic. You don't sound like the sociology students I meet. You wouldn't say "societal" instead of "social."

—. I wish I knew how to make it clear that I have always found the problems of sociology to be genuine. They interest me. They draw me into their conceptual possibilities. Anyway, I try my best. Just as I do with you. I want you to love me.

Perhaps, she said doubtfully. Perhaps they could really be in love and not just make love. She wasn't certain. They thought so differently that she couldn't be sure yet how it would work out. *How* was the important question. How could two people, so separated by their differences, make wholeness possible?

The little waterfall fell, over the crumbling, fissured rocks, swiftly into a mirage of doubtfulness. Ripples washed the shores, repetitively. The horizon stretched emptily away. (In this bright winter sunlight everything seemed sharp, etched, all two-dimensional.) How could anyone make sense out of such an existence? Chris thought about Moira and surged with festering bitterness. All responsibilities had become his. What to do next? How could he persuade a woman to love him? Find a situation that would make life more tolerable? Deal with hostile colleagues? Discover a way home to Melbourne? Make a son fasten his head on straight? Tell a daughter what she needs to know? The questions howled in his ears.

—. The truth is, Jennifer, that our bodies are always changing. If we know what is happening to us, then it is easy to accept. Only ignorance is frightening. Now you are entering a time in your life when you have to expect some fairly radical changes in your body. It's just part of growing into a woman.

—. Oh, Dad, don't be so groddy! Just relax, I know all about it. What do you think girls talk about at school? Social Studies?

Chris imagined the world as a hard, impenetrable sphere of unknowable substance. Over its orbicular surface investigators had drawn countless lines connecting all possible points with one another. Over those lines there were still more lines in different colours that other investigators had drawn. And over these were layer after layer of thin, meticulous lines, drawn by successive extrapolations of meta. Each time some points from the previous model were allowed to remain, but different ones were discovered and granted primary importance. Eventually, the unknowable sphere had been covered by this thick carapace of differing explanatory lines, its mere orbicularity encrusted by its metaphors, maps, and models until its outer shell, indefinitely separated from its substance, had become entirely knowable because entirely conceptual. The world had become a maze of ruptured surfaces, puzzling in abrupt planes and unexpected facets. But painfully unreal. The solution to its mystery had been deferred indefinitely, perhaps infinitely, by the efforts to discover it. How does anyone, he wondered, explain even the simplest things?

Chris remembered Durkheim's observation that the investigator could never investigate himself. He could never fully incorporate himself into what he wanted to understand. How could he ever grasp even the surfaces of things? How would he avoid leaving himself behind?

Imagining What Is Not

Several hundred years ago, a heresiarch of QueAng-QueAng spoke of the future. Soon he began to acquire many followers, all of whom were persuaded by his doctrine that there would be time to come. The future, he preached, must be different from the present otherwise it would be, as the orthodox doctrine of QueAng-QueAng has always held, merely the past's dreary reiteration. Present time, which is only the reiteration of the past, constitutes the very condition of the future for which, ineluctably, it will become the past. Many of his followers journeyed out into the countryside of QueAng-QueAng, even into the most remote deserts and mountains, to preach the heresiarch's message that there would be a future and that it would be unlike the present. Often, they carried small kaleidoscopes as symbols of the ceaseless unfolding of time. Usually, these were made from brass, incised with symbols of change, such as the stars, the moon, or waves. Occasionally they were made from wood, lovingly carved with figures from the Babylonian zodiac. Peasants would peer into the kaleidoscope, turning the cell as the prophets had instructed them to do, and would see the shifting patterns of bright glass as the image of future moments. See, see, the prophets would urge, time, too, can change. The future will come.

QueAng-QueAng was, and has remained, a theocracy dedicated to the principle that there is no future, only a past endlessly relived in a succession of specious presents. Nothing new is possible. There are no new ways: neither discoveries nor inventions exist. Thus the ruling thearchs of QueAng-QueAng hated the prophets of the future with the intensity with which they loathed time itself. They devised excruciating punishments for the prophets and, as if to show that only the past counted, the most awful were those that were recorded in the most ancient chronicles or which had survived in the garish tales of QueAng-QueAng's forlorn peasantry. The First Prophet was killed by having his skin flayed in tiny, slender strips beginning with his toes and inching upwards to his scalp. As each strip was cut from him, it was placed in a pile near his head so that he could watch it grow. From time to time, the executioner asked him gloatingly how many small strips of flesh would be needed to make a future. His followers were mostly executed in the time-honoured fashion reserved for blasphemers. Small groups of citizens crouched around them as they lay staked out upon the ground and sucked their blood with metal straws. The dried husks of their bodies were wind-blown across the empty horizons, into oblivion.

The prophets who survived the extermination of the future found hiding places in the lava caves of Slaa-M'an and along the skirts of the always-smouldering volcanoes. Each time that a volcano erupts, the prophets claim that, because it has been a surprise, it demonstrates the actuality of the future.

Clinks and Thuds

Chris had a quick, clear image of her diminutive female body dressed in a Brooks Brothers jacket, a subdued silk tie carefully knotted against her striped Hugo Boss shirt. She was walking along Rush Street with a group of young women, all laughing in a pre-theatre glow. He could also imagine her comfortably at home in Rio's Copacabana, in La Bolsa especially, or else in Ipanema somewhere along the Rua Farme. He could not as easily imagine the man prancing Melbourne's streets, not even in St. Kilda, wearing drag. Yet there the young man had been, as opposite from her as calculation could manage, in his blond dreadlocks and purple-flowered harem pants, tightened snugly at the ankles. Chris could see her more easily in Rio's gay districts, in a transvestite bar or along a beach-side street, then he could on Lake Titicaca, where he had actually seen her. Sylvia cracks into his imagination, vivid within its bubble of consciousness, with one of her boilerplate worries.

—. Challenges are important for the health of relationships. No challenge, no growth.

Chris tries to look serious, intent on following Sylvia's point, but his mouth purses, the under lip slightly stuck out. His lips always pucker when he is about to be sarcastic. Sylvia knows this.

—. Challenges make love better.

—. Like bungee jumping? From a space shuttle?

—. Like the couple we met on the Lake. They had been taking big chances and you could see how much they loved each other.

—. So if I wore my hair in long plaits down to my waist, you would love me more? Better? What if I snorted coke off the back of my hand?

—. That's not the point, and you know it. We should take chances together, you and I. We are, both of us, too risk-adverse.

—. I should have thought that taking the Christmas Vac in Bolivia was challenge enough. There're quite a few chances, risks too, in travelling here. But I'm not going to wear my hair in plaits. And I don't do drugs, not even something as *sympatico* as coke.

Sylvia has begun to look literary. Chris recognizes this transformation. She will begin to quote or, much worse, to allude. As she opens up, expansive into remote fictional worlds, Chris will close up, face tightly drawn into an austere rejection of all things literary. He likes to think that his analytic social scientist's mind, bearing his Melbourne training into the world's distant parts, simply cannot abide fuzziness. If it cannot be quantified, Blacklaws had told his fourth-year Honours students, face hitched sidelong in a characteristic taunt, it cannot be thought. Sylvia teases him that he is merely unimaginative, stuffy before the possibilities of life, as obdurate as an old bison.

The summer dusk has been thickening for some time now. Looking northwest over Lake Titicaca, they can still see, backgrounded by distant Peruvian mountains, fading sun-glimmers reflected unevenly upon the dark surface. Copacabana has already begun to cool, the blistering Andean sun sunk. Chris hangs his white Tilley hat over his right knee, relieved that for the next few hours at least he will not have to feel his brains broiling in the ultra-violet light. Sylvia evokes her personalized worried look, the one she likes to use during academic papers or when someone else is presenting a seminar report.

—. Don't you hear it?
—. No. What is it?
—. That clink. The clinking sound.

Chris can't hear it. He concentrates hard. The people at the next table are speaking in rapid Chilean accents, syllables clipped and cut, the word *ratito* repeating over and over. Only half listening, Chris works out that they have business of some kind in La Paz, but they are not clinking their glasses. No. He looks fixedly into Sylvia's eyes for the joke. No. He hears nothing clink. There is no clinking. The other tourists in the restaurant are locked deep in quiet, intimate conversations.
—. Listen more carefully. Sometimes it gets louder. Keep listening and it will turn into a clank or, more precisely, a thud.

Chris is puzzled and, very stupidly, looks about him as if he might see what he cannot hear. No one seems to be making clinking noises, much less thudding.
—. No, I can't hear anything like a thud or even a clink. What the bloody hell are you talking about?

He puts a heavy stress on the syllable "talk" and snorts intelligently. Sylvia has always been too literary for his mind. He thinks of her, with affection, as a bookish drongo, even though he often likes this quality in her. Sometimes he responds to it, but most often it frustratingly eludes him. Now he senses that there must be a punch line to her impossible query, some scene that he has not seen, words forgotten or never heard. A learned allusion waits in her throat to be spat up into his face.
—. I'm talking about fate driving iron wedges, Chris. It's what happens to lovers. Everything seems to be going well, lots of talk, smooching, good sex, and then suddenly there is a wedge being driven between them. A split, a gap, then lots of space opens up, plenty of light shining through, and finally a vast distance. And then each person walks separately into the lands of lost content.
—. What have I done now?

He can hear the unpleasant whinge in his own voice. Still puzzled, he glances at her once more, though now for a different reason. A wintry breeze nips his heart and apprehension, like early fog, crawls up his back.

—. Listen carefully, Chris, which you don't usually do very well, and you can hear lots of little clinks, a couple of thuds, and then, whacko, there'll be a big iron wedge between us. And it will be fatal even if it's not fate. So when it happens don't just blame things out of your control, like the opposition of the stars. Think about the disconjunctions of our minds. It's what you don't do, like listening, that's the problem. It's the way you hold back feelings. You manage yourself. Like one of those undead deans. Or some rotten research fund.

He puts on his distraught, worried face. How? Hadn't he held her hand most of the day while they were out on the lake? Hadn't he kissed her passionately, his tongue poking softly along her upper gums, there on the Inca steps, when no one was looking?

—. On the lake. That young man was Australian and he even came from Melbourne. But you wouldn't talk to him. Because he had long hair? Because he had the wrong accent? And you're so self-righteous, prim actually, about a little snort of coke.

Chris had felt a gut revulsion towards the young man with the coarsely plaited dreadlocks reaching down to the small of his back. The coke hadn't mattered, except that it was so flagrant, so carelessly in the open, as if Bolivia had no laws of its own, nor prisons either. What a way for a Footscray lad to end up. The broad, uneducated accent (pretense or not) wouldn't have mattered either, though this just had to be what Sylvia thought. She wouldn't see that the dreadlocks, phony and blatantly out of place, were stolen. They hadn't belonged to the young man anymore than a bowler hat, bought from an Aymará woman in La Paz, could ever belong to Sylvia. Once she put it on to wear, it would be stolen. So it had mattered. He despised, had to despise, cultural appropriations. Now Sylvia gazes at him thoughtfully, misreading the irregular flutter of his eyelids, seeing shame where there is only imagination, as he remembers the afternoon.

—. And what about the American girl he was with? I could tell you were jealous. I bet you sat there all afternoon, as secretive as Poldy Bloom fantasizing Gerty MacDowell, lusting after her naked skull, or maybe dreaming displacements, wanting to lick it.

He had not wanted to lick the girl's skull or any other part of her. But he had wondered at the deliberate counterpoint to her Australian man. She had been dressed entirely in men's clothing, her shaven head partly hidden under a Brazilian army garrison cap, dungarees tucked into surplus combat boots. She could hardly have arrived from Chicago dressed like a renegade from the Brazilian army, but she might have landed with habitual strategies for cross-dressing. The Hugo Boss shirt has narrow burgundy stripes against a pale blue cloth. Her silk tie is wide and the same robin's-egg blue as the shirt. Her hips, unswivelling, are steady ahead as she jaunts along Rush Street, a small mob of friends laughing in her audacity.

—. Chris, for God's sake, think. He couldn't have grown those dreadlocks in Rio. He had them before he arrived, at least he must have had hair to his waist. Hair takes time.

Sylvia had taken two steps up the Inca stairway, the wide stone steps climbing parallel to a down-rushing stream that fed into a fountain (also, it was said, Inca) towards the crest where Aymará women held alpacas for the tourists to photograph. He had put his hand out to touch her hips and, as she turned back, he climbed level with her, rubbing his lips against her left cheek. He had kissed her with conviction.

—. Are you happy? I am.
—. I think it's sad that they lost their ocean. I mean that monument we saw in Tiquina, the old man on his knees reaching out towards the ocean. It was really affecting. A tattered coat upon a stick yearning for lost immensity.

She had taken Chris' hand and squeezed it. His blood had begun to pulse more strongly. She would have said, he knew, that his heart had raced or skipped, some inaccurate poetic fiction or other. The social scientist in him had asserted itself. Bolivia had lost its seacoast in the War of the Pacific and, he was clear on this historical point, it had been more or less Bolivia's own fault. If now Bolivianos felt that they lived in a mountainous cloister, that was too bad, but it was their own historical decisions that had made it so.

—. They didn't lose it so much as let it slip. Too much unregulated immigration from Chile before the war, too great a continuing obsession with traditional Andean mining interests, too much indifference. They simply didn't care enough.

—. Oh, Chris, I bet they cared. You're so cynical. With no understanding of affects. Unless you can quantify them. They cared, but Chile had a better army and a bigger navy. So they lost. They lost their ocean. It wouldn't have been at all like that Peter Carey story where the country falls away in chunks just because the people don't love it. That's just a another myth of Australian insecurity. Yours is the only country in the entire history of TV to have had a prime-time series about tow trucks.

Chris had experienced a quick flush of irritation. He had scarcely heard of Peter Carey. He did not feel, had never felt, insecure. He had never even watched *Kings* when it had shown. Neither tow trucks nor towies had ever fascinated him. Not ever. Although definitely rational, Sylvia could never resist sadness or longing, hers or someone else's. She wrote articles on tragedy. She read poetry for pleasure. He had become used to her remorselessly defending his ex to him. Even in bed she might suddenly exclaim that Moira must miss him terribly. He could count on her to see, with all the resources of literary psychology, the reasons behind his Canadian colleagues' hostility. Yet she behaved as if she felt he was different, sexy in his taciturn down-under way.

—. At the time of the War of the Pacific more than sixty percent of the population around Arica was Chileno. That's bad management. The Bolivian government couldn't have cared less who lived along its littoral or what they did there so long as they paid their taxes.

Sylvia had started up the steps again. Chris took two steps at a time and caught her hand once more. The Aymará woman, her face cool beneath her bowler hat, was already urging these new tourists to take photos of her alpaca.

—. Perhaps their history is sad. But Titicaca is beautiful. This part especially. Over there, behind the Island of the Moon, you can see Illampú.

She had given an indifferent glance following Chris' pointing finger and walked quickly towards the woman with the alpaca. Over the lake, glittering in the December sunlight, the Andean peaks thrust massively through scudding lambswool clouds. Illampú was only one. They must try to get to Sorata, difficult as the bus communications were likely to be. Briefly he wondered what a taxi from La Paz would cost. His mind drifted and for a couple of moments he ignored Sylvia tugging his arm.

Through Titicaca's light-dazzles, Chris had seen the equally bright, but more agitated, surface of Port Phillip Bay. In Australia, nothing had ever been lost, only found, unless you were aboriginal. And what the aborigines had lost, everything, had not been through lack of caring. Drinking in the Rob Roy, Franky (who might have been a leader, and who did have status of some kind since other people would listen to him and take his opinions) had said that he could imagine Australia without Europeans. The sun was brighter, the air more clear. The people went where they had always gone and fished or hunted as their ancestors had. In the evenings no one drank, but they told stories and laughed. Franky could gaze into a stone, an opal perhaps, and see the world that had been. The colours, striations, chips, even the smallest nick, all took shape, and then the skies flushed with bright birds again, bright flowers sprang thickly from the dry earth. In this light-soaked wholeness, the people found food, told stories and danced in vast gum forests and along unmurky billabongs, all when it seemed right to do so. A striation, a glint of colour, a nick, would open up and become a horizon. Each colour became the shade of a different time. Each aspect of the stone was a mark of fullness. Now when Chris remembered Franky, he might think that looking into a stone had been like seeing Port Phillip Bay or the beach at Lorne in the Canadian snow and ice, only more rich and varied. Chris knew, had learned from Franky and other aborigines in Fitzroy, that detribalization is the worst kind of exile: a deprivation of all social forms and an excision of sacred space. Franky's vision had been of light and emptiness, but also of belonging, of place and identity. That imagined emptiness might also be a fullness, the overwhelming presence of everything that had been lost. The Aymará and the Quechua of the Altiplano had lost, but never so totally as the aborigines back home. They could still cross the western Cordillera, following their solitary latitudes, and find the ocean, even if the Europeans and the mestizos could not. For them little had changed, except a few trade patterns. The seacoast was where it had always been. Chris had felt Sylvia's tug at his arm.

—. Chris, wake up. Let me have five Bolivianos to give this woman, I'm going to take a photo of her llama. It's got a name, too. She calls it Goni.
—. Goni? The president's nickname? Anyway, it's an alpaca, not a llama.
—. Well, it's camelish for sure. Look at that smirk.

Behind them, the Australian man with the dreadlocks and the polled American woman in army boots were climbing towards the alpaca. Chris had turned quickly away, putting Sylvia between himself and his compatriot. Once she had taken the photo, he had pulled her up the path over the terraces towards the ruins at Pilco Kaima. At that moment Sylvia had resented him and made a face rather like the alpaca's.

On the little boat that had ferried them from Copacabana, Chris had heard the Australian man explain to a group of their countrymen that he had worked in Banff for nearly two years. He would have grown his hair there, but that was hardly the point. What bothered Chris was cultural appropriation. The dreadlocks came from Rio, from a black man's shop, and they imitated a shaman's cultural distinctness. Cultural appropriations were the worst sort of theft. Those afternoons at the Rob Roy, Franky had revealed that he missed his lost culture even more than the land itself. Detribalization, life on Gertrude Street, was like having had the culture lifted, pocketed, and walked away with. Having it stolen and dissipated, swamped in the rush to acquire and cultivate land, was sufficiently horrible, but seeing others carrying bits of it around, a dilly bag or a toy boomerang, was like having the heart squeezed. The young man in dreadlocks, his face screwed constantly towards haughtiness, must be carrying about a bit of someone else's culture, though Chris didn't know which one or from where other than Brazil. What about the cross-dressing, he had wondered, where did that come from? Standing above the lake at Pilco Kaima, he had asked Sylvia. What's the point to the queer get-up? Just youthful arrogance?

Sylvia hadn't known. She didn't think that the young man looked haughty, only self-confident. And, after crossing the Amazon, why shouldn't he? The American girl looked intelligent and strong. Back in Copacabana, eating pink lake trout, Sylvia feels certain that they were cross-dressing because of the challenge.

—. You "feel" that, sure, but you can't know.

—. It's the challenge of cross-dressing together that brings them closer. Couples need to do things together.

—. Cross-dress? Through the Amazon jungles? Across 4,000 kilometres of Brazil and Bolivia, all the way here to the Altiplano, just to see if they can survive being killed?

Chris remembers that, according to Amnesty International stats, five gay people are murdered each day in Brazil. Why would the lopsided couple have taken on a challenge that might mark them out for violent death? Perhaps they had made a bet with some rich person in Rio. He imagines the wager, made across a table with salsa or fados in the background, the rich person smoking a Maria Mancini or long cigarettes with gold filtres from an enamelled Russian box. (But this is so unlikely that Chris abandons the idea as soon as he has thought it.) It is more reasonable to suppose that they are both habitual cross-dressers who have happened upon each other in Rio's international ghetto. Banff would have provided the young man many opportunities, whatever Melbourne had offered, while the American woman strutted along Rush Street or down the Golden Mile in plaid shirt and black boots or in a worsted jacket and silk tie. They had met in La Bolsa, bumping into each other along the Avenida Atlântica or seeing each other dance at Jumping Jack's or Frutos do Bar. Chris can see it happen, but he doesn't believe in it. It is a clumsy narrative broken by one gaping hole. In the midst of many transvestites, why would either one have stood out? In Rio the man would have been just another Barbie. So they might have fallen in love at Frutos, struck by the brilliant image of each other across the crowded room. He knows immediately that this is a worthless hypothesis. Having decided to share a sleeping bag across the Amazon, two heterosexuals would not cross-dress unless they had a very special reason. At that point he arrives back at the beginning. Strolling purposefully through Rio's seaside districts, peering into the gay bars in La Bolsa, hanging back just out of sight as the customers dance in crowded cabarets, Chris tries supposing that the man is gay, but the woman straight. That scenario leads him somewhere.

The Australian Barbie dances powerfully to samba music in one corner of the floor. He wears a black leather mini skirt and a white blouse. No. The blouse might be right, but the skirt is simply outré. He wears loose fitting, pleated trousers, a white blouse, and a brightly coloured alpaca wool Bolivian vest. His long hair whips and curls with the music. He coils, uncoils, and dips again to the fierce rhythms, the muscles in his legs taut and massive beneath the flaccid slacks. A short woman, her broad hips rolling within her tight cotton skirt, joins him and for a few minutes they dance in mutual solitude until they begin to recognize each other. Her long brown hair, tied in a single plait, flicks to the music like an angry snake's tongue. Their heads come up and they move slightly closer, still keeping the samba beat. (Chris does not know much about the samba, but he believes that all South American dance music is mostly fandango in spirit. This casual conviction allows him to imagine music that he only barely understands.) A blue light has picked them out now and an admiring cluster begins to encircle them. Later, sprizzers in hand, they talk. Yes. This is the right scenario. She has wanted to see Machu Picchu passionately, but her friends like Rio too much to leave. Anyway she must be back in Chicago by early January. Chris sees them having dinner the next night at a bistro in Ipanema that he remembers well from a conference that he had attended in Rio only last year. They have lots to talk about, but sex doesn't seem on. He can like women, he says, but he never desires them. Their conversations would have been intense. Affection, instant in strange places, frees the heart, though not always the libido.

—. I think they wanted the challenge of being close. The other challenges, like crossing the Amazon, like cross-dressing, would have followed.
—. Perhaps. But suppose they were cross-dressing only to make their challenge possible.
—. You're losing me, Chris. What intellectual paradox are you framing?
—. Suppose it was just a *modus vivendi*, a means of relationship between two people with different sexual orientations.
—. Chris, that's sick. You think that because her head is shaved, she has to be a lesbian?
—. No. Not like that.

He sees them working things out gently, over dinners and drinks, dancing. In the *gafeira* at the old Hotel Gloria, they dance bossa nova, the lambada someplace else, perhaps at Carinhoso or Sobre as Ondas, but always returning to the samba. Their minds dancing too, hearing the music of possibilities. He scores some coke and offers it to her. No. Chris doesn't like that storyline. There may be coke, but it will not be an important thing, not something that he must imagine. It would be more like drinking *maté*, a part of the ambiance, a simple aspect of things. They plan the trip to the Altiplano and along the Inca Trail. Chris understands how tentative it must seem, how much fun to imagine, how difficult to believe. Then one day she meets him with her hair cropped close to the skull. He rubs this boy's head, roughly in play at first and then more softly, in camaraderie but with physical affection, subtle questions in his eyes, spectrally present. She begins to dress deliberately in boy's clothes. Yes. It must have been something like this. He has his hair plaited in a hairdresser's shop in Baixo Leblon by a man who has wrought this transformation many times before. He buys a couple of pairs of harem pants and blouses. She completes the job on her hair and has her skull shaved. Lovingly, if not actually sexual partners, they take a bus to Brasilia. Two weeks later they have reached Culabá. People make fun of them in the little Amazonian towns, calling out coarse suggestions and even coarser designations in the blunt South American manner. Several times he is nearly drawn into a fight. Once in Carceres, just short of the border, a gold miner in dirty jeans and bare feet shows him a knife, nothing more but it frightens him. Yes. Chris imagines that it would have been challenging. And Bolivia would not have been much better. In a small town, perhaps San Rafael, some men try to kidnap her, but they fight their way clear. Probably they are lovers by now, although Chris cannot actually imagine this explicitly. However, he does imagine her, in fragmentary glimpses, on her knees, her small breasts dangling but uncaressed, presenting herself like a monkey, or a boy. Yes. It would have been this way. In Santa Cruz, they stop several days for the nightlife, dancing and drinking weak cocktails again, like sprizzers. There must have been coke, in Santa Cruz there could hardly not have been, but Chris doesn't find that interesting. Then upwards into the Altiplano. Chris sees them riding a succession of microbuses, ascending into Cochabamba, on to La Paz, and then to Titicaca. Yes, that would have been the path of their journey. They grow closer and may even, he remains undecided, have become romantic lovers. Perhaps. They had seemed like lovers on the lake this afternoon, though that had struck him then as improbable, too bizarre even to imagine.

—. Not like that. No. It would have been more that he is gay and she was trying to accommodate him.

—. Chris, sometimes I think you must be mad. There was no reason to suppose anything of the kind. It's just more of your Australian minimalism.

—. Take it as a challenge. I'm yours. You're mine.

—. I don't want that. I want a mutual challenge.

—. It takes two to samba, remember. And that's a very solitudinous dance.

—. Tango?

Franky dances a solitary jig, a bottle of bitter, its green label winking with the rapid movements of his arms, clutched by its neck in his right hand. Chris knows that a jig is something he can only have learned in Melbourne pubs. A tin whistle chirrups unsteadily from the farther end of the counter. Franky flings himself about with increasing violence while his mates laugh and roar their accompaniment. His light footfalls sing, like a proclamation, an expression of revolutionary purpose, of liberty. Chris remains silent on his barstool, pretending to clap faintly in rhythm, his mouth slit in awe. Sylvia ignores it all. She sits at a table by herself writing in her journal, an open book shoved dramatically to one side. The Barbie dances to samba music in the shadows of one corner. His powerful movements mock Franky's. They seem less elegant, but more confident in their fluidity. His feet strike the floor like sledge blows, his body straightening and rising like a spring. Sinewy and aloof, Franky steps out like a brolga. The two men's reclusive movements, though hardly mutual, hold the eye. No one, least of all Chris himself, would seriously think that the watching eyes are partners in the dance. Alone, caught up in the movements of their cleidoic dances, their bodies call out for consorts. Sylvia refuses to look up from her hermetic text.

—. Tango or samba. I reckon there is more illusion of being together in the samba. But, whichever, it takes two.

—. But only one to break the dance.

QueAng-QueAng's Tales

In QueAng-QueAng, the people do not read. A traveller reports that once they did read. In that time they had many books, beautifully written and produced, which they cherished. Centuries ago, they taught themselves to forget how to read. Reading, they believe, always creates problems that cannot be solved because they have different solutions. One of their wise men discovered how to tell stories from strings. Now they take many lengths of coloured string and braid them into patterns that they have learned to interpret. These narrative nets are highly colourful and often very intricate. Bits of bright colour twist together in dazzling sequences. The inhabitants of QueAng-QueAng know by heart every possible sequence and can always say what it means. Foreigners cannot understand these patterns, even when they have studied the techniques for string-writing. The cardinal rule, which foreigners have much trouble understanding, insists that all patterns must finish at the same point. All the patterns possible in braiding strings lead to a central knot of black string. Sometimes the string-writer will use a piece of black rock or obsidian. The effect is the same. The patterns of string are spliced into the black knot or tied to the piece of rock. The inhabitants of QueAng-QueAng say that this shows that all problems have the same solution. All stories are meaningful because there is only a single story.

Smoked-glass

> You're told time and again when you're young to write about what you know, and what do you know better than your own secrets?... A little autobiography and a lot of imagination are best.
> —*Raymond Carver*

Here is one way to tell a good story.

Slowly, past endless tight-meshed shacks, the pedicab wound through alleys and half-streets. Twice it cut across a bazaar bustling with people preparing for the next day's skirmishes. Several times the bright, vertical machines of a *pachinko* parlour slashed the night. The pedicab threaded unhurriedly through the mazes of light. Caterwauls of reed-pipes pierced the autumn air.

Sitting tensely on the edge of the cramped seat, the boy squinted into the flowing shapes about him. Hardly aware, he was being overcome by apprehension. Every few minutes, as if prompted by the fear that he might suddenly find himself alone, he glanced at the woman beside him, obscure in black kimono. She leaned forward, hissing, towards the old man straining against the pedals. The man was crouching forward, his spread arms holding his body away from the handlebars, the saddle losing itself and then reappearing in the folds of his smock with each jagged push. One of the pedals clinked repetitively against the cycle's frame on its loose upwards swing. Without turning his head, the man threw back a curt *hai*! It was the single word of Japanese the boy understood. Yes.

He hadn't a choice. Jumping from the cab would be even more stupid. How would he find the harbour? He was up a shit-creek now. And no paddle. Directions had become tangled, forgotten in the increasingly distorted web of the strange city. He was forced to trust the woman. He had to keep going on. Shoals of kimono plashing among the laden benches of a fish market surprised his gaze. An acrid stench filled the air. Plump, spent cuttlefish dusted with blue, like pale lichens, swam beneath reefs of opal lanterns while long, fluttering signs sprinkled their ideographs groundwards.

That boy is me. I try to imagine his uncertainty and apprehension, but it is difficult. He can not suppose what is about to happen, the decision, unconsidered and unreflective, but utterly compulsive, that he is about to make. Nor can he guess the immense problems he will eventually confront in writing about the experience that he is creating for himself. I imagine him now, stiff with anxiety and yet flooded by a kind of joy, and I try to recall the reasons that have led him to go with the old woman, his state of mind, the qualities of his perception, how he, even at this moment, is trying to remember what he is experiencing. I am amazed at his ignorance and his blind egotism, but I am also touched by his romantic faith that experience can be sought, even solicited, and then remembered to be written about. He is narrow, a fool no doubt, but far from being perverse. He writes in a certain, knowing manner and out of an easily recognizable motivation.

In what I have written in my first two paragraphs I try to imagine his experience, his perception, and the casting of his future memory (which is also mine but, evidently, not altogether mine), and I have tried to write as he would have written then. I have tried to capture the words, the cadences, the shape itself of sentences as he might have shaped them a few days later, a month or so perhaps, in the fo'c'sle or in a cheap hotel in San Francisco or Sydney. The romantic faith in experience leads one to purpleness, to overwriting in rendering even quite ordinary things such as dead fish. How does a dead fish look? Like a lump of congealed slime? or like a slack cord of sticky snot? But to call those plump cuttlefish "spent" is to overwrite. They *must* be spent since they are, so clearly, dead. The fault is not in his experience but in his manner. He seeks the correct word, a language that is accurate and precisely given, for his brilliant, but dark, experience, and he gets it wrong. Too much romanticism, I find it easy to say now, but it is also a bad case of having read too little for the task. He has read Conrad, London, Marryat, Sabatini, some others no doubt, but nothing of his own time and place, the middle 1950s. He has not learned spareness.

Yokohama had shimmered with the poised expectancy of an unstruck gong. An hour before, he had whistled down the ship's gangway, hands thrust jauntily into pockets, the quickness in his body leaping forward. It was his first night ashore since they had sailed from San Francisco and, bearing purposefully beneath the Golden Gate Bridge, dropped everything familiar off the port quarter. He had been eager for something right to brag about, heady with the joy of things to happen that might appeal to his youth. As he had hurried from the ship, fingering a smudged, scribbled pass from the mate on deck, the evening had begun to close upon the bay. Gliding in the distance, or nestled among piers, the riding-lights of other ships had glinted on. The twin red glimmers from the lips of the breakwaters that shelter the inner port from the outer roads had marked the verge of night. Seamen, hungered or satiated by the flickering images of the city, went and returned.

The hubbub, a counterpointed din of winch, falls, boom, and chains clanking or creaking against the intermittent rumble of a ship's horn, had rung almost unnoticed about his ears. Before reaching the gangway he had stopped by the inshore railing just aft of the bridge, put one foot rakishly on the head of a bitt, dug swiftly into his hair with a comb, and turned to look back upon the scramble of gear. The midship hatches, gulping at the hoisting slings of cargo, were smothered up to the coamings. Beyond the ship, felt rather than observed, so powerful was its habitude upon him, the vastness of Tokyo Bay surged and, farthermost, the spindling skeletons of the shipyard cranes arched out of the industrial areas, nearly swallowed in the dusk, of Chiba. A last obscene jest from the able-bodied seaman of the watch chasing him down the gangway, he had scudded through the pier's warehouse to the streets. Do or die, the AB had yelled. Pass in hand, he had gone out into the city. It was, the United States (which wasn't really foreign) excepted, his first exposure to human difference. The richness of the instant drove through him. His bones had sung.

I find it easier to imagine his eagerness and joy leaving the port than to describe his fear and apprehension later. (He would have said to himself, and then confidently written, that his bones "had sung.") His feeling that he is about to have a rich, unique experience is touching, but his romantic conviction that "rich" and "unique" belong only to exotic experience is embarrassing. He would not, at this time in his life (he is, perhaps, nineteen), think that he might write about growing up in Hamilton, about the port there, about seamen other than himself, about the ordinariness, the acts of ordinary people, of human life in a Canadian port. He is certainly proud of his seafaring experience, proud that he has sought it, and perhaps one can forgive him for that. It is not so easy to forgive the false future-yearning that drives his deliberate efforts to remember, to achieve feats of memory, and, later, his intense wilfulness about writing. Those exotic moments in foreign countries etched in memory, he wills fiction into being. It is possible to observe the writers whom he has admired inscribed both in the way he writes and in the way he shapes his experience even as he is having it. The attention to detail characterizes his idea of memory and of writing, but one can note that it is always exotic detail or, at least, the kind of remembered fact that might surprise, even startle or bemuse, readers who have stayed home. The running-lights of ships and the red lights at the lips of the breakwater are precisely noted, and he pretends to remember the cranes of the shipyards in Chiba across Tokyo Bay. Could he actually have seen Chiba? At this remove, I can't know for certain. It may be that he could see lights and that someone told him that they were the shipyards of Chiba. In either case it is an important detail, and precisely the kind that he wants to remember and to use. He observes the sounds of a ship's deck with impressive accuracy, but it is the kind of detail that he has learned from the fiction that he has read. (It sounds striking that the longshoremen hoisted the cargo in "slings," and that is a pure Conradian touch, but the cargo must actually have gone up on pallets.) Behind the shipboard detail that he remembers are the details that Conrad chose to evoke in his writing: remember the paragraph in *The Nigger of the Narcissus* which describes the many types of nails, all jumbled together after the storm. His idea of writing fiction is inauthentic. He has read too little but what he has read counts for too much. He misses, obliviously, stories at least as good as the one he wants to tell.

His muscles and nerves tired as the jostling of the pedicab sapped the rigidity of his body. He was growing impatient, worried. He felt cold fingers jab, twisting, in his gut. The woman, her English scant, fixed to a few precise situations, could not understand his questions. How much longer? Were they nearly there? She threw him off. O.K., Joe. O.K. With annoyance, some desperation, he began again, deliberately. Fresh to the barriers of language, slowness of speech seemed important.

Mamma-san, how much longer? he asked, word by word. He had to get back to his ship. There would be shit flying if he wasn't on deck by four to help clear the after-hatches. The mate had laid that on him when he signed the pass. Did Mamma-san savee the ship? O.K., Joe, little ways. Her tongue slid the syllables wetly through her teeth. O.K. He sat back, quiet.

The streets had narrowed and fish-netted. The cab jolted up into the hills west of the port. Once girls jammed a window under a glaring greenish neon, laughing and watching. Whores, he thought to himself. He studied the woman but she was looking away towards the hulk of a gutted building. Silently, he damned her. The variousness of the city had ceased to interest him. It seemed to have blended totally into a single antagonist. Numbly, he dreaded its on-rushing, unpredictable bulk. Each fragment of flowing life, held and lost within the uneasy quicksilver of night, pounded against his blunted senses. Explicitness in things withdrew. The boy's mind could grip upon only the stifling regret that he had followed the woman.

She had stood out from the swarm of pimps and whores that fluttered around the cabarets in the first approaches to the harbour.

Perhaps it had been the kimono. The other women, in skirts and sweaters in order to appear more familiar to the sailors leaving the ships, had seemed dangerously counterfeit. So he had chosen to go with the old woman in a black kimono. It was a dumb thing to have done. If he had chosen one of the westernized girls in sweaters, she would have had a pad there at the port.

After he had passed through the warehouse at the end of the pier and walked out onto the streets, he had crossed the financial and office district fronting the docks until he reached the Tsurumi. Small and fetid, crosshatched by barges and outlandish sampans, the boy had not known whether it was a river, canal, or sewer. On the far bank, the bazaars had stretched, like a puzzle in lights, inciting. Garish neons had spieled, in Latin letters, the delights of minuscule cabarets and honky-tonks. Leeched to every doorway, girls had gestured encouragingly. He had felt his breath catch, felt himself prickle. Small, pretty girls, mouthing softly, caressingly, had set upon him. And men in double-breasted blue suits had waved photos of their merchandise, crying its wonders. Smiling, muttering polite negations, turning his head aside, he had kept going. The foretellings of desire had worked strongly, but the evening had been too young, everything too strange, he too unsure.

Pressing through the shifting crowd along the footpath, he had confronted the old woman. She had scurried, uttering moist, low spittle-sounds, from the entrance to a souvenir shop, its windows cramped by bric-a-brac. In an attempt to block his path she had crossed, with clipped, hobbling gait, scissor-wise, in front of him. The shop window had bulged with figurines and chess sets: whaletooth samurai wheeled above kowtowing pawns. As he had ducked towards it, trying in a single long stride to edge around her, his glance flashed upon a large, polished Buddha sprawling in frozen uproar. Monkeys! They were tearing at the figure. The woman had swung back closer to the shop hastily, cutting him off. He had raised his eyes to confront hers.

Shrivelled, her hair drawn tightly over her head, she had sweated urgency. Sensing this, the boy could not have sensed the bleak necessity, the want, that shaped her manner. But he had hesitated, snared in her need. Clutching, she had taken his arm, a bird snapping, and spoken rapidly, in English, to hold him. Did Joe like girl? Nice girl. An embarrassed, Maybe, had risen funnily in his throat. Not in business. Nice girl. Cherry girl. Joe like? Cherry girl.

His desires had quickened, but skeptically. Not cherry, not in Yokohama, but she might be clean. There were some weird diseases a guy could catch, some even doctors hadn't heard about. Hadn't the second cook swollen up like rotten cheese on the last swing? So he had heard. He had felt his spine turn queasy when his fellow seamen had told him about the Hong Kong clap. He had felt an acute terror, which he continued to feel even as the woman excited him with the bait of a virgin whore, that his cock might puff up like a goddamn blowfish and, like the second cook, he would have to have it reamed out. If it didn't fall off first. Long before they had reached Japan, he had learned, in stories, what he must expect.

Stung, intimidated, feeling vaguely committed to the woman because he had given her the chance to speak, he had doubtfully watched her call to the waiting pedicab. Led by the sleeve, he had climbed up, assuming a forged jauntiness, an air of worldliness that he had wished he felt. Until the cab had begun to move the woman had prattled encouragement, then she had fallen quiet. And then the city had drummed against him. Only the brusque, strained happenings in the city around him penetrated his consciousness. A child hunched in a doorway, still wearing the day's school uniform, shrilled frenetically upon a *shaku hachi*. A one-legged man, lurching along at an angle that barely failed intersecting with that of the pedicab, looked up from under his skullcap, the scored tallow of his face wrenched into a yell, and belligerently swung a crutch. Jagged fragments of experience wheeled. The pedicab stopped.

I cannot entirely dislike this early incarnation of myself. His voice is inauthentic, heavy with stolen cadences, posturing in Conradian gestures. (I read him now and those unmistakable echoes of Conrad's normal precision in the use of the past perfect tense grate like a schoolmaster's chalk along a blackboard.) And, yes, he is sick-making in his borrowed desire to startle, to achieve those feats of memory and make a chiselled record of his experience, to mark himself off. Yet he is serious, dedicated, determined to become a writer. He is too serious about himself, of course, but that is only a passing disease. For him, the self must be fashioned in heroic proportions, neither distance nor irony can play a role. (In something that he writes about this time, the following sentence appears: "Big with his fabled self, he had laboured his dreamworld out." Serious, dedicated, *heavy*: neither irony nor distance.) Yet he does have a good story to tell. The first of anything, puberty, entering the menarche, first sex, even the first goal, is always, and already, a good story. He might call it "Cherry Girl" or even "Cherry Boy" if he could write differently; instead, he calls it simply, in still another Conradian gesture, "Tale." There were (I think now) many good stories for him to tell, perhaps some even better than what he actually writes. He is blind both to irony and to the ordinary. He can scarcely observe, other than as background detail, ordinary people doing regular things.

Here is another way to tell a good story.

Quickly, he shut the door behind him. The hall was a single room. It was very deep and poorly lit. He saw into it like looking through smoked-glass. Some men sat around heavy wooden tables playing cards. Later he would learn that it was not poker but canasta that they played. He went up to the man behind the counter. The man spoke with a slushy, unfamiliar accent; his nose was splayed to the left and he had a cast in his right eye. The agent was out but he could wait if he wanted. Jerry would be back in a couple of hours. Behind the counter a blackboard listed scribbled job notices. There were two jobs for porters going and one for an oiler. There was nothing for an ordinary seaman. He sat in a straightback chair along the wall and pretended to read a copy of the union newspaper. The man with the cast stared at him from time to time. He felt uncertain, stupidly alien. What would he tell the agent when he returned? That he was a Canadian? That he had sailed on ships manned by the Lake Carriers Association? Or that he had never sailed? Perhaps he would say that he had crewed on an uncle's tug. Something too small to attract the union's attention. If he wanted a permit, he would have to say something that indicated he had experience but hid the fact that he had been a scab. Chicago made him feel wonderful. He loved the buildings and the wide, open views of Lake Michigan. But it made him feel foreign as well. If he had been born here would he still feel so insignificant and cowed in the cool, shadow-closed spaces between the buildings?

A large, muscular man in an Hawaiian sport shirt came into the hall. He was bald with a fringe of red hair. His face was flushed and his thick, pockmarked nose was crimson. The man with the cast whispered to the big, reddish man and then made a curt beckoning gesture to the boy. As he came up to the counter, he observed how both men stared at him, as if measuring the roll in his walk. The man in the sport shirt bulked over him by several inches. This is Jerry, the man with the cast said. The boy sucked in his breath. I need a permit. I want to sail S.I.U. Jerry looked fixedly and hard. Something was being measured. Bearing, muscles, voice? Then he smiled coldly. Can you fight? The boy felt weak. The back of his knees trembled. Hell yes, he said. Come on out on the street and find out. The two men laughed. The boy felt like running out the door and down the street to the Illinois Central station as fast as he could. Then Jerry began writing on a slip of paper. SS. Judd, he said. She sails tomorrow morning. She's unloading coal at the Youngstown mill. You can board her tonight. Later, Coast Guard Z card, permit, job, and future in his grasp, he learned from other sailors that the agent, Jerry, had been a professional boxer. He had lasted six rounds with Jersey Joe Walcott. There must have been something special in his laughter. Affection perhaps. Or a tolerance for the absurd.

He might have done fascinating things with that story. The old men playing canasta, for example, who were they? Did they watch him? Why was the room so dark? Was it to mimic the dim lights of forgotten fo'c'sles and passageways? What about the man with the cast? That slushy accent, what was it? What did Jerry see in him other than a clumsy fool? Suppose that I, now, were to shift the narrative focus to the rear of the long room and then look forward *at* the boy. How would that change things? He could not write that story then.

The pedicab stopped. Dismounted, the old woman exchanged pistol-quick words with the man who now rested off the saddle, slouching upon the handlebars. The boy hesitated, then swung his legs over the footboard. There were no streetlights. The houses were lit, here and there, by lamps. Steep wooden stairs pointed up the side of a hill, and clinging to the top, perhaps a hundred feet above, orange flickerings sketched the outline of other houses. The two Japanese stood eyeing him as if awaiting some obvious decision. Like a man thoroughly spun around, directionless, he remained awkward before them, his right hand resting on the pedicab's cowl. O.K. Joe? Pay. O.K. Joe? The woman bent towards him, skew-eyed. He dug for his wallet. How much? Mama-san, how much? Pay thousand. O.K. Joe? A thousand yen! That was nearly three dollars. He would spend that much in a single hour, easily, on beer in San Francisco. Five hundred, he blustered. That will goddamn well do. A thousand's too much.

Unaffected by his loss, the man took the money with a deferential shrug. Surprised that his firmness had been accepted without protest, the boy followed the woman. They climbed up the stairway towards the crest. Rickety, slippery with dirt, the handrail broken in several places, it was clearly much used, indifferently repaired. It proclaimed poverty. From the last step, the boy gingerly behind, the woman picked across a thin line of wooden chocks, smooth in puddles like discs of mud glittering. Amber reflections from half-hidden lamps crinkled on their dark surfaces. A slight rise in the hill remained, and at the end of the walk he could see a squat, darkened shack. The woman led him into an unfloored porch that was screened with wickerwork. The night breeze had turned cooler on the crest and the boy twitched with the chill as he zipped his jacket up to the neck. Inside, there were three steps up to the main room. Someone lit a dull lamp. The woman crouched to remove her *zori*. She placed them along the bottom step with several others. Another woman, younger, but he couldn't tell by how much, came from the inside room. Both of the women now smiled at him encouragingly. Feeling raw and unskilled, hardly knowing what he should do first, he started in. Shoes Joe! Unexpectedly sharp, the command frightened him. He drew back, confused. The two women, all smiles and bows, tried to reassure him. He must come in, only he must take off his shoes. It was clean. He obeyed.

Once inside, the two women caged him aggressively. Clucking and gesturing hospitably, they edged him to the rear, closing between him and the door, so that he was left, the uncertain apex of a triangle, facing the door from the far side of the room. Sparse, neat, it ran rectangularly the breadth of the house, but he could see that the house itself was deeper. Through a crack in the wall where a panel was partly slid back he could make out another room. There were a few spare decorations, cushions, and a couple of stubby tables. The old woman had hunkered down, poking intently at a brazier in which a few embers glowed darkly. He remembered how, precisely in that manner, the longshoremen had squatted about the deck that afternoon, calves to hams, feet splayed, elbows on knees, rocking slightly. On the walls of the front room there were a few faded hangings: a fish swam through a handful of reeds, some plucked landscapes of hillocks and firs. Only the short time in which he had looked around had been enough for him to understand that he had come in among a family, or what was left of one. He felt hesitancy and impropriety, as if he had been caught at something shameful, swelling within him, though he knew that he was doing only what he believed a sailor in a foreign port should do.

Then the younger woman broke the momentary silence, wrenching his shyness into attention. She pointed sharply into the shadows of the second room. It was lower than the large room in which they were standing. He could make out little in the dimness. On the right, curled snugly within a quilt, there was a small body sleeping on a mat. Son. The younger woman waved with her forefinger. She pointed, lightly, to the left. He would sleep there. She would call her daughter now. Something like shock waves rippled through him. Look, please, Joe. You like. Sure, he thought, sure he would, bring on the goddamn joy-san. The mother lifted her voice, strong, liquid, and commanding.

A girl came forward from the recessed shadows of the sleeping room. As he twisted his head to face her, she nodded her body gracefully towards him. She wore a white kimono with patterns of yellow flowers. Little ducks glided around her *obi*. Her smooth face, like toffee, was set off in a wreath of dense black hair. He looked quickly into her eyes, dark brown, glistening, smiling. Twelve, fourteen, he couldn't tell. Could the mamma-san have told the truth? It wasn't likely, but he felt his groin swell with the rush of blood. Joe, he heard her whisper, and in her upper teeth a gold speck glinted. He had bought this lovely thing-child to fuck but he would have to do it on the mat next to the other child, the boy, her brother, while the two women waited. Indecision knotted itself. Loneliness, the fear that he wouldn't make the ship on time for his watch, the sense of being an intruder, feelings that had worked disparately, fused now. He felt himself utterly foolish, standing before these strangers in his socks, one toe protruding ignominiously upon the matting.

O.K. Joe? Did he like? The mamma-san would call a cab in the morning. O.K.? The old woman leaned forward, a note of finality in her voice for the first time. The second woman, the mother, took the child's hand and offered it to him. But he shuffled back, fishing in his pockets. Couldn't stay. Really sorry. His ship, see. Had a watch to stand. He spat the words out. Shitty luck for them. Oh, fuck them. His brains floated. Here. He thrust a ten dollar bill into the mother's hand. He could not see the girl's expression, but he felt the bewilderment. The old woman snatched the bill, nuzzling it. Probably it was more money than she had ever seen at one time. Its very queerness must have been exciting. Pushing past the two women, he stepped out onto the porch, stiffly slipping back into his shoes. The cold leather hurt his feet and, flustered, he looked back to apologize once more, only to stammer.

Hurrying, his mind skimming backwards, he found the wooden stairway. He looked up at the stars shining dimly through a thin veil of smoky clouds. Once more, he felt as if he were floating. Below, a sheen of light thickened coldly towards the port. Icy wedges, flecked with crimson points, distorted, but revealed even so, the hidden forms of ships. Twice he nearly fell, stumbling from step to step. He felt regretful, relieved, a bit pissed off with himself, happy to be heading back to the ship. Reaching the bottom, he saw a small hut, lit by a fire inside, that might be a cab stand or a policeman's post.

I like that ending but it doesn't work for him. He needs something weightier, something solid exhaling its symbolism. I think that his character should run towards those frozen wedges of light, uncertain, confused, and distraught, towards openness. Then nothing more should follow. But he wants (so acutely that he will write and rewrite his conclusion) a lapidary closure. Well, let him have tightness and weight. Let him have symbolism. His story can bear that unsteady cargo.

As he ran towards the police hut, he saw that his shoes were still untied, the trailing laces caked with filth.

Academic Advancement

At the university of Ultima Thule, a number of academics have made it their custom to gather each day at the faculty club to drink. They have been disappointed in their career hopes, and their dissatisfaction shows daily in their conversation. They mumble and growl. They are notoriously anti. They are default iconoclasts. Then one day, a member of the group, the Sly Man, younger and more vigorous than the others, proposes to establish a new discipline. If only the furniture were alive, he observes, we could publish research about it. Thus begins the development of the study of Living Furniture. Eventually, they have a newsletter; later, a journal. They found a professional association known as the Canadian Association of Living Furniture. They have conferences and an annual meeting. They gain rapid incrementation and promotion. Young academics write theses upon the theory of living furniture. Some members of C.A.L.F. become famous. One or two are interviewed on TV and radio. They are said to have had impact. The Sly Man becomes a guru and earns income from media appearances. Yet their discipline depends upon keeping the door closed. No one should ever be admitted to the discipline who might ask stupid (or embarrassing) questions. Much of the success of the new discipline lies in keeping the gate. Only those who will express an interest in the theory, and help to develop the study, of living furniture are allowed in. Everyone thrives.

Parable

Once upon a time, not so long ago, nor so far away, in a village on the pampas, on the prairies, along interminable Pacific beaches, there lived two brothers. They were like commonplace real-life brothers who got up each day and did what they were used to doing: eating normally, walking in more or less straight lines, feeling the winds of air and heat that blew, seeing within the variable translucencies of light, and living in the linear unfolding of time. Then one day they grew tired of this ordinary existence. It came to seem dun-coloured, dreary, and ever so scruffy. It was dismally predictable. And so they each began to invent a fresh existence. The first brother began by asking whether it was truly necessary to walk in straight lines from one point to another. Perhaps, he reasoned, it might make more sense to walk in curved lines, since they might prove to be more interesting, or even (in the long run) quicker. After all, he reflected, the universe sometimes appears to be composed of chunks of curved space, so curved lines might make more sense than straight ones. He went on to think about other things that he had been taught to accept, all very ordinary matters, but which might be only assumptions that could be changed: the notion that one line, and only one, might pass through a given point; that distances between points are constant; that planes have surfaces; that time passes linearly. All these workaday assumptions about human existence could be inverted and then strange, but profoundly exciting, innovations would follow. New Worlds would emerge, open to exploration yet blankly closed to the commonplace vision of the rejected assumptions.

Meanwhile, the second brother began to weary of the undeviating predictability of life. He grew tired of the heaviness of gravity, of the solidity of substance, of the tedious on-goingness of cause and effect, and of the sensation of heated air that seemed to be the blowing of the wind. He began to imagine worlds in which things floated at will, in which substance dissolved and then flowed together again like quicksilver, in which events called out meaningfully to, but did not accuse, one another. He began to suppose that all human experience could be counterfactual. Suppose (he mused) that the wind were made of light. Suppose that the sky could be made of flowers and the clouds were bundles of soft petals, then rain might be the perfume of roses or of poppies. Let us suppose that the winds blow (or illumine) the embryos of desire.

In this way the two brothers began to reinvent the world. But it is important to remark that they did so in very different manners without paying much attention to others, precursors perhaps, who had similarly tried to reinvent reality. The first brother began by assuming a single proposition that was contrary to reason and to the likelihoods of experience. The propositions that he invented were often antirational, but he was able to draw from them fascinating consequences. Once he had made them, it seemed, extraordinary worlds became possible, and narratives about these worlds, before unimaginable, now flowed in his voice. All the it-goes-without-sayings that he had grown up believing began to fade (either into insignificance or into the vast volume of literary conventions). Thus he was able to assume that a library could be infinite, that a man might lose his ability to forget detail (and hence to make abstractions), that God might suspend time for one man but not for others, that a coin could have only one side, that a book might have as many pages as there are grains of sand, not one of which could ever be found again, or that there might be a world in which existence arose from having been perceived. Once he had invented these propositions, they began to function in his fresh accounts like axioms in fantastic geometries. When one accepted them, one could not avoid where they led.

Now the second brother shared the desire to begin freshly and to discard what had become dustily familiar. But he followed a different method of reinvention. He began by imagining spaces in which common and uncommon things existed side by side: folks died, grew old, had children, were born, yet flowers rained from the skies, human persons metamorphosed into animals or exotic plants, ghosts and chimeras abounded, and the mind lent the structure of obsessions to things so that the world became, in its speculative constitution, a labyrinth of emblems. In the second brother's narratives there were no single axioms from which everything descended, or from which the world hung, but there were instead two codes that were fiercely interwound, twisted in a grip closer than blood and mind, in a tight choreography of clinging antitheses. The one code put things into place quite normally (naturally and routinely) so that people were shot dead, had ambitions, were deserted, became lonely and sought sublimations such as, say, making gold fish. The second code organized events so that any number of strange things might occur: butterflies might follow a man everywhere, another might swim to the bottom of the sea and find lost villages where life continued or where ancient turtles snoozed by the thousands, still another might build a lighthouse out of ice. In the imagined space of the second brother's narratives, the possibilities of two worlds were always co-present (their codes snugly spliced) and clung to each other inextricably, like substance and reflection.

Both brothers learned to tell stories about their reinvented worlds with a straight face, without shrugs, secret winks, or other hints that it was, after all, just a tale (the world had not been reinvented, only temporarily disguised). Some people thought that their talent as storytellers was simply this knack of telling about their newly imagined worlds without drawing attention to them as out of the ordinary, of giving their worlds narrators who could never raise the question of how it could all be the way it is, who never raised problems or suggested that anyone should look for explanations. There never were any explanations because none was ever required. Their worlds easily generated their own illusive conviction.

No doubt there are always people (more than policemen, politicians, and pedagogues care to admit) who would like to reinvent the scruffy earth. If they cannot do it for themselves, except in sleep or when the fog is thickest, then they beg others to do it for them. And so the two brothers quickly gathered disciples, followers like scattered knights, who swore to reinvent their own worlds according to the rules the brothers had created. As their followings grew, the number of disciples increased, many uncertainties stuck to the brothers' fame. They became associated with strangers, their origins lost, and (worst of all) they became confused with one another. There were some adventurers among the new worlds who claimed that the brothers were actually just one person who possessed a single magic spell; others, that they lived in this place or that, making gazetteers of all the real world's invisible cities; still others, that they were impostors, panvestites, masters of bunco and Buncombe. As often happens, a myth, or a network of little myths, sprang up about the brothers and they became at once more and less than their true disciples knew them to be. They were everywhere and everyone spoke much of them and of their power and influence. But who are they, really? everyone asked. Really, who? An exciting sphere of strange boundaries now encompassed the world: a space of dissimilitude and striking deformation.

INFINITE PLURITUDES

QueAng-QueAng's most ancient doctrine held that there was no where else. Only QueAng-QueAng existed. Later, compelled by the evidence of travellers and merchants, it was found necessary to admit the existence of other places, but the learned insisted that these were all, even if they appeared to be different, one place. QueAng-QueAng could be deformed by shifts in perspective, but it remained a singularity. Other scholars argued that the apparent differences outside QueAng-QueAng were genuine, but that they had the force of negative exempla. The other places which travellers reported were obscure variations, always corrupt, perhaps evil, of QueAng-QueAng itself. The former group, who might be called the orthodox, were known as Monists while the latter, the unmistakably heterodox, were called Pluralists. In this way a bitter theological dispute arose. It was made more intense by the mutual acceptance of an unexamined first premise: QueAng-QueAng was single, both unique and total, and always undifferentiated.

The first examination of this unexamined premise occurred when a radical heresiarch proposed that QueAng-QueAng must be divisible. If, he reasoned, all things and places are divisible and QueAng-QueAng is a place, then it must be divisible. And if it is divisible, then it cannot be always the same, always an undifferentiated totality. If it is divisible, the orthodox Monists countered, then each part must be identical with every other part since QueAng-QueAng is always the same. The Pluralists replied that different parts might be false images of other parts, perverse replications that had, even so, only a single reference. The heretics argued that each part must be different since size itself constituted a difference such that even if each part were a total QueAng-QueAng (which could only be assumed, not proved), it would still be distinct from all the others, and each from one another, following a descending scale. This led the orthodox to formulate the Fallacy of Differentiated Reiteration, according to which it was fallacious to ascribe difference to parts that are reiterated within a whole. QueAng-QueAng reiterated itself, but it did not differ from itself. The heterodox Pluralists then proposed that QueAng-QueAng's divisibility must be infinite since, if it were not, there would have to be a necessary indivisible part, the final atomistic QueAng-QueAng, beyond which analysis could not proceed. This ultimate monad (however many of them there might be) would have to be superior to all the other parts, and certainly different, since it alone would be incapable of division. If there were no infinitesimal, but only an infinite series of increasingly smaller, QueAng-QueAngs, then no individual monad would have to be counted as final, and thus superior. However, each monad, because of its difference in size, might be a deformed, or at least a cause of a deformed perception of, QueAng-QueAng. The Pluralists then reformulated the Monists' fallacy as the Paradox of Undifferentiated Reiteration.

The heretics, those who had not been strangled by black thongs or sucked dry by mobs wielding metal straws, insisted that the arguments only showed that the unexamined premise of all thinking, whether Monist or Pluralist, was wrong, even unsustainable. They argued for a principle of difference within reiteration and held that each divisible part of QueAng-QueAng must be distinct simply because it would not be any of the other parts. There are many QueAng-QueAngs, they claimed, all distinct from one another, even if they cannot all be perceived. Few inhabitants of QueAng-QueAng have ever read their writings. Fewer still have been able to heed them.

POSTLUDE

Every book owes acknowledgements. It comes into existence, whatever its eventual fate and future entanglements, with a prior history of tentacular connections. Many things will have been read, others will have been heard, people will have made observations, thoughts will have passed from mind to mind, and all of this will show up, refracted, deformed, and reshaped, in the book. *Boundaries, and Other Fictions* is no exception. I owe a vast debt to numerous writers from whom I have learned too much easily to record. The editors of literary magazines have been occasionally supportive, occasionally helpful, and insofar as they have been, I owe them my gratitude. I have given many intellectual IOUs, perhaps never to be satisfactorily redeemed, to friends who have often made comments that have registered with me. Birgitte Larsen demonstrated, within the rigours of actual space, the importance of impossible limit-cases and disturbingly fuzzy boundaries. Garry Sherbert gave me the phrase "carnivalesque emblem" which I have used in the metable "Self-Enhancement" and which may resonate in (I think) interesting ways in other stories. Similar acts of intellectual generosity have abounded and are, indeed, too numerous to name. Long ago in

Melbourne, Leonid Goncharov told me that all my fiction seemed to involve characters lost along the inside of curved lines, trapped in concavity while stubbornly seeking convexity. And they never, he added, winking, quite succeed. I found his words wonderfully liberating. I no longer needed to worry about writing stories that particularly concerned first loves, hockey, fishing, growing up in small towns, or last rites.

I would like to express my thanks to various other friends. Elizabeth Hollis Berry, Chris Bullock, Deirdre Crandall, Brian Edwards, Jonathan Hart, Edward Milowicki, Sandra Morris, Greg Price, Wilm Robertson, Imre Salusinszky, Peter Steele S.J., MaryLynn Scott, Elena Siemens, Lynn Weinlos, and Bobbie Rae Wilson have all discussed literature with me and made comments upon fiction that I have found rewarding. I would like to extend my heartfelt thanks to the University of Alberta Press for having made this book possible. And I owe special words of gratitude to the general editor of the *cuRRents* series, Jonathan L. Hart, and to the always helpful and informative editor of *Boundaries, and Other Fictions*, Leslie Vermeer.

A number of the stories in *Boundaries, and Other Fictions* have been published previously, mostly in very different versions. Often these early versions were published under different *noms de guerre*, an authorial strategy that, holding overmuch to neither identity nor boundaries, reflects the conviction that all writing is nomadic, usually piratical. I would like to thank all the editors and publishers who have given space to my fiction.

The second of the two "Metafictionist Metables" served as an epigraph to the final chapter of *In Palamedes' Shadow: Explorations in Game, Play, and Narrative Theory* (Northeastern University Press, 1990). "Boundaries" was first published in *Mattoid* 34 (1989). In a very different form, "Paracursions" appeared initially in *Coming Attractions 2*, eds. David Helwig and Sandra Martin (Oberon Press, 1984); rpt. *Green Eyes, Dukes & Kings* (Quarry Press, 1985). "Understandings" appeared, untitled, in *Shakespearean Narrative* (University of Delaware Press, 1995). "Making Do" is a fused variant of two fictions: "Surrogations," which was published in *Alberta Rebound*, ed. Aritha van Herk (NeWest Press,

1990), and "Making Do," in the *Dalhousie Review* 70 (1990). "On Intolerance" appeared as "Shultz On Intolerance" in *Green Eyes, Dukes & Kings*. "Rethinking Ludopolis" has been significantly rewritten since its original appearance as "Ludopolites" in *boundary 2* (Fall 1986-Winter 1987); rpt. *In Palamedes' Shadow*. "Mapping Toronto by Darkness" first appeared in *Boundless Alberta*, ed. Aritha van Herk (NeWest Press, 1993); rpt. *Mattoid* 48, "The Disgust Issue" (1994). "Self-Enhancement" was published, without a title, in "Tattoos: Play and Interpretation" *Textual Studies in Canada* 3 (1993). "The Scarlet Crab" was first published in the "Crossing Cultures" issue of *Mattoid* 52/53 (1998). "Evidence" appeared in "Hyperplay, or How to Beat The Sly Man," *Journal of Literary Criticism* 7 (1994); rpt. in a footnote, disguised as a "thought experiment," in *Shakespearean Narrative*. "Smoked-Glass" was first published as "The Dark Backward: Yokohama" in the *Dalhousie Review* 66 (1986-7). "Parable" appeared for the first time in *Magic Realism and Canadian Literature: Essays and Stories*, eds. Peter Hinchcliffe and Ed Jewinski (University of Waterloo Press, 1986); rpt. *Magical Realism: Theory, History, Community*, eds. Lois Parkinson Zamora and Wendy B. Faris (Duke University Press, 1995).